THE HATCH

MICHELLE SAFTICH

Copyright © Michelle Saftich 2019

All rights reserved. No part of this book may be reproduced or transmitted by any person or entity, including internet search engines or retailers, in any form or by any means, electronic or mechanical, including photocopying (except under the statutory exceptions provisions of the *Australian Copyright Act* 1968), recording, scanning or by any information storage and retrieval system without the prior written permission of the publisher.

Published by Odyssey Books in 2019
www.odysseybooks.com.au

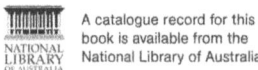 A catalogue record for this book is available from the National Library of Australia

ISBN: 978-1925652857 (paperback)
ISBN: 978-1925652864 (ebook)

Cover design by Elijah Toten

PROLOGUE

FEATHERS—SLICK, BLACK, TWITCHY THEN STILL. EYES—unmoving, piercing, with a stare as sharp as its beak. The crow...

Not the symbol she wants to see, though it is the one in her mind and horribly she knows it does not symbolise magic, or mystery, or change of life; it speaks to her of death.

We're not going to survive this.

Amelia Tate breathes in and rubs her lips together. She is on a spaceship, minutes away from making a jump through a Hatch.

The crow's eyes turn red, its feathers transform into tattoos. Mandon! Of course! He wants the weapon and will kill them for it. His security forces are waiting for them on the other side of the jump.

Damn. Why hadn't she seen all this before? Is it too late?

Urgency breaks her connection. She has to stop her crew from making the jump. Eyes open, she slaps her cheeks, trying to fling off her meditative state.

Secured tight in her seat like the rest of her small crew, she takes in the view out the front display screen and observes their rapid approach to the massive, cylindrical Hatch; rotating, charging, waiting...

The central computer announces, 'Two minutes to Hatch entry.'

Their ship shakes. Peering to the right she observes androids busy at the ship's controls and knows instinctively they are taking the ship to him, to Mandon. They are with him. They will take them through the Hatch, transcending time and space, to deliver them into his hands. Programmed by the World Council, the droids were always going to betray them at this moment. If they were human, she perhaps would have telepathically picked up on their plans much sooner.

At least, her foresight has granted them this last-minute warning. The immediate future is always easiest to see.

She swipes at a sensor near her waist and the seat's locking mechanism releases, lifting the frame. Her crew members look to her and she swiftly lifts a finger to her lips, begging them with her eyes and the gesture to remain silent.

Squatting, she reaches beneath her seat and slides out two Apexa guns.

'What?' Shanen lets slip. She casts a scathing look at her first officer, but the androids have been alerted. They turn.

'Tate. Return to your seat. Hatch entry is in ninety seconds...'

She fires a white, hot stream at the android that spoke. Its fabricated skin melts away, leaving a metallic chrome mould of its face and neck beneath its now lopsided helmet. She fires a second stream at it, burning out its central control system. The other two make a grab for their weapons affixed to their waist belts.

'Don't,' she screams at them, waving both guns with trembling hands. She is outnumbered.

'Captain! What are you doing?' Shanen yells. 'The Hatch...'

The ship is vibrating so violently, Amelia can hardly hold her stance. Sweat has the guns sliding in her hands. She grips tighter.

'Mandon's turned against us. I've seen it. I've seen it,' she cries desperately. 'We go through the Hatch, we're all dead.'

One of the androids tilts its head. 'Coordinates for the jump are set.' It smiles. 'One minute to Hatch entry.'

'Is she telling the truth?' Shanen asks of the grinning, bald android. 'Mandon will kill us?' Her first officer can't take this in. In the past, her prophecies have proven accurate, but he had put those outcomes down to lucky guesswork or coincidences. He has always been more in line with the doubters when it came to the psychic arts. In this case, the World Council is the sponsor of their mission. He can't imagine why they would turn on them. They've succeeded in bringing back the weapon. It doesn't make any sense. Needing more evidence, he wastes precious seconds in seeking it.

'Will Mandon kill us?' Shanen yells at the android.

Compelled to answer a direct question, it replies, 'Yes.'

Amelia shoots at the android and watches its face melt away. The last remaining android fires its gun. Knowing which way to leap, she throws her body clear of its stream, while Veenan, the ship's engineer and the youngest member of their crew, has already freed himself of his restraints and wrenched out a weapon. He returns fire.

Within seconds, all three androids are destroyed, left smouldering in their seats.

Amelia hurries to the controls.

'What are we going to do?' Shanen asks, gripping the back of his seat to hold steady against the ship's shuddering. 'Choose another human settlement?'

'They are all run by World Council security.'

'Go back to Nattalia?'

'They'll hand us over. They only let us leave because they knew the androids were delivering us directly to Mandon.'

'Thirty seconds to entry.'

'I know of another Hatch,' Amelia says. 'Not man-made, near no human settlement.'

'What?'

She looks to the others and takes in their shocked expressions. 'It's a long way out,' she tells them.

'How far?' Veenan queries.

'Far.'

Shanen's head is shaking. 'Not man-made?'

'Whatever made it, are they friendly?' Veenan asks.

'Yes.'

Amelia looks to the controls and speaks into the computer. 'Jedder, set the coordinates for Parsec Zeta, three-one-two-zero, dash, five-five-six-three-nine.'

Shanen's eyes are bulging. 'What! Why that... that would have to be billions of light years away! Are you sure?'

'Yes. I've seen the red Hatch.'

'Seen it? As in one of your dreams?' Shanen has never openly derided her prophetic abilities before, but this is different. He can't let that nonsense cast them into the far reaches of space, well beyond the map of human knowledge. Based on what? Some notion of a red gateway that can't possibly exist.

The Jedder computer informs them, 'Coordinates set. Ten, nine, eight...'

Amelia hasn't got time to argue with doubters. She had known he was sceptical; had always sensed it. Fortunately, she is the captain and it's her call that counts. 'Get back to your seat,' she shouts at the young engineer while clambering back to her own. Veenan slams his body in and their restraints lock against their chests as the brutal shaking begins.

Shanen, seeing it's too late to alter course, looks as though he's staring death in the face. Amelia closes her eyes against his fear and bites down on a mouthguard, hanging from a cord before her. It's not her first time through a Hatch, but this jump will definitely be the biggest and the riskiest.

There are several long seconds of remorseless shaking, then it's over.

They are through.

All is calm and quiet.

Amelia's heart pumps hard, feeding her trepidation. She is coated in sweat. What has she done? Where has she sent them? If only she had had more time to think. But there was nowhere else to go. Mandon had them. He had had years to prepare for their capture and they had only two minutes to plan their escape. Two minutes and they are now forty-five billion light years away from their home planet of Earth. *Oh, what have I done?* she thinks.

'Look,' Shanen calls. 'It's flashing.'

Amelia opens her eyes and sees a blinking three-dimensional blip on the hologram receptor. Her crew are out of their seats and at the controls.

Shanen points. 'We've picked up a Hatch. It's pinging a signal at us. We just have to lock on.'

Amelia takes a shaky breath, hardly able to believe it herself.

'You were right,' the youthful Veenan says, letting loose with a laugh of relief.

'There's really a Hatch?'

'You had doubt?' Zantha, their onboard medic, throws her a critical sidelong glance. 'You brought us this far out on a hunch?'

'Wait. We have a problem,' their heavily bearded pilot, Rogan, butts in. He is manically swiping at screens. 'I don't understand. No.'

'What is it?' Amelia asks, swiping her seat's release.

'We've got major disturbances in this sector; gravitational anomalies, a pull. We're being drawn in.'

'Into what?'

Amelia and her crew look out the viewing screen. They see an expansive black field, like a giant has swiped out a large scoop of stars. The chilling darkness spreads across most of their view. They all feel it; a humming, but not the low humming of the Hatch. This is different, visceral, more intense and all pervading, like it's playing in their bones.

'What's that?' Veenan asks. 'Some kind of black hole?'

'Not a black hole,' Rogan says. 'But I don't know what it is. Look at the readings. Never seen anything like it. It's indicating the space-time continuum is extremely unstable.'

Amelia scans their instruments. 'Doesn't make any sense.' She feels the first twinges of alarm. 'Pull away. Just move it. Engage primary drive. Get us out of here. Punch it, Rogan. Punch it. Now!'

The thrusters fire up. There's the familiar low frequency resonance as the huge primary drive engages and ramps up to full power. Even though the anti-gravity buffers are working overtime to stop them from feeling the massive G-forces, Amelia and her crew are tossed off their feet and sent tumbling around the cabin. They are left scrabbling for a hold.

'We're not going anywhere,' Rogan says. 'If anything, we're slipping back.'

'Engage secondary drive.'

Rogan glances at Amelia. 'Captain, you know that's dangerous with the primary going.'

'Do it.'

The control panel starts to fuse and there is the unmistakable smell of electrical burnout. Rogan follows her command and scrambles to hit the right combination. The ship shudders.

'It's working. We're making headway.'

Amelia nods, well pleased, but aware they are still a long way from safety. After a minute, inevitably, the secondary drive gives out, but it has bought them their escape. They are removed from the influence of the mysterious void.

'Bring primary drive down to nominal levels,' Amelia orders. 'Keep us going positive.'

They hear the drive power down to a less frantic burn.

Amelia looks to their pilot. 'What's the status? How did we fare?'

Rogan won't answer. He strokes at his beard while assessing the instruments.

Amelia sees a slight tremble in his hand. 'What is it? Tell me.'

He can't meet her eyes. 'It's fried. We've suffered critical damage to our operational controls. The circuitry's been fused on a lot of our sub-systems. Can't tell you in detail yet, but it's bad. Put it this way, we're not up to any kind of Hatch jump.'

There is a long silence as this shocking realisation sets in. Without a Hatch jump or any human settlement for billions of light years...

'You mean we're stuck out here?' Veenan pipes up, suddenly sounding much younger than his twenty-one years.

'Can it be fixed?' Shanen asks.

Rogan doesn't want to give false hope, but he doesn't want to be the one writing their funeral notices either. 'Like I said, it's bad. I don't know, I have to do a full assessment. On the face of it, I don't think so.'

'What are we going to do?' Veenan appeals to his captain.

Amelia absorbs the situation and, given the tension around her, struggles to find her usual calm. She is reeling from a full appreciation of the devastating consequences of their mission failure, not to mention the personal consequences of never going home, never seeing her children or husband again. She shakes her head. They have no spare parts for repairs, no capacity for communication, no way of signalling for help... Signalling! There is one way. She can communicate telepathically. She thinks of her eldest son, Jem.

'I will get a message to my son,' she tells her distressed crew. 'Tell him where we are, our status, and that we have the weapon. I'll advise him to inform the head of EASA, Treesa Breenswick. She alone can be trusted and will know what to do. Our mission can't and won't end here.'

The crew members fidget, shuffle, avert their eyes; they are not convinced. They know she can communicate through other planes, but they doubt she can make meaningful and detailed communications with her son on Earth, forty-five billion light years away. They wonder at the speed of thought, not appreciating the concept that there is no space or time on the other side.

'How old is your son?' Shanen asks.

Amelia tries not to hesitate, though she knows her answer will not do anything to allay fears. 'He's fourteen.'

'You're trusting our planet-saving mission and our lives to telepathic communications with a young adolescent across an unfathomable distance?'

'Yes.'

'I don't think—'

'You have an alternative plan, Officer? Any of you? If you do, let's hear it. We sure could do with another solution. Anything?'

'You shouldn't have brought us...' Shanen starts, taking an accusatory tone.

'But I did,' Amelia says. 'If I hadn't, we'd all be dead right now. Mandon's security forces would have taken the weapon and believe me, with what we know, we would not have been allowed to just walk away.' She sees that they get this. 'It was a risk, but we're alive, we've taken no injuries, we still have the weapon, and we've still got time.'

'But we've mashed our ship!' Shanen cries. 'We're on the edge of whatever that void is. Who knows what's out there? Do you? Do you really know everything? I mean, what's a Hatch doing out here and what built it and why?'

'Check your stress, Officer, and know your place.' Her words are as sharp as a slap.

With clenched jaw, he murmurs through tight lips, 'Apologies, Captain. Of course, we are safe in your hands.'

His sarcasm bites at her but she chooses not to react. 'I will contact my son and help will come. We can survive a long time in hibernation.'

'What if you can't contact him?' Veenan puts in. 'Your son?'

'Then I'll try to contact someone else or something.'

'Something?'

'That's right.'

She sees their faces. They are drawing on shock as a numbing agent to help ward off debilitating fear. She expects at least one question, but none come.

'This rescue may take some time. I support going into hibernation,' their medic states.

They are uneasy. Hibernation will render them vulnerable. They would rather stay conscious and hug their weapons.

'We will do what we have to when we have to,' she says, her voice husky with strain. 'Now excuse me. I've got a call to make.'

She leaves the cabin in search of a quiet space, determined to meditate for as long as it takes to reach Jem.

CHAPTER ONE

IT'S A COFFIN-LESS FUNERAL.

I watch the ceremony from my front-row seat. We're burying Mum. She went on a mission for the Earth Aeronautics and Space Administration, better known as EASA, and never came back. They say her ship exploded.

The leader of the World Council, Mandon Allic, is present. He is a scary man with red, synthetic eyes and red and gold tattooed stripes across his face. I don't like him, even though he speaks well of Mum, telling those gathered about how brave she was, representing her planet in support of global security. Of course, he doesn't say anything specific because Mum's mission was a secret.

I'm not farewelling a body but a memory. I haven't seen Mum since I was six. That was five years ago. I remember long, caramel hair that smelled like nutty fudge and a lovely smile full of love. She was not pretty in a flowery way but still beautiful, like a big cat; a black cat, because she used to wear black. They all do at EASA. That's their uniform—a shiny, tight, black suit. I don't like it either and I promise myself, then and there, that I'll never wear it.

The funeral is over. We are ushered into a neat room and served round bread patties with sugar. The sweet food is a luxury and I eat two, quickly and greedily, making my throat dry.

Jem, my older brother, eats one, slowly. He is always trying to act like an adult these days, doing the right thing, being polite and all that. He has Mum's hair, that caramel shade, which reminds me of the sun shining through light chocolate. He also has her proud walk and so much courage. He's the bravest person I know. He's always trying to protect me, even from things I don't need protection from, but it's nice to know he cares. Sometimes, I wonder if he cares too much.

My younger and rather tubby brother, Neath, eats four patties! I see him, stuffing them into his pouch at his waist belt, then one by one popping them into his mouth for a hurried chew and swallow. It's impressive to watch. I wish I could eat four, but annoyingly, my stomach has already had its fill. Neath is three years younger than me. We are all aged three years apart. He was only three when Mum left. I suppose he didn't have much memory to bury today.

Dad doesn't eat any of the patties. He's too sad and angry. He doesn't like EASA or the World Council—blames them for Mum's death. He says if they didn't let her go on the mission, she would have been home all these years, being a mother to us.

Given Mum wanted to go on the mission in the first place, I have to assume she didn't want to be a mother so much. She chose to go. I know she did. She told me before she left that she had to go because she had an important mission to carry out. She was doing it for us, she said.

I wish Dad wouldn't be angry. He should just be sad and eat the nice patties.

Jem approaches a woman. She's a broad woman with closely cropped black hair and a wide forehead. Her features are dark and heavy. Everything about her is dark and heavy, including her mood. The tight, black EASA suit stretches awkwardly across her mountainous chest and rounded hips.

Jem starts speaking with her. He is speaking fast. What he has to say takes ages and he seems worked up about it. I watch him closely. He is relaying information, not conversing. It's him doing all the talking. She's listening with all her might. What's he telling her, this stranger?

I weave between EASA uniformed personnel, trying to get closer.

The woman's face is oddly fixed on a neutral expression. She is not reacting to what Jem is saying and yet, I can sense she is deeply disturbed. Why is she hiding her distress? What a good job she does of holding her face still.

I push closer but as I come within earshot, Jem stops mid-sentence and turns.

'Britta, go back to Neath. You need to make sure he's okay.'

'He's okay. He ate four.'

'Then help him eat five.'

'No one could have that many. They fill you up.'

'I need to talk in private.'

'A secret?'

'Yes. Now go away.'

I stare at the woman. 'Who are you?'

She doesn't answer.

'This,' Jem says, 'is the head of EASA. She's a very busy person and you're wasting her time.'

'I'm not. I just got here. Don't mind me. Keep telling the secret. I can keep a secret.'

'I think I've heard enough,' the woman says briskly. 'Jem, I think it best we bring you in. You're young but I know you have the same qualities as your mother. We need you at EASA. I'll talk to your father...'

'You want to take Jem? For training at EASA?'

'Britta!' Jem is furious with me. 'Go away now.'

'Yes. We want your brother trained. He will be good at missions, like your mother.'

'Mum wasn't good at them. If she was, wouldn't she still be alive? Her spirit hasn't even come to talk to me yet. I figure she must still be sad about the mission.'

'You talk to spirits too, like your brother and mother?' The woman is suddenly interested in me, staring.

'No, she can't,' Jem says, stepping his foot on mine and applying pressure.

'Ouch.'

Jem glares. 'Go away right now.'

'All right, all right.'

I move away with an exaggerated hobble and a loud sniff, feigning physical and emotional hurt. There goes Jem, protecting me again. He knows I have the language of the spirits. I'm better than him at it. Why didn't he want the head of EASA to know? Isn't it a good thing?

* * *

When we get home from the funeral, I wait until Jem is alone and ask him about Mum. He doesn't want to answer me. I sense secrets. 'Well? Do you talk to her?'

'Yes,' he says.

I look sad but sound angry. 'Why can't I see her?'

'She doesn't want you to. She doesn't want you to get sadder.'

This I understand. I'm very upset that she's died and not coming home. I nod. 'Okay, Jem. Tell her I say hi and... and nothing.'

'I will.'

* * *

A week later, EASA takes Jem away. The giant, large-handed men in their black suits arrive at our little apartment unannounced.

Dad lets them take him, though I know he's angry—angrier than when Mum went away.

Still, he doesn't try to stop them. Poor Dad. He doesn't eat dinner or breakfast the next day.

Neath and I eat his share.

We're sad Jem's gone, but like with Mum, I can tell he wanted to go.

* * *

Because he's only fourteen, Jem is allowed to visit home once a month for the first year of his EASA training. Dad cooks up a feast for these visits. We all love seeing Jem. Though EASA's changing him. He is getting stronger and quieter.

On some of these visitations, he brings home a friend. His name is Cal. Cal has a carer family. I'm not sure where his real parents are but we know he doesn't like his carer family, so he chooses to visit us on his day pass out.

Cal is shy and unsure of us at first. He regards us with large, brown eyes—such serious eyes. His hair is shorn, like all EASA personnel, but I can see it is dark and fine; a soft spread over an evenly shaped head. His face has fine features, with a nicely curved chin and boyish cheeks. It's a friendly face, not imposing or cross or mean. I like that he's taller than Jem, and a bit older. I pretend to be his little sister too, shadowing his every move and asking him endless questions about EASA, questions that nearly always go unanswered. Everything to do with EASA seems to be a secret.

Cal is sweet about it though. He doesn't tell me to go away. He tells me some things, such as how physically and mentally hard the training is, how afraid he is that it will hurt when they enhance his hands and how much he's looking forward to exploring in space.

I often find myself staring at his hands, horrified that one day they will be synthetically altered. His hands are exquisite with long fingers and strong, shiny nails. I tell him I wish he could keep his hands, that they are too perfect to enhance, and, in return, he compliments my hair that runs down my back to my waist. I notice he doesn't praise the colour. No one ever does. It's a mousey brown, boring colour. I wish it was something brighter, something richer, like caramel. I want to print-dye it.

I tell Cal.

'What colour?' he asks.

'Green.'

'Why green?'

'I like plants.'

'You want to look like a plant?' He is laughing at me and I withdraw. I shouldn't have told him.

'Green will suit you,' he says, his eyes settling into that serious regard that I like so much.

'Next time you visit, it will be green,' I promise.

'I look forward to seeing it.'

Jem doesn't like it when I talk to Cal. He always tells me to go away. He's always trying to protect me from things I don't need protection from.

'I can look after myself,' I tell him.

'I know,' he says. 'I just...'

'What is it?'

'Don't let EASA come for you. You need to study plants and become a grower. You should look for a soul mate, a hard worker to love and have children with. Have a happy life.'

I want to tell him that I've already found my soul mate, but I don't dare. He doesn't like it when I talk about Cal like that. Instead, I ask him, 'Why shouldn't I go to EASA? You're there!'

'It's not safe.'

'Why not? At EASA I can train my senses.'

'Why would you want to?'

'Because Mum said it was important.'

'When did she say that?'

I reach over to Ray-Ray, our animatronic pet. Ray-Ray is part dog, part Panda. He's all black except for large white patches around his big eyes. He's never far from my side. I tap in a code at its collar to start a recording that I play often. It occurs to me that I have never played it for Jem and suddenly I want him to hear it.

Mum's voice plays. 'You have to understand, I have to do this. With technology becoming so complex and overriding ethical boundaries and our ever-expanding push into space, we have to develop our senses to their fullest potential. We have to evolve faster.'

The recording ends. I look up at Jem. 'See it's important to train. That's what she meant, isn't it? All right, she had been drinking, but I think she meant it.'

'When did you record that?' His face is pale.

'The night before she went away. She was talking to Dad... more like arguing.'

'I see. Well, yes, it's right, it's important to train, but you can train yourself. You don't need EASA.'

'If I go to EASA, I'll be with you.'

Jem looks downcast.

'You'll be there, Jem?'

'Sure.' He looks away.

'Jem, are you going into space? On a mission?'

'Don't tell Dad.'

'You're not going to tell him?'

'No. The home visits will stop and he won't know I've gone. I don't want him worrying.'

'Should he?'

Jem looks into my worried eyes. 'No. Everything's going to be all right. Though Britta?'

'Yes?'

He lowers his voice to barely a whisper. 'You know how we sometimes talk to each other in our minds?'

'Yes,' I whisper back.

'Well, when I go, listen out for me, okay?'

'You'll talk to me? From space?' I'm excited. Jem never lets me in on anything.

'Shush. If I need to.'

I frown. Only if he needs to, not that he wants to?

'And listen out for Mum.'

'Mum? She doesn't want to talk to me. I've tried.'

'That's just because she doesn't want to upset you.'

'I'm upset that she won't talk.'

Jem smiles. 'Mum has your best interest at heart. I love you,' he says, and he sounds sad.

'I love you,' I say back enthusiastically. He walks away and doesn't see my tears.

My big brother takes his leave. The visits stop. Jem and Cal don't come again.

I print-dye my hair green and they don't get to see it. Maybe one day...

* * *

Not long into the New Year, Dad gets a drone-delivered message from EASA.

I hear him yelling, 'No, never, no. Not again. Not her. Not her too.'

I come into the kitchen where he is crying.

Dad looks up at me. His pale, papery cheeks and thick-set lips are wet with misery. He hurries over to sweep me into his arms, pressing kisses into my green hair. He is a tall man and bends to lift me to kiss the top of my head. I know that combination of sadness and anger and I know that my lovely, soft dad, with his slight build and long thin limbs, won't eat tonight or probably tomorrow. I hope he will eat again, for he loves me very much and he's already lost too much weight. I don't want him to fade away.

It's my turn to go.

Tomorrow I turn thirteen. Tomorrow they will come.

Our apartment may be no more than a concrete-walled cell, seven floors below ground, but it is my home. It's all I've known; the only bed I've slept in, the only room I've called my own. I don't want to move out.

Jem had told me not to let EASA take me. Yet I don't have a choice. Didn't he know there would be no choice?

Here, I have my dad and Neath and Ray-Ray. I love them all. I don't want to leave them.

I want to stay and learn more about plants. I love our kitchen pantry, which has shelves crammed with lettuces, herbs, bell peppers, radishes, dwarf apples, and berries, all growing well beneath artificial heat lights. It's my job to keep them healthy. I also work in an above-ground garden inside a small dome house. Anyone from our building can go there, but I only see droids come in to operate the water spray and other sprays, re-seed and pick things. I'm the only human doing that kind of stuff. I grow not only plants to eat, but flowers and shrubs, as they are so pretty.

It's when I'm in the garden alone that I get brave and try talking to Mum.

Sometimes, I think I hear her, telling me when to stop watering, when to start pruning. She seems to like helping me with the plants. Maybe Jem was right. Maybe she has my best interest at heart and my best interest is gardening.

Perhaps that's why I like green. Green gives me the strength to be with Mum.

Is EASA taking me because I told them I talk to spirits? I shouldn't have told them, I see that now.

At least, Dad won't lose Neath. They'll let him keep one child. Neath isn't like us. He can't talk to spirits. He's lucky. He won't get taken and trained in all the things that Jem told me about; things such as astral travelling, psychic interpretation, psychometry, telepathy, as well as the science stuff, like interstellar warfare, planet exploration, space station technologies, rocket engineering, weapons deployment, and alien biology. Ironically, Neath is jealous. He wants to learn those science things. I don't.

Ah, here comes Dad with my birthday treat. He's bringing it himself rather than letting the drone deliver it. We are celebrating now; the night before. We won't have my birthday together, so this pre-celebration is it. Thirteen. I don't feel grown up enough for what's ahead. If only I could be twelve again for another year or two.

Dad pours from a tall flask a dessert of soggy, sweetened bread into a large indent in the table and hands us each the ceremonial straws. His hands shake throughout the task. He is taking it hard; this last birthday before I go.

'There you are, Britta,' Dad says. 'Just how you like it, like Mum used to make it. Your mum would have been proud to see you all grown up.'

Neath sucks up the sweet at a fast pace, like it is a race. When he stops, his flabby cheeks wobble as he chuckles. 'Not with the green hair!'

Dad comes to my defence. 'I think your mother would have liked it. It's very you.'

'Yeah. You, like a cactus.'

'That's enough Neath. It's your sister's birthday and...' Dad doesn't finish. He doesn't have to. We know what he means, that we don't have much time left together. Neath takes the hint and tries to be nicer.

'Your plants will miss you,' Neath says.

It's nice of him to say, but that thought makes me sad too.

Dad then steers the conversation and we talk for a little while about memories of Mum and Jem and of when we bought Ray-Ray.

Ray-Ray watches us with his exaggerated cuteness and non-smelling pant.

As I expect, Dad doesn't eat his dinner or the ceremonial dessert.

At last, I go into my room and open my sleeping capsule. My silver sheet shines, catching the light from the illuminated ceiling. I climb in. Dad and Neath stand in the doorway, staring at me.

'Good night, Britta,' Dad says. 'Try to get some sleep.' He says this because he knows I won't. He can see how nervous I am.

'Good night,' Neath says too, which is touching, because he never comes to my room to say it. Ray-Ray's tail is wagging behind them.

'Thanks, Dad, Neath, Ray-Ray. Good night.'

They leave. The ceiling slowly loses its glow. Just before darkness claims the room, I look at my packed tube filled with everything I could stuff in it. Inside, carefully concealed is Gemma, my netwire doll. Once upon a time, it could answer questions with an inbuilt knowledge system, glow in the dark, and tell me the time. Now it's broken. She's got long, matted hair and grubby arms and legs. She was my last birthday gift from Mum.

'Goodnight, Mum,' I say into the dark.

* * *

The next morning, three people clutter our tiny entry at the front door. Their eyes are covered in mirrored visors and their skins are coated in gleaming blast-proof fabric that showcase muscled bodies. So bulky are their builds and so perfect their stance that they could be machines. Maybe they are. Hard to know the difference sometimes.

Upon their bodies is a range of impressive weaponry; one long gun, one short; several explosive devices and a fold-out shield. I wonder if I'll have to be weighed down like that one day.

'Britta Tate.'

I step forward with my tightly packed cylinder. I don't say anything. My courage is failing. I couldn't speak even if I wanted to. Not so, my inner voice. It's screaming, no, no, no. Yet I squash that voice down too, like the stuff in my tube, pressing down, down. Quiet.

'We are here to escort you.'

'Goodbye,' my father and brother say formally.

They do this because they don't want me to make a fuss. They don't want me to cry.

I nod at them.

With my long, green hair blending against my bright, shimmering green dress, I follow the officials with their weapons, their enhanced hands, their bulk, and their slick black suits. I know they will want me to become one of them and fall into uniformed line. But as my scrawny arms hug my cylinder against my chest, I doubt very much that that is going to happen. I'm too green, inside and out.

CHAPTER TWO

I AM PROCESSED.

First, I get a new name. 3249. At least it ends in nine. I like nine.

I am given three more things. A nano-band, to wear around my wrist, which holds my training schedule and will keep track of my location. A chip is inserted into my arm. It grants me access to the student areas, classrooms, exercise yard, and shower facilities, and no doubt will keep track of me too. Lastly, I'm issued a black EASA suit. I hang it over the crook of my arm; the arm that now sports a band and a chip.

At the end of a tour of the place, where I pass lots of older teenagers dressed in black, I am shown my sleeping chamber. It is in a steel hangar where over a thousand capsules are stacked on top of each other. The sight reminds me of a shipping yard. Each capsule has a dome-like door and all of them are shut. Mine is in the purple coded section, and to reach it I need to go for a ride on a platform. The platforms run up and down in between each column of capsules. I want to ask for a bed in the green section, but my voice fails. Purple is not so bad.

'Please surrender your pack,' the faceless droid tells me. It is in human form, all silver with a silver mesh face and a muffled voice. Its face looks more like a speaker on our hologram device and I want to swipe it to sharpen its audio. But I don't. Instead I focus on finding my own voice and making it loud and clear.

'Do I have to surrender my pack? Please, can I keep it?'

'It is not allowed,' comes the waffled reply.

'What will you do with it?'

'Disintegration.'

'No.'

The droid faces me. A red beam extends from a disc on its forehead and runs across my face, scanning my emotions. I gather it won't like what it reads.

'Why won't you surrender your belongings?'

'I like them. They are important to me.'

'I will take up your protest with my superior. For now, give it to me.'

I'm too afraid not to. I hand it over. I draw on what's left of my failing courage to ask, 'Is my brother here? Jem Tate?'

'No.'

That's it? Just no? 'Where is he?'

'That's classified.'

Another secret, of course. Tiredness descends.

'I want to rest.'

'Soon you must report to astral training. Your band will vibrate two hours and eight minutes from now to alert you.'

'I will be alerted. Yes.'

'Your band has geo-guidance. Just follow it.'

'Follow. Yes.'

'You may retire to your capsule.'

Bed. Good. I move away from the droid and ride the platform. I enter my designated capsule one leg at a time before pulling the door shut. I'm alone and yet I'm sure there are cameras on me. Although it is dark, I feel watched, recorded.

The slippery flooring inside is soft and clean. I sink into it and feel it mould around my body and limbs. As I turn over, it moves in a rocking motion.

I try to keep still. I try not to cry.

The next thing I know my band is vibrating. It wakes me and rattles my senses. I rock and slide about. Astral training. I don't want to go. But I take it that my band isn't going to stop its urgent style of vibrating until I do.

Back on the purple platform, I swipe at my band for geo-guidance. Little red lines light up on screen, pointing my way. I follow the flashing vertical and horizontal lines, which lead me out of the hangar and through a maze of criss-crossing corridors. As I walk, I pass students—tall, strong, young people—who stare at me. I suppose my green hair and clothes do stand out. After a few minutes, I arrive in a small room where two faceless droids are waiting.

My band ceases its jittering.

'3249?'

'What?'

'Tate?'

'Britta. Just call me, Britta.'

'3249, why are you not dressed in your suit?'

I look down and see the soft material shimmer like dewy grass in the sunlight.

'I like this dress. I like green. Don't you?'

'It is not the uniform. Next time wear the uniform.'

It suddenly occurs to me that when I take this dress off, it will be whisked away from me and not returned. It is all I have left to remind me of home.

'I prefer...'

'Strap in. It's time we started. You were late.'

I look at the table and see straps, supposedly for my wrists. They are metal, as are the gloves that appear to be hooked up to a power source.

'Electricity?'

'It helps increase your vibration and astral connection.'

I'm surprised and anxious. 'I don't need it,' I assure them quickly.

'You can astral travel without it?'

I don't know if I can, not on command. My astral travelling is more random, unpredictable. In fact, it often happens when I least expect it. Still, I don't like the idea of being constrained and zapped, perhaps at painful levels, to activate that state.

'I don't want straps.'

Again, there is a red beam crossing my face. I know this time they will be reading fear and defiance.

'We will report your protest to our superiors. Now get on the table.'

I look from the droids to the table. 'No,' I say very softly.

'You must.'

'I won't go astral. I won't. You need a willing mind and mine is not willing. All the electricity in the world won't work. You'll just have to fry me!'

The droids summon their superior, who summons their superior, who summons theirs.

Until, on my first day at EASA, I find myself once again meeting the head of the organisation, Treesa Breenswick.

Her suit still appears too tight for her, her schedule too busy, her expression too heavy. Yet, I see intelligence and reason in her eyes and I relax. Despite her impatience to be elsewhere, there is the possibility of gaining some empathy and understanding.

'You won't cooperate?' she queries, getting straight to the issue.

'I won't.'

'Why not?'

'I don't like pain.'

'There is no pain. The electricity is very light. You will hardly notice it.' She turns to the droids. 'Why didn't you explain that to her? You know she's younger than our usual interns. Give her more information.'

'Yes,' the droids respond in unison.

I look to the controls and see that the electricity can be turned up. Once I'm strapped in, I'll be subjected to their will. Treesa follows my line of sight and reads my expression. 'You don't trust it?'

I shake my head.

'Your brother and mother did.'

'They were brave.'

'And you're not?'

'No.'

'It takes courage not to cooperate.' She walks closer to the table, runs her hand along it. 'You know, your mother was very good at astral travelling. She learned how to use electricity, how to master vibrations. You could be good too.'

'I am not them.'

'No. I can see that.' She straightens. 'What if you were to hold the straps? You could let go if it became too much. Retain control?'

I look at the table and concede, 'I could do that, but it still won't work.'

'Why not?'

'I have to be happy for it to work.'

'Happy? You're not happy learning such amazing things?'

'No.'

She's growing more impatient and I sense she needs to resolve my problem quickly so she can go do more important things. 'All right. What would make you happy?'

'I want my pack back. I want to wear my own clothes. I want to do gardening. I want books, recordings, music.'

She holds my gaze and I read her judgement. She thinks I'm spoiled. Still, she nods. 'Done.'

'Really? I don't have to wear black?'

'If you don't mind being the only twig of colour in the whole place.'

'And I want to visit home once a month.'

'For the first year only. After that, no. Ongoing home visits are non-negotiable. They will generate too much resentment from the others. But your other demands—gardening, books, music, your own clothes—such things won't elicit envy.'

I'm surprised. Why wouldn't the other interns desire such privileges?

As though reading my mind, she explains, 'Gardening is too hot and arduous. Entertainment is preferred in the virtual gaming room and people like the uniform. They like to blend in.'

I absorb this, though I'm still mystified. Gardening is wondrous, and the heat is not so bad beneath the glass domes. How can anything replace the magic of books and the sound of a good tune? As for clothes...

'Now you will have all the things that make you happy.'

'Not all the things,' I say, thinking of Mum and Jem, and Dad and Neath and even Ray-Ray.

Treesa sees my pain and softens her tone. 'No, not all. But with all the things that we can give you, will you be happy enough to get on that table and show us what you're capable of? You know, we need you more than you know. Your skills are valuable in times like these. Your mother and brother would be very proud.'

I feel it then. Her impatience is not to be elsewhere but with me. She needs me to work. She needs what my skills can bring. Her eyes are resting on me and, I sense, will do so until she gets from me a promise to try my best. She is trying not to put too much pressure on me, yet I can see in those dark eyes a strong measure of hope. What is she hoping I will do, or see, or learn? Funny, that in a time of such incredible technologies she has a desperate need for my skills. Seems Mum was right. We have to train.

I nod.

'Good.' She gives my arm a firm pat with her big hand. 'If you hear from your brother or mother, let us know.'

'I usually only hear from Mum in the garden,' I admit. 'Not much though. We don't talk, really.'

Treesa considers my words for a moment before looking to the droids. 'Bring plants in here for the next session.'

'Flowers, if possible,' I put in.

The droids' faces glow green with affirmation.

Treesa smiles at me as best she can. I gather she doesn't usually smile, and I can see the action pulls on unused muscles and looks awkward. She walks to the door and turns back to me before leaving.

'You know, we've never prescribed happiness and flowers for our training sessions. I hope it goes well.'

I hope so too. I hope I get to hear more from Mum!

CHAPTER THREE

TEN YEARS LATER

I AWAKE IN THE SAME COFFIN-LIKE CELL IN THE PURPLE section to the sound of my wrist band emitting its nerve-rattling buzzing.

I can't say I'm happy, yet I know I have it as good as it can get at EASA. At age twenty-three, I'm in my final year and graduation is finally within reach. It has been a long internship.

I haven't been home since the end of my first-year visitations. Communications happen once a year in the shape of a brief exchange via holograms on my birthday. I miss Dad, Neath, and Ray-Ray. Occasionally, I astral travel to them. They don't know I'm there and can't talk with me, but it's enough to put my mind at rest as to their wellbeing.

EASA says it isn't healthy for us to hold on too tight to home, to our past, saying it won't serve us when we later go on long-range space missions. I think they just want us completely under their control and influence.

Ironically, my privileges have given them a lot of power over me. There is much they can take away if I do the wrong thing. I should have expected that. Not that I want to do the wrong thing. I've kept to my promise to try, and it seems my efforts have not gone unrewarded. My results have surpassed those of my mother and brother. I can predict events up to ten days ahead with acute accuracy and can foresee more significant happenings within a six-month range. I have discovered six new planets that could sustain human life simply by astral travelling to them. My reports on my findings have been remarkably detailed, impressing EASA's astrobiologists, biometeorologists, and exogeologists.

Treesa visits my sessions regularly and I sense that despite my excellent achievements, I'm not giving her what she needs. Sometimes she approaches me, wanting to ask something specific, then changes her mind.

'It will come,' she mumbles. 'If it's meant to.'

'Meant to what?'

'Nothing. Are you sure your mother doesn't visit you or Jem? Surely you want to hear from them?'

I always answer the same. 'Of course I do. I guess they don't want to upset me.' Treesa doesn't understand this, she doesn't know how protective they are of me. They want me safe. I know this, somehow. I do feel them. They watch me... from a safe distance. I can't watch them. They won't let me, which isn't fair, but it is the way it is. I let them in, they block me out. I don't know why.

Treesa leaves the sessions with rounded shoulders. I leave frustrated. What am I not seeing? What does she want me to learn?

Today, when I awake in my familiar cell, with that irritating buzzing in my ears, it is not disappointment or frustration that clings to my thoughts but dread. There's a shift, a downturn. Something isn't right. Change is in the air and grave news is on the way. I brace for it. I hope it's not about Dad or Neath or Jem. Don't let it be about them, I think; not them.

With this ominous mindset, I join the morning queue for the hygiene showers. We walk through an alley where jets on either side, high and low, squirt us with cleansing fluids that blast away bacteria, dead skin cells, grime, and sweat from our clothes and skins, deodorising both.

I'm the only strip of blue, white, and green in a long line of black. Today, I've chosen a blue skirt, with bunches of material beneath it, giving it a bubble shape, and a pearly white top that is more like a strap across my chest, leaving my waist bare. My green hair has been cut short. I'm not permitted to grow it long. At least I'm allowed to print-dye it.

Everyone else is in standard uniform; their hands are unnaturally large and their heads are shorn.

My first-day happiness pact meant that at age sixteen, I didn't have to undergo the painful, intraskeletal enhancement procedure that increases the size and strength of people's hands. And once a month, I escape the razor caps for hair shearing. As far as I know, I'm the only intern who has been granted these exemptions.

As I shuffle along with the walking black train to the communal dining station, I keep an eye on the ceiling where the drones are at rest. I expect one will drop and deliver an ill message at any moment. I see this happen so clearly in my mind that I am surprised when I reach the station and eat a breakfast of sloppy grain without any drone intervention. Maybe I've got it wrong. Maybe I've tuned into someone else's troubling news. No. That's can't be right. There's been too many signs: an upset stomach, accidentally smashing a glass tube, kicking my toe and cracking the nail in the shape of a cross, dreaming of a bird whispering at my ear... That is a clear sign, very clear that news is on the way. A black bird means the news will be bad. I've been dreaming about a crow.

My nano-band buzzes again. I'm late. I hurry to the astral training room.

'Ready to begin?' one of the droids asks.

'Yes.' I slide onto the table, not wanting to keep them any longer. The walls can't be seen for the plants, which have grown high and wide over the years. Growing out of huge, green pots and offering a pink bloom, they are taken outside once a week for replenishing and right now I can sense their craving for sunshine. It must be the end of the week.

'I'm not myself today,' I warn.

'Does that mean you need more or less electricity?'

For the past month, each session has taken my astral self to a dark place where no light bleeds in. I have risen from my body only to find myself in an obsidian opaqueness that my many years of experience and my natural abilities cannot penetrate. In this absolute darkness, I hear whisperings; like leaves trying to talk, a rustling of words that convey no meaning. Each time I visit, the whisperings seem faster, more urgent, more intense. I feel failure. I'm disappointing the whisperer or whisperers. It's as though I'm not quite tuned into the right channel and am just getting the static of it. I wake in a sweat of frustration and loss.

Treesa has begged me to decipher the whisperings, to try harder. I keep letting her down.

The droids are looking at me expectantly. 'I don't think it matters what level you apply,' I reply honestly. 'I'm not that happy today.'

'Should we bring in more flowers?'

'No. Let's just start.'

As soon as the electricity is turned on, I leave my body. It is easy for me now. The electrical currents from the straps help me to jolt free of myself and I lift out. Looking back, I see my body on the table, my hands holding the straps. My spiritual being is still attached to my physical body by way of an ethereal cord. I know I can always follow the cord back, no matter how far I travel, or how dark and disorientating it becomes. Travel is easy for me on the astral plane, for here I lose all sense of the human construct of time and space; in fact, I lose all senses and am pure existence, able to warp space and bend time.

I seek answers, wanting to know why I feel such dread, but my soul simply plunges into the darkness. I'm stuck on that suffocating channel and can't change it. I wait there, waiting for the whispers that always come, but this time I'm astounded to hear words, actual words, soft and faint, and I understand them.

'Help. Help. Find Tasma.'

My cord whips me back into my body like a long elastic band of light, and I wake to the faceless droids and their questions. What did you see? Where did you go?

As always, these simplest of questions are hard to answer.

'I heard it. Jem's voice. A message from my brother.'

Treesa is summoned immediately. She forces herself to slow her pace as she marches in.

'You've heard from Jem?'

'I think so.'

'What did he say?'

'Help. Find Tasma.'

'How do you know it was Jem?'

'Tasma was our first animatronic. He loved that pet most of all. Tasma was his favourite.'

'Why would he want you to find some old animatronic?'

'I don't know.'

'He asked for help.'

'Yes.'

She pales and leans heavily against the table.

'Is everything all right?' I ask, registering the depth of her worry.

She doesn't look at me. 'Thank you.' She stands and leaves.

* * *

At first, I think hearing Jem's cry for help is the reason for my earlier dread, but as the day continues, my anxiety only increases. There must still be bad news on the way. I wait for it impatiently, and, finally, in the early evening, a drone descends. Relief. It's happening. I'm ordered to visit the office of an EASA superior for a special communication. The news must be terrible if a human is to deliver it.

On my way to the office, I picture black birds following me overhead. The door opens on sensing my arrival and I see two EASA officials. The younger of the pair looks familiar.

Seated opposite them, perched on swing-style seats that hang from the ceiling, are two civilians that I know straight away.

Dad and Neath.

As I approach, they spring out of the swings and wrap their arms around me. I don't know how I don't cry. Why didn't I sense them coming? It would have been good to prepare.

Neath is now a bear-sized twenty-year-old. I stare at his thick, brown hair and long, baggy jacket of mustard yellow. After years of looking at shorn heads and black suits, he appears so... beautifully covered. He has grown into a handsome man. He's lost the weight that liked to hug his middle and, fortunately for him, it has relocated to his back and shoulders, giving him a nice, broad spread. He's not muscular, not in the hardened, rock-style formations of EASA's trainees, but he's toned and appears capable of heavy lifting. His face has slimmed out, his cheeks losing their puffiness, and so now his eyes shine and dominate.

'You look good,' I say.

Neath shrugs off the compliment. 'You look good too, though you don't look like one of them!' He says this while looking over at the EASA officials.

'True. It's me, the same me. Oh, it's so good to see you both.' We embrace warmly, kissing cheeks, holding hands.

Dad is in his work clothes, suggesting he came straight from the hospital. He is wearing a long white coat with a silver collar. His greying hair is in two awfully untidy ponytails; one on top of the other. The hairstyle is required of all robotic-guiding surgeons, though I have to wonder if he did his hair the day before and slept on it overnight at the hospital. He still looks painfully thin. His coat does not hide from me his depressed chest, protruding hip bones, and long, skinny legs.

'Why are you here?' I ask, wanting to get to the bottom of the visit.

'We'll get to that now if you can all sit.' The younger official, the one who looks familiar, speaks with authority. I sit and examine his face: straight forehead, fine nose, rounded chin. Intelligent, serious, considerate... Then it floods back to me. Cal! He was Jem's friend at EASA. Strange our paths have not crossed again until now. He's filled out, taken on the build of the typical EASA minion, yet there is an inquiring air about him, which possibly indicates an independent mind, and I see he still has that kindness of heart, that soft side that made him not dismiss the non-stop questions of a curious twelve-year-old.

'Hello Britta. Sorry to summon you without notice,' he says. 'I'm Cal Granton. You may remember me? I was a frequent visitor to your home, thanks to the friendship of your brother. Let me introduce you to Commander Moro, somewhat of an EASA veteran.'

Moro, who appears to be aged in his early sixties, glances up at me and I see his eyes narrow critically. He doesn't like my attire. I know. I've seen that look a lot.

'Hello, Commander,' I manage, trying to look unassuming, but as I take my seat, my bubble skirt pushes up around me, broadcasting indulgence.

'We should get on with it,' Moro says. My eyes fix on his cynical mouth, perhaps shaped by years of service with not much to show for it. I'm disappointed that from such a mouth will come the news without care or sympathy.

Cal shifts his weight. His restlessness makes my throat

constrict. No, this can't be happening. Not again. Not like with Mum. Please don't. Bad news. The crow. The cracked nail. Help.

'Jem is missing,' Cal says.

Missing? Yes, he is. He needs help. It makes sense. I turn to Dad and Neath and see them reeling with relief. They had expected to hear the worst.

'What do you mean by missing?' Dad asks. 'How worried should we be?'

'Jem was assigned to the human settlement on Nattalia on a mission. The planet's security scanners show Jem stealing a long-range ship and leaving the planet.' Cal stops and clears his throat. 'It seems he told no one of his plans, gained no clearance. Just left his post, abandoned his mission, his crew, without explanation.'

I consider this. No wonder Jem hasn't been letting me in. He's been trying to keep his mission from me; a mission he's kept secret even from his own crew. But this morning he reached out to me. Did he do that because something has gone wrong? I remember him telling me he would talk to me from space only if he needed to.

Dad sounds distressed. 'That doesn't seem right. He wouldn't...'

'Well, your son has,' Moro says. 'They've been interstellar scanning in all adjacent quadrants. Nothing. They've waited for him to make contact. Nothing. He's vanished without a word. We can't even track his nano-band. I don't know how he's managed to block it.' Then mumbles, 'Unacceptable...'

'Easy,' Cal advises. 'I know these people. These are good people and so is Jem.'

'So where do you think he is?' Dad asks.

'That's it. No one knows.'

'How long has he been gone?'

'Over two months.'

Two months. It was about a month ago when I started seeing

the dark and hearing the whispers. Has Jem been trying to reach me after he stole the ship? Did something go wrong?

'Two months!' Dad cries. 'And you're only telling us now?'

Moro's mouth hardens. 'A couple of months is less than a blink in space.'

'Communications across such distances take time,' Cal says.

Dad shakes his head. 'The information isn't right. Jem's a rule keeper. He wouldn't desert his crew. Is a search party looking for him?'

'EASA will go after him, if only to get back the very expensive piece of hardware that he's stolen, though to be honest if you think mounting a search party to find someone on Earth is difficult, you should consider looking for a missing person in space. Hopeless.' Then, as though we wouldn't fully grasp the hopelessness of it, Moro adds:, 'It was a state-of-the-art craft built for long-range missions with hibernation sleepers and an ion drive engine with Hatch capacity. The latest model, it had enhanced zillet layering, level seven, to protect it from broad spectrum radiation and space-time flux, meaning he could take it just about anywhere.'

'I don't suppose any of you have any ideas, know of any personal missions or vendettas that could explain...' Cal puts to us.

Dad turns up his hands. 'I hardly think so. His visitations stopped a long time ago. The boy I knew followed every rule. If he's gone rogue, it isn't my fault.'

'It's no one's fault but his own,' Moro says.

'Britta?' Cal looks directly at me. 'Any idea why Jem's disappeared?'

I recall my training session that day and my belief that Jem was calling to me for help. I try casting my mind forward and stretch out my senses, hoping to glean more. Darkness again comes to mind.

'Britta?'

'I think he needs help. He's in trouble somewhere.'

'How do you know?' Cal asks.

'I just know.'

'What kind of trouble?'

I shake my head apologetically. 'I don't know anything more, except that it may be dark there and has something to do with...' I'm about to say Tasma but halt. That's not much of a clue.

'What?'

'Nothing. I've got nothing more.'

'Miss Tate,' Moro says. 'It doesn't surprise me that he needs help, and of course it's dark where he is. He's in space. Aren't you meant to be one of those gifted interns? Psychic or something?'

I glare at him. He is a doubter, and if there's one thing I've learned about them is that they don't like to listen.

'Let her be,' Cal says. 'She's trying.'

'She is?' Moro snorts. His eyes rake me from my sparkling blue shoes and pale bare legs to my small soft hands and vibrant green hair. 'If your brother dresses anything like you, we might have a chance of finding him after all,' he mutters, brandishing a smirk.

Dad comes to his feet, pulling up to his full height. He may be on the lean side, but his imposing stature and fervid expression lends him a respectable strength. 'I hope you do find him. Don't let us keep you. You must be busy putting that rescue crew together.' He turns to Cal. 'Look, we've come a long way here to learn my boy is missing and needs help. We're grateful that you told us but we sure would like to make this visit a little more palatable... that's if you could spare Britta for an hour or so to have dinner with us. It's been a long time between meals with my daughter.'

I too turn to Cal, widening my eyes. 'Please, can we?'

Cal glances at his commander.

Moro straightens. 'It's not customary or regulation or normal...' He takes a breath, peers at me, sees my agitation rising. 'But you're not one for regulations. Anyone can see that. Why not? Have dinner.' He leans in. 'Tell no one.'

I beam a smile. He does have a heart.

Cal smiles too. He seems genuinely pleased for us. 'Enjoy your time together,' he says. 'You can go into the breakfast station. No one will be there at this hour. I'll get something hot sent over.'

'And dessert?'

'I'll see.'

Cal opens the door for us. Before we pass through, he says, 'Ah, Britta, if you become aware of anything at all that could help find Jem, please let me know. Is it okay if I send you my band access code?'

I nod, surprised. It is the first time anyone at EASA has offered to give me their code. While the offer is in relation to helping find Jem and not an act of friendship, I feel strangely flattered and uplifted. I leave the room with Dad and Neath, and the single code saved to my band's contacts.

* * *

We are served salty soup in a bowl with a curved lid and rolled up flat bread. The bowls and matching lids look like moons. 'Three moons,' I start to say in my mind, over and over.

Dad and Neath lift their lids, releasing steam.

'How's Ray-Ray?' I start, wanting news of home.

Neath smiles. 'Hasn't changed a bit. Major upgrades have been pushed on us, but we haven't installed them, only the essentials. He's perfect the way he is.'

'Good.'

Neath looks around the sterile room and glances at the row of drones plugged to the ceiling. 'Go on and tell us, what's it like here?'

I see Dad scrutinising me, wanting the truth.

I, too, know the drones are there... listening. 'I'm treated well,' I say.

'Look at your arms,' Neath says. 'What do they make you do, lift droids?'

I hold them out and see clear cuts around my muscles.

'We work out,' I say, thinking of the hours of navigating moving obstacles in the dynamic feedback gym, lifting weights that automatically grow heavier to suit your capacity, paddling in tubes filling with water, running in dark spheres that roll in every direction, wrestling droids, climbing never-ending terrain simulators and conducting heavy weapon manoeuvres that sometimes go askew. Two trainees have been killed by such misadventures. I'm lucky I'm given leniency, but I'm not excused from participating in basic training.

'Know how to fire an Apexa gun yet?'

'Yes.' I don't mention that I'm the best in my class. It's not something I'm particularly proud of or want to be especially known for.

'How big are the fins on the bullets?'

'Big enough.'

'What about your specialities? The reasons you're here?' Dad asks.

I don't want to tell him about the astral travelling and my frustrations with it. I don't want to mention the solitary, month-long meditations in crystal rooms that involve severe fasting and aura cleansing rituals, or the psychometry testing using alien plants and animals and the insights I had gained from them, or the regular automatic writing sessions where I often start to write in languages foreign to my own. I don't know how much he'd believe or is ready to hear.

Instead, I offer him a light shrug and say, 'I've made progress.'

Neath lifts his eyebrows. 'Can you read minds yet?'

'Not exactly. I read faces, sense thoughts and feelings, receive images, more like symbols. It's hard to explain. It's more like developing a language that takes time to learn and decipher.'

Neath frowns. 'Can you sense where Jem is? What he's thinking now?'

'No.' I lower my eyes. I'm annoyed at this. Why can't I? If Jem's trying to contact me now, why can't I pick up on him?

'That's okay.' Neath tears at the bread. 'It will come.'

'I hope so. What's the point of all this training if I can't even hear from my own brother!'

'Can you see my future?' Neath asks.

I look at him, softening my gaze, and soon see a goat tugging at his shirt, tearing the fabric. A grey shirt with a water pattern. I don't know what this means so I just say what I'm seeing.

Neath's cheeks become blotchy.

'Neath?' Dad asks, laughter in his eyes. 'What's with the goat?'

'Not a goat. A girl. She's annoying. She ripped my shirt when I tried to get away from her. My favourite grey shirt! She's a goat all right. A silly goat with a face like one.'

Neath looks at me, his expression one of admiration and apprehension. He is nervous of what else I might see.

'Are you sure you can't see anything more around Jem?' Dad asks, looking too hopeful.

'I'll keep on it.'

'And then,' Dad says firmly, 'you tell that young man, Cal, everything you learn. He was Jem's friend at EASA. I can tell he really cares.'

'I think he does too. I will.'

'Do you have friends here?' Neath asks. I know he is wanting me to introduce him to some nicely built EASA girls, but I don't think I can help him there.

'People like me don't have friends,' I say and resist a melodramatic sigh that should probably have accompanied such a statement.

'Why not?' Neath looks confused.

I shrug and have a stab at explaining it. 'People just want me to see their future or to astral visit their families and report back about them or to hear from their passed relatives. They don't see me, just what I can do, and do for them, which is fine sometimes, just... I get tired and need my space.'

Dad and Neath are quiet.

'We love you very much,' Dad says at long last.

'We do,' Neath agrees.

'I know. I'm not lonely.' I smile at them reassuringly. 'I know we are all in this together. Though, it would be nice to have a friend, a proper one that likes me, for me.'

'We like you for you,' Dad says and Neath agrees.

* * *

No dessert is served. I knew I had been pushing my luck in asking. The meal done, we are soon set upon by droids who escort Neath and Dad out of the institute. Saying goodbye is hard on all of us. We had such little time together. It makes me crave more, much more. Unhealthy contact is what they would call it. I don't regret it though.

It is approaching time for lights out. I return to my capsule and lie down. I want to pat Ray-Ray, to tell this girl to leave my brother alone, to make my dad a nice dessert. Mostly though, I worry about Jem.

Where is he and what made him abandon his crew? What's he up to?

I think back to Mum's funeral when he was talking to Treesa. Their conversation had looked intense. He had not met her before then. What had they discussed? Soon after, EASA had brought him into training. Why?

Then, despite wanting to focus on Jem, I start to think of Mum.

She's close, watching over me, caring... I feel her now. I want to reach out and hold her. It's as though she's right in front of me, like there's a thin veil between us. I soften my gaze, trying to see. A swish... a flick of caramel. Mum? It's gone so quickly I am left wondering if I just imagined it. I want to see her so much.

I'm getting stronger, I say. *You can talk to me now, if you like. Let me in. I can take it...* But even as I think this, I doubt my own strength. I'm crying!

'Mum, are you there? Mum?' She doesn't respond but I assume she can hear and so I push on courageously. 'Jem's disappeared. Though you probably know that, right? Whatever he's doing, please help him. He needs help. Just... don't take him. Not yet. Let him come home...'

I stop the sob before it can happen and roll over. I bottle it up: my worry, fear, frustration. Exhausted, I seek sleep, long for it, and invite it in—a soothing friend at the end of a long day.

Surrendering to the sea of my subconscious, I ride over waves, float far. Dark, gentle, rocking waves take me out on a starless night ocean. There's an image on the water. I peer closer, refocus. I'm in space, on a ship. Someone is at the controls, staring at a view presenting a starless expanse. He's in EASA uniform. His hair is short and thick. The way he sits, one shoulder lower than the other, is familiar.

Jem.

My view swings to the left and I see his face closely. It is him. He looks drawn with deep stress lines that point to sunken eyes. He's aged; time has ravaged him well beyond his mere twenty-six years.

Where is he? Where's he going? I want to bring my focus closer to the control panel, to see what his navigational monitors reveal.

It's then I see it: a faceless, androgynous droid. It's rifling through a storage container to the rear of the cabin. Suddenly, it casually lifts out a hefty Apexa gun, one of the older models, then turns and takes aim.

It is pointing the weapon, projecting a red dot on the back of Jem's head. It can't miss.

What? No. Jem! Jem! I'm screaming in my mind. Behind you!

CHAPTER FOUR

I wake. I'm in my capsule. My sheet is over my face. It's hot. I'm breathing hard, my heart rate is high and my skin wet. I wipe my face with the sheet and sit up.

No, no, no. What have I seen? Was it real? Was I really there? Does the droid get off a shot and kill Jem or does he turn and defend himself? Was I seeing the past, present, or future? If only I could cut off my emotions to get some clarity.

What should I do? I want to tell someone. The EASA droids who train me? No!

Cal? He had said to contact him if I had any ideas. Does this horrible vision count?

I feel so hopeless. Jem, Jem, Jem...

Calm down. I have to be calm and sense for him. Is he alive? Surely, I would know if he had just been killed, if his spirit had been blasted from his body. I would know, wouldn't I? Calm, calm.

I try to meditate, to lift myself out, but I can't. I'm too disturbed.

I look to my nano-band. I swipe it. Cal's contact code comes up on the narrow screen. Should I contact him?

I should.

The hour is late. He is not likely to receive my message until morning. This makes me feel better; the delay will give me time to settle, to gather my thoughts and highly charged emotions.

I think out my message and request it be sent.

I wait, wondering if he'll respond straight away, but after an hour or two of lying sleepless, listening intently for a message to drop in, I fall into a troubled, shallow sleep.

The sound of students activating platforms wakes me.

Instantly, my thoughts are haunted by that tormenting image of Jem with a tiny red dot on the back of his head. Why would a droid want him dead? A droid he trusted on board his ship?

I check my wrist. A star is twinkling at the bottom of the screen. A message. My first. I watch it twinkling for a while, marvelling at its presence, before finally thinking it open.

'Meet @ Moon Café space station precinct 9 am today? Tell no one.'

Space station precinct? It's above ground and out of bounds for students. Cal must know this. He must have much faith in my ability to dodge EASA's security droids! My schedule states I'm supposed to be at the gym at nine. Meeting Cal will require some creativity. I don't think I can do it. I can't see a way out without getting caught and punished, and yet I have to try. I reply 'yes' to Cal, then start to plan.

Wear white, I hear myself thinking as I ride the platform. White is for the streets and you are going out there. Fortunately, my storage crate contains white garbs: a sari with headscarf. It will do just fine.

I attend breakfast and, despite sitting by myself, four students at a bar nearby turn to ask me if I see them passing their climbing test that day. I look at them but don't see any passes or fails. 'There won't be a test,' I say with conviction.

They argue with me. They show me the test on their schedules, waving their nano-bands at me. I shake my head and repeat my declaration. 'No test. Maybe it will be postponed.'

They look at me like I'm crazy. In the history of the institute, tests have never been postponed. They are run by droids that never alter schedules. I must admit on this point I am starting to wonder at my own logic.

'Is that why you're wearing white? You think classes are being cancelled and you are going outside today?' They say it to tease, but I'm aware my choice of dress is conspicuous. I wonder if I should change clothes and just take the white sari for covering. I feel stupid. I'm no good at deception and I realise with dread that it's going to be impossible for me to skip gym without the droids noticing, no matter what I wear.

Just then everyone's nano-bands start to vibrate on and off. It means we must attend the front hangar area immediately for an all-institute communication. It is unusual. No communications were scheduled. Something out of the ordinary must have happened. I try to sense the nature of it but feel nothing. I gather it is not for me to know ahead of time.

The breakfast station empties and I reach the hangar as others are pouring in from four entry points. We are expected to stand in rows in order of our issue number. I step on to a fast-moving travelator to get to my spot. Above us a hologram is loading. The communication will come in this format. I dismount the rapid walkway and shuffle between rows, falling into my allocated position.

The hologram wavers. Everyone hurries. They must be in place when it starts. The travelators stop. A few students are left to run the rest of the way and slide into place, chests heaving.

Then a projection appears of Mandon Allic, head of the World Council. We hush beneath his bio-enhanced eyes and heavily tattooed face.

'Good morning. I have an important announcement to make that will affect you all. This is a major directive. To give you an inkling of how major... what I'm about to say will result in your training being disrupted for some years.'

Heads turn. Confusion is shared. Is it a mission? I hear this being speculated around me. Space missions often take years.

'Your superiors have been informed and can answer any questions you may have. This campaign comes after years of planning. It is yet to be broadcast outside these walls but soon will be.

'I'm referring to an Intergalactic Pro-Development Campaign. This campaign, devised by the World Council in conjunction with EASA, is aimed at stimulating the economies and increasing the gross domestic product across all eighteen of our human settlements in space.

'The World Council is calling on people across the globe to consider relocating to these settlements to increase their labour forces and help improve trade relations with our alien partners.

'As you well know, campaigns to do this in the past have failed, due to the unaffordability of space travel and the historic connection people have to our mother planet.

'To help overcome these barriers, we propose to offer free return space travel in the hope that people can sample life on another planet and become more open to relocating. Given Earth's fluctuating weather, environmental issues, and scarcity of food and water, we strongly believe the time to shift some of Earth's population is now.

'Of course, the campaign will involve an application process. We want to screen for those most likely to resettle. We will especially be encouraging families with older children and adolescent youth to apply. They are deemed to be more adaptable.

'So, I assume that right now you are wondering how you fit in? You, as trainees, will serve as advisers on these flights. You will also be expected to conduct Hibernation Assist, helping to place each passenger into a hibernation capsule. Your own entry into hibernation will be assisted by androids.

'During wakeful stages of flight, if problems arise, be that mechanical, technical, or of a security nature, you will be available to support a solution. It is your duty to ensure this campaign is a success, that the flights are safe and comfortable, and that we represent ourselves well to the rest of the universe.'

His lips curve in a cosmetic smile.

What is he saying? We're to serve as space flight attendants? All this gruelling training to nursemaid a bunch of civilians, mostly teenagers, on some peaceful mission? We're months away from graduating—will we not complete our internships?

It doesn't make sense. It will take years to fly to a human settlement and back. What will happen on Earth while all these people are away? How will these travelling teens be schooled? How can the Council afford to provide free travel? So many questions...

I look around. The trainees appear stricken. They too are grappling with questions. They have been trained for war; not just war, but battles in extreme and alien environments. Their bodies have been pushed, broken, and rebuilt; their minds stressed and tested to the edge of their psychological limits; and their memories stuffed with knowledge of weapons, defensive drills, and attacking manoeuvres and strategies. The minimum ten-year role as a flight attendant on some sightseeing trip is so far removed from what they expected that they are stunned into a shocked stupor.

'While some of you might get to engage in security enforcement on some of our outer settlements where alien tensions are still experienced, I expect most applicants will opt to be transported to Nattalia, our most liveable destination in space. This will mean many of you will be stationed there.'

On mention of Nattalia, I feel a tangible shift in the room. It happens quickly. Emotions switch from negative to positive and the first smiles break out.

Nattalia is best known for being a resort-style planet with a lavish dining and entertainment culture. Its residents are wealthy and fortunate, for the planet is both naturally beautiful and bountiful. Smiles radiate into excitement, which leaps from face to face. They are starting to understand what it means on a basic level. No more training! Space and adventure awaits, and... dare they hope, fun!

But unlike them, I'm not thinking of all Nattalia has to offer: swimming in lakes beneath the churn of waterfalls, taking out pretty boats on the deep blue harbour, or feasting on sweet fruits, fleshy seafoods, and tender meats.

I'm thinking of Jem. He was stationed there before he stole the ship and went missing. If I go, I could find his crew, talk to them and find out what he was doing and thinking in the days leading up to his disappearance.

I could start my search for Jem.

I don't know if the droid has already killed him or if it is yet to happen. If I was seeing it in the present, it's possible that he defended himself, that he turned and saw and fought back. Maybe he was injured and needs help... Help! Is that why he was asking me for it?

Mandon calls for attention. Eyes snap back.

'All classes are to be dismissed, effective immediately. Check your nano-bands for flight details, which will be sent to you in a few hours, along with information about remuneration for these works. I advise you to spend your next few days preparing for long-range space travel. All efforts will be made to maintain family cohesion, so if you wish to travel with your families, please get them to apply to book on the same ship to which you are assigned. Again, if you have questions, take them up with your superiors. I wish you well on your mission—the biggest one EASA has ever undertaken. It will involve tens of thousands of ships and a significant proportion of Earth's population. Your services are vital in making this campaign a success. Make your planet proud.'

The hologram fades out.

Chatter erupts. Those around me seek confirmation from

each other that they are going to be reunited with their families and can even travel with them. I hear shrieks of excitement as they accept this is part of the campaign.

While anticipation builds around me, I am rooted to the spot, grounded by my concerns.

Free return travel involving tens of thousands of ships? This is a massive and extremely costly exercise. Why the rush to boost human populations in space? I thought the settlements were growing at an adequate rate.

I look to our superiors, standing on the borders of the hangar. They are not smiling. Their eyes hold mistrust and anxiety. Their arms are crossed against their solid chests. Some trainees approach these senior officers and I see them shake their heads.

That sense of dread returns threefold.

'Are you all right, 3249?'

I turn. I see a red beam. A droid is scanning my face.

'You tell me,' I reply. 'What have you scanned?'

'My sensors tell me you are afraid.'

'Should I be?'

The droid's beam disappears. 'I'll let my superior know your query.'

'You do that.'

The droid hurries away.

The hangar has almost emptied. I remember I have a meeting with Cal.

Cal must have known about the dismissal of classes. He knew I could leave the institute and meet him outside today. Suddenly, I'm eager to see him. There is much I'd like to put to him.

Already dressed in white for the outside, I have a head-start on the others, who will have to report to corporate wardrobe for outside attire. I hurriedly pack my cylinder, my childhood doll going in last, and make my way to the departure bay. I am the first in the queue for a flight out, which doesn't seem to surprise the others, lining up behind me. No doubt they think I predicted the turn in events. I wish I had.

On schedule, a hovercraft carrier with its glass roof, black hull, gold trim, and red seating roars down. I board this gondola of the skies and take my seat. A few other trainees, with white coats thrown over their coloured clothes, board too.

Once all seats are filled, the carrier lifts and tilts to zoom out the bay's opening, rising to join a busy lane of air traffic. Natural light streams in and I pluck out my visors from my shoulder bag and put them on. All around I see drones, private pods, individual jetpacks, and other hovercraft carriers.

We are in a stream dedicated for north travel. Above us is south streaming, below us is east and below that is west. In between each stream is a transition corridor, where vessels are waiting to change direction from stream to stream. Well above all this are the long-range, supersonic flights, dropping off passengers via pods as they lap the globe on high rotation, stopping only to refill their pod stock.

I peer down to the ground. Thousands of wind turbines stand tall and dutiful like soldiers, feeding energy to the underground city secretly going about its business beneath them. Each turbine is topped by a ball covered in solar tiles. I become mesmerised by this black-headed army of spinning blades. Below them, mounted on high beams, are the rapid tubes, taking bullet-shaped transports from station to station at exhilarating speeds.

Apart from my gardening activities at the back of EASA's training institute, I haven't been outside in years and so I'm a little irritated when my above-ground observations of the city are interrupted by three EASA trainees in front of me. They spin in their seats and demand my attention.

'Britta, we need your advice. It's very important. Can you tell us if we go to Nattalia? Will we have fun? Can you see... you know, can you see our future?'

The teenaged girls are looking at me eagerly, awaiting my

answer. I decide it best to give them my impression as quickly as possible in the hope they'd then leave me alone.

'Let me see...' I look at them and open my gaze, but sadly I don't see any smiles or laughter in their future. Now I don't know what to say.

'Look. This might help,' the girl says, holding out her smart glasses. 'Glass up.'

I frown and can't help but remind her, 'Smart glasses have been linked to eye and brain cancer, you know, and there's still a long, three-year wait for cancer healings.'

'That's what makes them so cheap,' the girl says with a bright chuckle. 'Come on, a quick look won't warp your cells.'

I reluctantly put on her glasses.

On the back of the lens, images of a vast, natural waterpark come to life and a recording starts to play. It begins with a young shirtless man shooting down a rock slide that delivers him into the thundering rapids of a waterfall. He plunges into an iridescent blue lake set in a field of golden grasses. Other young people are swimming in the lake or floating on what looks like giant lily-pads with flowers that serve as umbrellas. The recording then zooms in on a cute furry creature with gentle eyes and a black button nose. It walks upright and is carrying a tray of drinks on its shoulder over to a group of people wading in the water. An alluring voiceover says, 'Nattalia, most liveable planet in the galaxy. Book your free trip now.'

'Ain't that the thing? It's one of many lakes on Nattalia. And that creature isn't an alien. It's just a cute animatronic—built to serve. Non-stop zinga!'

The trainees are smiling.

I take off the glasses and look at them again, trying to gaze forward, hoping this time I'd see them having fun.

'Well?'

The planet's imagery stays with me, clings to my mind. It is as though I'm there. I feel close to it as though I can reach out and touch it. But when I look at the trainees, waiting on my advice, I see only black birds circling in a stormy sky. It is not a good sign.

'I would perhaps choose another planet,' I say. 'The campaign is focusing on Nattalia, but I believe you can go to any human settlement. Inform your superior of your preference as soon as possible.'

They stare at me for a long while. Their faces hold disappointment. They don't argue though. 'Okay,' one says, nodding. 'I will.'

I'm stunned at how quickly and easily she accepts my advice. The others nod too. 'If you say so, Britta.'

'I say so. I'm sorry.'

'Don't be. I'm sure you are right. You always are.'

I'm uncomfortable when she says this. I'm not always right. I often get my visions confused, my lines crossed. Symbols can be hard to decode. Archetypes have many facets. And yet, on this occasion, the darkness around their future on Nattalia had been clear. I feel glad they won't go there.

Shortly, the carrier touches down, right side then left, on a landing bay at the city's leading tube station. I make my way from the bay through an air-conditioned tunnel to the relevant platform, swiping my nano-band at its entrance. As an EASA trainee, I can ride free. Before long I'm on my way, sitting on a hard seat while clinging to a bar as the cylindrical transport whistles through tubing, not unlike a bullet shooting through a dark barrel.

At my stop, I alight and keep to the enclosed walkways, but eventually I must exit to get to the next precinct. As I step outside, heat and humidity slam into me and I remain still for a few seconds, trying to absorb the sudden change in temperature. Consciously, I pull my sari over my green hair and across my chest, wrapping it close around me. White keeps city folk cool and allows them to blend in with each other. No one wants to stand out where crime is rife and brutal thanks to the hoard of above-ground homeless and unemployed.

Quickly, I choose a path shaded by towers used for refuelling craft. I press a button on my visors that darkens their tint and look to my nano-band for a temperature reading. Forty-one degrees Celsius—a cool day—and it is still early. As I spray my face with a cooling agent, I swipe at a directory on the outer wall of a government building. A map lights up and lifts out as a red-coloured hologram, showing the rest of the way to the space station.

I'm close. Sluggishly, I traverse the paved streets, coming at last to a huge tarmac. At its centre is a large white building with several viewing towers. All around it, baking in the sun, are powerful looking rockets, gleaming shuttles, squatting pods, and huge two-hundred-metre-long spaceships.

Across from this crowded launching pad is the city's only above-ground greenhouse zone. I see growers and farmers dashing from glass sphere to sphere like white, life-enhancing bees. Here, they work with mostly genetically modified foods that grow on trees. Most our food production still takes place underground, so this site has always fascinated me. I envy their occupation and wish I could work with them instead of at EASA. It seems strange to me that I harbour this desire but don't have the freedom to pursue it.

The café, built in the shape of a crescent moon, sits in between glass spheres. It caters for the space station personnel and the growers, gives them somewhere to go on a break for their workdays are long. I see Cal straight away, waiting at the steel entrance. He turns as I approach and I can't help but smile as the distance closes between us. He's not wearing white, but the fine, tight-fitting black uniform of EASA and a ranger-style cap. I find myself admiring his looks. The uniform seems to suit him.

My thoughts are cut short at his curt greeting. 'I should've arranged a droid escort for you.'

I bristle. 'I got here.'

'Yeah, but Jem would kill me if something happened to you.'

At mention of Jem, I lower my eyes, steady my breathing.

'Britta? Everything all right?'

'We should go in and talk.'

'Okay.' Cal steps aside to let me enter. At that moment, the café's door slides up and three large groups of people in white coats walk out, blocking our entry.

At this hold up, Cal sighs and whispers to me, 'No one has come in or out the whole time I've been waiting.'

His comment reminds me of something Jem had once told me: it wasn't random bad luck when people got in your way but merely a representation of energy flow. As we continue to wait for the people to exit and be tantalised by cool air escaping the café, I decide to mention Jem's theory.

'You know, if you were watching what just happened from above, you would see that the movement of people is not so different from the activity happening within an atom. It's just energy.'

Cal's eyes light up. 'Sounds like something Jem would have said. Okay. Tell me more.'

'Positive and negative charges, higher and lower energies, push and pull and influence movement. Like the electron moving around the nucleus. People are not much different. We, too, have energy fields that interact with each other. You see this all the time. No one in an airstream, then suddenly five crafts. No one in the aisle at the market, then suddenly a wave of ten shoppers. No one in a high-rise elevation tube, then three cram in. We are all interacting with each other, moving in waves of attraction and repulsion. We think we are in control…'

With hardly a blink, Cal responds dryly, 'I wish these people had been repulsed. I need a stimulant to drink if you're going to keep talking like that!'

'Come on, then. The way is clear.'

We go in and choose a balcony booth. A waitress in the form of a 3D-hologram appears. She is attractive with a warm, maternal manner.

'Booth forty-nine... can I take your order?'

'Barlo?' Cal asks me.

I nod. 'With three pellets.'

'Two barlos, both with three pellets,' he orders.

'Thank you,' the waitress says and vanishes.

'So...' Cal begins.

'So,' I echo. 'Jem.'

'Yes, Jem. What can you tell me?'

I suddenly don't want to say it. I'm afraid of what he'll think of me, especially after my energy pattern rant. It might be too much, but I can't stay silent. With a breath for courage, I tell him what I saw.

Cal listens attentively without interruption. At the end, he leans forward.

'And you're sure this was a real vision? Not a dream.'

'Not a dream. I was there, only, I get time mixed up. I'm not sure when that took place or what happens after.'

'What do you think happened next?'

'I don't know. You see, when you're involved, when it's your family, it's hard to stay detached and neutral and just impartially observe the communications. When my head and feelings get in the way, it's just a mess.'

'Britta, you have to wait until you feel calmer, got some distance on it, then check in again. You know you can do it. You've trained for this.'

'Yes. You're right.' I feel shame. I have trained years for this. I'm annoyed at myself, frustrated. I wish I could just order myself to get a grip on my fear, but I can't. It's my big brother... I take a breath. 'Why do you think the droid was trying to kill him?'

'I don't know. Knowing Jem, he was up to something, and whatever that was, someone was trying to stop him.'

A buzzing sound signals the arrival of our barlos, which are lowered to our table by an overhead spherical drone. The hot brew is served in two cratered spheres, replicating Earth's moon in keeping with the café's theme. A third moon is placed in between them. It holds the pellet sweeteners.

Three moons. Three moons. Such repetition, either orally or visually, tends to suggest a message in orbit around me. I know it will keep repeating or appearing until I get it, so, I utter, 'Tell me, does Nattalia have three moons?'

Cal looks up. 'Yes. Why?'

'There are three moon containers on our table.'

'Yes.'

'They're a sign.'

'They are?'

'Yes. I need to go to Nattalia.'

'You know that... from these containers?'

'And when I had dinner with Dad and Neath, we had bowls with lids that looked like moons—three of them.'

'I see.'

'Do you? You don't think it strange?'

'Jem used to see signs in things. They proved accurate for him. And you do have a reputation at the institute for being... clear.'

'I do?' I'm stunned that he would have heard of me at EASA.

'Yes. Your clothes are renowned too. They say you style them yourself?'

'Yes.' Now I'm embarrassed.

I tear open the seal of my moon cup and add a few pellets. Cal does the same and quickly takes a long, needy sip. I watch him. Stress. I'm picking up stress. What's unsettling him? My vision of Jem? No, something other.

He looks up at me. 'I know you're not sure about when, but any idea of where Jem was?'

'No,' I say flatly. 'The view showed a large dark expanse in space. There were no stars in his field of view. That doesn't exactly narrow it down though.'

'No.' He smiles. 'You mentioned the darkness before; perhaps a void in space. I don't suppose you can dream yourself there again?'

'I seem to have no problem visiting the dark, but I don't know if I can see Jem.' As I speak, I feel it: fear, a debilitating fear. What if I see Jem killed? I can't. I don't want to see.

'Britta?'

'I can try...' then mumble, '...my travels aren't always productive.'

'I know someone who can help. Someone who Jem used to see for instruction with his... dreams. A woman.'

'At EASA?'

'No, outside. She used to work at EASA, but not anymore. Now she works in secret. She'll trust you. We can go there after our barlos? It's a short walk from here. Unless you need to get back home. I'm aware you've been advised about the pro-development campaign.'

I gaze at him boldly. 'Yes. What do you make of it?'

He looks down. When he peers up, he looks serious, stressed. 'I can't say.'

'Can't? Or won't?'

'I've forgotten how headstrong your questioning can be.'

I smile and soften. 'I'm sorry. I just want to know...'

'We all do. It doesn't make sense... this sudden drive to boost populations.'

'Maybe we can ask this woman about it.'

Cal nods. 'I was hoping to. Ready to go?'

'Sure.'

Although I'm eager to go home and enjoy the freedom of being in the outside world again, I can't think of anything I'd rather do more than walk with Cal to meet a secret woman who used to work with Jem in a psychic capacity and who may be able to shed light on what I saw and why our world is being turned upside down.

It sounds like the perfect interaction to me.

CHAPTER FIVE

Heat slows our journey to the secret woman.

We walk one block in air-conditioned comfort before having to take to the outside and the crippling humidity. It is so hot that we don't speak and after a short while I take out my coolant spray and apply it to my white sari to dampen it.

In this part of the city, there is still evidence of the Deadly War. It raged over a century ago and was responsible for sending humans scuttling underground, seeking cover from drone-raids, smart bombs, and biological weapons. The war had taken so long that the underground settlements had become permanent.

I can't imagine living any other way, though I envy the images of the old cities.

Halfway down a dingy lane, strewn with industrial rubbish, Cal halts before a plain wooden door with no signage, no numbering, no handle. It looks strangely familiar, as though I've seen it before.

Cal knocks and the door opens. The occupant has been expecting us. Of course she has. We step in and I remove my visors. The room is small and lit by an orange glowing floor. Running the full length of the far wall is long, fluffy seating.

First, I rejoice in the cool embrace of the air-conditioned room, then in the embrace of our welcoming host. Slender arms reach around my shoulders and I peer up into smiling blue eyes; an indigo blue that must be the result of colour therapy. The woman's hair is long and black against pale skin. Studded stars sparkle on her lips and eyelids and lavender robes drape her tiny form. I wonder why a woman of such loveliness is residing in an above-ground, ruinous neighbourhood.

'Come in. I'm glad you've come. Welcome Cal and Britta.'

'You know me?'

'Yes. Jem spoke of you many times. You are his little sister. I would know you anywhere. I have seen you in his dreams. I'm Meela.'

'Hello, Meela. Thank you for seeing us. We are hoping you can help us,' Cal begins.

'Yes, I know. You want to find Jem.' Meela takes my hand. 'He needs your help. He is confused; lost, so very lost.' Meela strokes my fingers. 'Jem, Jem, such risks he takes. Such risks you will take. It won't be easy, young one. Your search will take you far. It will lead you down two paths; one easy to reach, Cal will get you there. The second path, only you can follow.'

Cal will get me there? I glance at the tall, large-handed, highly trained astronaut by my side but detect no enthusiasm radiating from him and my anticipation falters. He doesn't want that, I think.

'Can you help Britta see where Jem is? Connect with him?' Cal asks, swiping at his nano-band, authorising a payment to the woman.

'You pay too much, but yes, of course I can help her. She doesn't really need my help but I don't think she knows that yet, do you, my girl? Come, come.'

Meela leads us down a narrow corridor with a low ceiling. We walk through a doorway and emerge in a room where there are two glass-domed capsules. *Take the one on the left*, I hear inside my mind, and I move toward it.

'Well done,' Meela praises. 'Don't be afraid. Just climb in.' I see electrical wiring, the clips, the padding, the straps. 'I won't go higher than general static.'

Trusting in this woman whom Jem once trusted, I accept her assistance and climb into the capsule.

'Lie down and put your hands in the cases.' I follow her instruction and feel my fingers resting on metal pads. The glass dome slowly starts to close overhead.

'What will happen to her? Why the wires?' Cal questions abruptly. He has obviously not seen EASA's training rooms for the psychics.

'She is perfectly safe.' Meela smiles. 'This is how she will be helped into a deeper sleep.'

The dome clicks shut and I'm sealed in. 'See you after. Come, Cal.'

Soft lights dim further. As I begin to relax, I hear a voice inside my head. Close your eyes. I do. Breathe slow and deep. Focus on the inner space behind your forehead. Imagine a screen there. Look not with your eyes but from within the centre of your mind. I know how to do this, but her voice is so calming that I feel my mind's eye open almost immediately.

The air around me is becoming warm and humid, like a sauna. This is different. EASA does not use humidity. There is a humming sound and I feel an electrical charge flowing from my fingertips through my body. It almost tickles. I wonder if I'm smiling.

'Your vibrational levels are lifting,' I hear in my mind. 'Just allow it to flow. Go with it.'

I know what to do and I accept the light charge and relax with it. There is no pain and I am calm and receptive to the tingles running along my arms. Gradually, my thoughts begin to change. I am no longer thinking about the pads at my fingertips, the dome, Meela or Cal, but instead I welcome the sight of lights, flowers, fruits and plants; all in vivid colours. I am colour, I am a smile, I am peace. My mind empties, the colours recede, and I am rising. Floating with the vibrational white hum, I watch with an eye that is strong within me. Shapes materialise on the screen in my mind. Show me Jem, I command, knowing instinctively what to do in such a relaxed and heightened state. As I make this demand, I feel my fear rise like a wall, blocking my sight, and I hear in my mind: watch the fear, let it fall away. You are stronger than it... Float over, float over.

I watch my fear fall away. I rise. Like a camera zooming in, the shapes form a face, Jem's face. As the focus sharpens, the image becomes startlingly real, breathtakingly so, and without breath there can be no connection. Breathe, my higher voice kindly reminds, and I take air in and out.

It is dark. He is sitting, knees to chest. He is no longer on a ship. He sees me.

'I'm sorry,' he says. 'You've been told I'm missing.'

'Yes. Where are you? Are you okay?' I breathe in, breathe out.

'Britta, you have to leave Earth and convince Neath and Dad to go with you.'

'Dad won't. You know that.'

'Make him.'

'Why?'

'Trust your instincts.'

'Jem, where are you?'

'I've gone, Britta. I'm sorry. Tell Dad and Neath, I'm sorry.'

'Gone?' I repeat.

He looks at me gravely. 'I've passed over. I'm not coming back.'

The shock of his reply breaks our connection. Walls rise and

Jem fades. No! It wasn't long enough. I want to call him back and, in desperation to reconnect, I start breathing hard and fast. It's useless though. I can't resettle. The current is cut and the dome lifts, letting in a rush of fresh air. I gasp at it, hyperventilating.

'Hey, easy now. Calm down,' Cal says. He helps me out of the capsule and, as I struggle to find my balance, he places an arm around my waist for support.

'You okay?'

I don't answer. I'm flustered and hot, too hot. Burning tears roll down my cheeks.

'What is it?' Cal asks.

I glare accusingly at Meela. 'You said he needed help, that he was lost, but it's too late. He's gone.'

'Gone?' Cal's face tenses.

I look to Meela, hoping she can explain.

'He is lost,' she says. 'You will go to him.'

'I'll die too?' My voice is thin. I don't understand. Is he alive or not?

'Listen to your heart. What do you feel in here?' She rests a hand on her chest.

'I feel he's alive because I want him to be. My heart's not exactly reliable. I know better than to listen to it.'

Meela's expression is one of sympathy. 'You will come to trust in your heart. If you feel he is alive, he is. Now, what did Jem tell you?'

'He wants me to leave Earth, with my brother and father.'

'Then you should.'

'But why? Surely, you know. You must know what's going on.'

'Meela, please. We need to know,' Cal says, adding his plea to mine.

She breathes out and presses her fingers to her cheeks. 'All right. I'll tell you what I think I know. It is not a good time for our dear, old planet. I have seen an evacuation. Children and the young first. Earth is facing a threat. It comes from far away. It is coming closer. It's a threat that could destroy all life-forms upon it. I know this. I feel it. You do need to go. Both of you.'

CHAPTER SIX

A FLOCK OF BLACK BIRDS CIRCLE MY HEAD, THEIR FEATHERS flapping, shrewd eyes glaring without falter. I block out this image and try to focus on what Meela has just told us.

'What is this threat?' I ask, wanting to know more.

'Alien life-forms?' Cal asks.

Meela shakes her head, her expression uncertain. 'I don't know exactly.'

'The pro-development campaign!' I say on a sharp inhale. 'EASA knows and is offering free space travel to get everyone away. It's an evacuation.'

Cal doesn't look surprised. 'I thought as much. Nothing about the campaign makes sense. I gather they're doing this to avoid mass panic.'

'But we have to tell everyone,' I say.

'Tell them what?'

I stare at Cal dumbfounded. 'The truth.'

'The truth? What? That you dreamed your brother told you to leave Earth? That some above-ground psychic predicted a catastrophic threat to Earth and, from that information, you have concluded that EASA is encouraging people to sample life on other planets and boost populations as a screen for a mass evacuation? What do you think that sounds like?'

I'm hurt at his tone. He is ridiculing not what we know but how we know it. He has been surrounded by doubters, for there are many at EASA, many who prefer to ignore the evidence and outcomes of the psychic program because it doesn't fit well with their own grasp of reality. He obviously feels their influence and judgement too acutely.

'The truth is the truth. We can't just know it and not tell anyone. What do you suggest we do? Just save ourselves?'

Now Cal looks hurt. He doesn't like what I'm insinuating—that he is putting pride before the protection of others. He releases his hold on my waist and straightens his shoulders. 'EASA is executing a plan to get everyone out minus the panic. Let's leave it to them. For now, talk to your family and friends and tell them to apply to the campaign. You too, Meela.'

'I'm not going anywhere,' Meela says.

'Why not?' I ask.

'The people who fail to evacuate will need support. I want to be here for them.'

I am awed by her response.

'But you two go,' Meela urges. 'You will go to Nattalia where Jem went, you know this.'

'I'm already assigned to Nattalia,' Cal says.

'You are?' I lift my eyes to his. 'Do you know Jem's crew? Are they still there?'

'Yes, I know them. Yes, they are.'

'We should speak to them.'

'We?'

Meela smiles at him. 'You will need Britta more than you know. She and her brother are closely connected. When I look at their futures I am blinded by the sun. It is not often I see such light. Look after this girl, my astronaut friend. She is walking a well-lit path, a path of global significance.'

Cal peers at me and slips on his tinted visors in jest. 'All right, bright one. Let's get you home and booked on a ship to Nattalia.'

* * *

I go home. Ray-Ray greets me at the door with all the enthusiasm of a long-left pet. I can't help but smile at his antics: rolling, flipping, playing jingles, puffing smoke rings, clawing scratches on my back. I could take his programmed affection all day.

Neath enters. 'Britta! What are you doing here? Why...?'

I decide not to tell him about my recent astral encounters with Jem or the threat to Earth. EASA's story is good for him. I square my shoulders. 'We were all released. Should be on the media streams soon. EASA's offering free return space travel. They want to fly everyone into space to check out other human settlements. I want you and Dad to be part of it.'

Neath looks at me as though I've just changed form. 'Dad? Go into space? Are you some new form of crazy?'

I give him one of my all-knowing glares. 'He will leave Earth.'

'Enlighten me, big sister. Why would he give up his comfortable apartment, his respectable job to go somewhere he loathes?'

'Because I will talk to him.'

'Ah, you learned mind control? Is that it?'

'Not quite.'

He grows serious. 'I don't know, Britta. Dad blames space travel for what happened... you know... to Mum... and now Jem.'

'I know. Don't you want to go to Nattalia?'

Neath's smile is back and broadens. 'Nattalia? Oh yeah. Most zinga planet ever. Everyone wants to go there. Can we go there? For free?' Suddenly, he is interested, keen. 'You going to talk Dad into that? Please Britta, do it!'

'I'm going to try.'

'Can you come with us or do you have to go back to training?'

I squeeze Ray-Ray's nose, hesitating before revealing, 'I'm coming too.'

'No way. That's the best news ever,' he says, then drops his voice to add, 'Jem was on Nattalia.'

'Yes.'

'Wouldn't it be great if he came back and we could all be there?'

'That would be perfect... or is the right word, zinga!'

Neath grins. 'That's the word. Good luck convincing Dad of its zinga-ness though. He's hard to shift.'

* * *

When Dad comes home in the early evening and finds me at the dining table, drinking barlo with Neath, he is stunned.

'What?'

'Surprise.'

I'm in Dad's arms in no time, his grip tight and warm.

'How long for?'

'Until we leave.'

'Leave?'

'I'll take Ray-Ray to my room,' Neath announces, making a quick exit to leave me alone with Dad.

'A barlo?' I ask.

'No. I don't understand why you're here.'

'Take a seat.'

I tell him everything. The truth. It's the only way. I tell him about Jem, my meeting with Cal and Meela, and that EASA is likely rolling out an evacuation plan. Dad sits, eyes glazed, taking it all in.

'So, what do you think?' I stop talking. I'm exhausted.

'What am I to think? That's a big story and yet, one part makes sense: the government's never given anything away for free without an agenda.'

I smirk. How I've missed him.

'Jem told you he's gone. And what you saw supports that. But you don't think he is?'

'Meela told me to trust my feelings. You see, I always thought I would sense his passing. There is a strong bond between us and I just know if it were to break in the physical world that I'd feel it. Dad,' I look at him with tears welling, 'we're still linked, and I know it doesn't make sense after everything I've seen and heard, maybe it's me just not wanting to let go, but... I do think he's still alive.'

Dad gulps and his body is racked by sobs. 'I know what you're saying. I know too well. I'm doing the same thing right now. Believing he'll come back to us.' He rubs his chin. 'So, you want us to go to Nattalia?'

'It is just like Earth centuries before the Deadly War—even better. It is clean, temperate, with plenty of oxygen and water and comfortable gravity.'

'I've seen the advertisements, Britta. I just don't know. Space hasn't been kind to us.'

'Earth is in space,' I point out.

His tone hardens. 'I know that. I know. It's just... All right. Let's do it.'

I blink. What did he just say? I thought I'd never convince him to leave Earth, and yet here he is quickly agreeing to go. He believes me, has believed everything I've said.

'You want to go into space?' I ask, needing confirmation.

'If you think Earth is in trouble, then I don't want you and Neath here and if you're both out there, I'm coming too. Besides, who knows... Jem could return to Nattalia. It is possible, yes?'

I nod. 'Dad... thank you. Thank you.'

'Now, before you rush off to pack your bags, there is something I have to tell you.'

'There is?' I see him waiting for me to calm and I struggle to do so. Eventually, I manage, 'Go on. I'm listening.'

He searches my eyes, watching for my reaction. 'Nattalia is where your mother was stationed before she died. I didn't know that was where Jem was placed until they told us he was missing. She went there and never came back, and now Jem. It's not just space—it's that planet.'

I take this in and my thoughts blur. What? Jem and Mum... Did Jem know Mum was on Nattalia? He must have.

'You think Jem went there... to find out what happened to Mum?'

Dad shrugs. 'I know as much as you—next to nothing. EASA likes its secrets.' Dad closes his eyes. 'I wanted to tell you about Nattalia straight away, after we were told about Jem, but I was afraid. I thought it would only make you want to go there too, to that cursed planet. It's our family's black hole, that's what it is. And now we're all going there.' He shakes his head with a sad laugh. 'Tell me you think it's safe. For every particle of my being tells me it won't be.'

His eyes challenge mine.

I feel forward. Blackness. I'm in the dark, a whisper at my ear. 'Help.'

What does it mean? Dad is waiting. He has seen my confusion. I sense his fear escalate.

'I don't know,' I mutter. 'I just know we have to go to Nattalia. That somehow, it's about helping Jem. He needs my help.'

'If that's what you feel, then we will go.'

* * *

I contact EASA.

'I'd like to be assigned to Nattalia.'

'You want to follow your mother and brother?'

I am surprised at this question. I stammer, 'Yes.'

'Why?'

I decide it is best to be honest. 'I want to investigate my brother's disappearance from that planet.'

'Our sources tell us he is gone.'

I inhale sharply. What sources? What do they know? Their choice of the word 'gone' is too much of a coincidence. I look around the ceiling of our apartment searching for pico-drones.

'I won't believe he's gone until I have proof,' I say.

A very long silence follows.

'Wait. Transferring you.'

I wait for a few minutes. A familiar voice breaks the silence. 'Britta Tate? You are requesting to go to Nattalia to engage in a mission to find your brother?'

It is Treesa Breenswick.

'Yes, with my father and younger brother and animatronic.'

'Approved. You will all board the Aquila Forty-nine. We'll send details.'

'Thank you. I appreciate this opportunity—'

My nano-band stops glowing. The call has been terminated.

* * *

The next few days are spent packing and making plans for a long absence.

I go into the city with Neath to shop for supplies. Top of my list are comfortable shoes and fresh toiletries. As we wander the underground mall, I start to realise that many people have signed up for the free space travel. Many are buying travel items and we encounter long queues at vending and 3D printing machines.

I'm relieved to see it. There is certainly a determined air among the shoppers that it is time to go. I'm impressed at the calmness of it. The underlying current of change is efficiently herding everyone to safety. They must leave; they know it and feel it. There is no need to shout for everyone to get out with the threat of a catastrophe. They are going. A subconscious fear packs their bags and stops them from asking why.

As we wait to be served, Neath meets friends and I overhear them echoing the same sentiments that we are hearing everywhere: what a great opportunity, what a wonderful campaign, how great it is to be going on an adventure. Doesn't Nattalia look like paradise? Most liveable planet in the galaxy! The chatter sounds a bit forced, a bit overdone as though they are just mimicking the government-run advertisements showing on wall-to-wall screens along the mall corridors. It is the human way to hope for the best, I think.

Yet, not everyone is leaving. Over the coming days, I become aware of several families in our apartment building opting to stay. I try to talk them out of it, going so far as to warn them of a possible disaster, but they won't hear me. They don't want to. They love Earth and are not interested in going anywhere else. They'd rather go down with it.

On some level, I admire their loyalty and courage. What we have on Earth is unique and humans have evolved with it over countless millennia to suits its rarest of rare conditions. I, too, resonate with Earth and am not ready to say goodbye to it forever. Earth must keep its place in the orbit of the sun, as it has done for billions of years, keeping company with its solitary moon, doing what it does to stay home to humanity. That's its place in the universe. I give up trying to scare them into abandoning their way of life, all they have ever known, and wish them well.

I wish Earth well.

I watch its horizons, its skies, the way humans fly across it. There's a vibration here that fits with us, I think. I'll miss it.

Days later, it is time to go.

The space station is a flurry of activity with over a hundred craft of various sizes and shapes lined up along the vast stretch of tarmac. Inside the four-storey underground compound, thousands of people are milling about; eating last-minute foods, slurping vitamin shakes, listening to music via ear implants, watching holograms, chatting with family and friends, spraying cleaning fluids on their clothes and hair from testers at vending machines, ordering around droids, swinging on seats, jumping over low-flying drones—all savouring and enjoying Earth-bound activities that may be hard to come by in space. It looks like organised chaos.

We use a high-speed tube carrier to get to departure gate forty-nine.

At the gate, we are among a crowd of hundreds of nervous space travellers of all ages, mostly families. In front of me is an old woman who looks close to stress-related collapse. She is dressed in many layers of clothing, overlaid by a long, shiny, thick coat, which she no doubt couldn't fit into the limited luggage space we were allowed. She is clinging to her husband, who is pale and drawn. They don't appear to be seasoned adventurers, more like apartment languishers, and I feel sorry for them. Like many others, they are only going because their family is going; their adult children and grandchildren, who are standing with them in a group. Given the ten-year return trip, if they remain on Earth they will miss seeing their grandchildren grow up and perhaps not live long enough to welcome them back.

The more I glance around, the more agitation I see. The exciting notion of free space travel is starting to be outweighed by the thought of leaving everything you've ever known. It will be a long time before they will return and when they do, they will be different, shaped by the experiences in front of them.

I can't help but notice there aren't any babies. Where are they? Have they been assigned to a ship built for infants?

A projection of a black-suited man materialises, interrupting my brooding thoughts.

'Gate forty-nine boarding now.'

We lurch forward. That lunge toward the gate ushers in life-altering change. I feel it. This boarding, this highly charged walk down a congested, enclosed corridor alongside my dad, Neath, and Ray-Ray represents the transition between our familiar life on Earth and something unknown.

Immediately, I struggle to take in the sheer magnitude of our ship. The docking bay is several storeys high and the size of a sporting arena. Along the back wall is a series of verandas, marking each level of the spaceship. People are standing on the verandas; some deign to offer us new arrivals a wave of welcome. I see Neath wave back.

Everything seems clean, shiny, and new. Reflections are bouncing off many surfaces and with so many people milling about, it is like the bay is swaying.

Breathing hard, I follow Dad and Neath to the end of a snaking queue for processing, and after over an hour wait, we are stamped with number forty-nine, representing our room number, and told to attend induction in compartment forty-nine.

Forty-nine! Again? That number seems to be haunting me. Didn't we get booth forty-nine at the Moon Café, and we are on ship forty-nine, boarding via gate forty-nine...

'Neath, don't you think it strange?'

'What?' he asks, his eyes following a young woman in snug EASA uniform walking along a balcony.

'The number forty-nine. We keep getting it.'

'Yeah,' he says absently.

'Need help?'

I startle. It's Cal. He's in formal EASA uniform, inclusive of black gloves and solid boots. As always, he looks impressive. His dark eyes are penetrating mine.

'You made it,' he comments, dropping his heavy hands by his sides.

'I did. We did. You remember my father, Dr Freenan Tate,

and my brother Neath. Oh, and Ray-Ray—you haven't met our pet. How did you see us in this crowd?'

Cal smiles. 'Have you seen your hair and dress?'

I look down to the lime green, shimmering, metallic material, forgetting how eye-catching it can be.

'No uniform? Not even for a mission?' Cal asks. There is a teasing note in his voice, which at first rankles, then wounds. I don't know why I let it get to me... why I care, but I do. I wonder about my appearance then. I'm average height and slim from all my training. My face is pert, I'd say elfish, with a nose that points up. My eyes are the same dull brown as my natural hair, though the green dye in my hair has helped to bring out the green flecks in them. My eyes are at least bright, or so my mum used to say. Am I attractive? Attractive to who? I query, then tilt my face up to Cal's, who's still waiting for my response.

'I don't want to wear black,' I state so passionately and profoundly that for a moment he's taken aback.

'I see. What about the unity and equality we get from a uniform? Don't believe in it?' He's not letting the matter go. I wish he would. I'm uncomfortable and baffled by his argument and his desire to press it.

Neath responds for me. With laughter dancing in his eyes, he blurts, 'Hey EASA man, we're all equal under the clothes, aren't we? I'd imagine once we get into space you're either human or not. That's enough of a unifying factor, isn't it? Our humanity?'

Cal turns to my brother and immediately smiles with him. 'True enough. Well said, young Neath. Welcome aboard the Aquila Forty-nine. I see by your stamps you're on the sixth floor. Let me show you the way.'

'You know this ship?'

'I boarded yesterday. I've got a feel for the general layout.'

'How many does she carry, Cal?' Dad asks.

'I believe around twelve hundred.'

My dad produces a low whistle. 'That's a lot of humanity.'

Cal leads us into a glass tube and, after the glass door slides into place, the floor rises, gliding us up six levels. We exit on to one of the verandas and are now overlooking the bay and seeing other people filtering out through corridors from gates, their heads turning as they do so to take in their vast surrounds.

'You're at the end of this corridor,' Cal says. 'It's not much of a space. No window. Just for sleeping really. Want me to show you where your belongings have been stored?'

'Why don't you go with Cal and see?' Dad says to me. 'I wouldn't mind a rest before induction.'

'Okay. Want to join us, Neath?'

'No. I want to shut down Ray-Ray. Don't want to overuse his power supply. Not sure about recharging facilities on board.'

'Make sure to ask about it in induction,' Cal suggests.

'Will do.'

'Come on then, Britta. Let me show you round.'

We ride back down in the glass tube and exit on floor three. Cal leads me to a storage area where large, crate-sized boxes have been assigned; one to each room number. I look inside and am comforted to see all our belongings are there. A digital beeping prompts me for a password. I apply one and the box is secured.

'Want to visit the flight deck? All EASA interns are meant to check in within the first twenty-four hours of boarding. You'll learn that at induction too.'

'All right. Let's check me in.'

Cal weaves in and out of corridors and I'm soon disorientated. We emerge onto a mid-deck, with windows to the front and a series of control panels to the sides. There are several uniformed people monitoring the controls and crosschecking information that's blinking on their nano-bands.

In the doorway, we pass a tall, dark-skinned man on his way out. His uniform is as formal as Cal's, though there are more badges on his chest and sleeves. He smiles warmly.

'Good afternoon, Officer,' he says to Cal. Cal smiles back. They seem to be friends.

'Afternoon, Garth. This is Britta. She's an EASA intern. Jem Tate's sister, in fact.'

'Sister? I see the resemblance, though you're much better dressed.' His eyes light up on my dress.

'Thanks,' I say.

'Have a good launch. I'm sure we'll be seeing you on deck, especially if Cal has taken you under his wing.'

Garth leaves us. I glance up at Cal, liking the idea of being under his wing, but he is looking elsewhere. I follow his line of sight and see he is watching a young woman of mixed heritage. She is slender and supple with muscular arms and thighs. The EASA uniform clings well to this admirable form.

She sees him and smiles.

'Cal.' She holds out her hands and he takes them in greeting.

'Britta, this is Tilly,' Cal says. 'She tops our athletics program at EASA. We trained together.'

'Not that we'll be requiring athleticism for this peaceful jaunt,' she says rather sulkily. 'So, Britta, what's your speciality?'

'Mine?' I hesitate. I don't like talking about it.

'She's in the psychic program. She's like her brother, Jem Tate,' Cal says.

'I see. I liked your brother. Never quite understood the program, of course, but his heart was always in the right place and he was a good pilot too.' Her face crumples with overtly expressed sympathy. 'I'm sorry, missing, isn't he? I hope he's found soon. Perhaps your speciality will help with the search.' She proffers a smile that I can't help but find condescending.

'Believe me, I'm on it,' I say and force a smile.

'Good for you. Of course you are. First flight then, intern?'

'Yes.'

Tilly adopts a confiding whisper. 'When you come out of

hibernation, just sip the foul-tasting drink they give you, don't gulp. It'll make you vomit. Just sip. Remember?'

'I will. Thanks.'

'Anytime. I've got to get to stores. I'm sure to see you again soon.' Tilly leaves us and for some reason I'm glad. I didn't feel much warmth coming from her.

'And over here is Beck.' Cal walks to a screen where a woman is scanning a series of scrolling digits.

Beck. Black, glossy, short hair hangs by a beautiful face of perfect alignment. Well-toned, her legs are tall and shapely; her bust is pert and high in her tight-fitting black uniform. I'm about to have a rare attack of envy when Cal introduces her as their trusty android.

Android? I look for the tell-tale mark on her wrist but can't see one. Beck's expression and eyes are so human-like that I find myself staring in awe. She is a stunning synthetic; a work of art.

She looks at me, or should I say assesses me, then asks, 'What induction compartment have you been assigned to?'

'Forty-nine.' I answer quickly as the number is uppermost in my mind. I'm intrigued by its repetition and have noted it as a sign.

'Forty-nine.' Beck swipes at numbers, dragging and dropping a name into a table. 'There. I've just organised a swap. I'll take your induction class.'

'You didn't have to... go to any trouble,' I say, surprised she would want to do that.

'No trouble at all. I prepped Jem for his mission. He was smart; one of the more capable trainees. I was sorry to hear of his disappearance. Anything I can do for you and your family, I will. So, I'll see you in class.'

'You prepped Jem?'

'Yes.'

'Did he ever mention why he signed up for that mission?'

'He didn't sign up. He was assigned.'

'Do you know why?'

'That mission was classified.'

'I understand that. But surely...'

I feel eyes on me. I turn and see Moro in the doorway. As on our first meeting when he informed us of Jem being missing, he looks me up and down, noting my choice of dress with disdain. I gather he's been standing there long enough to hear our exchange. I see he is wearing the pin of Commander in Charge. Really? Of all the EASA personnel to lead our mission, it has to be that ill-mannered, cynical, miserable...

'Welcome aboard my ship, Miss Tate,' Commander Moro says, approaching us. 'So, still don't know where your brother is?' he asks, not hiding the amusement this gives him.

'I'm working on it.' I'm beginning to feel like the class joke.

'You do that, psychic. Maybe when we get to Nattalia, you may have a better chance of picking up the scent.'

'Yes. I'm confident I will. I'm hoping to speak to his crew.'

Moro purses his lips. 'That might not be possible.'

'Why not?'

'Another missing report just came in. Seems they were sent on an exploratory mission to the uninhabited side of the planet. They failed to return and we've since had no contact from them.'

I didn't know Nattalia had an unpopulated side. Perhaps they were going to cover that in induction too.

'How long have they been out of contact?' Cal asks his commander.

'Long enough for us to know they've met trouble.'

'What kind of trouble?'

Moro's expression flattens. 'Not a single scouting group has returned from that side. That's why it remains unoccupied. Of course, we've sent drones, low-flying craft. We've got plenty of recordings showing nothing but the same majestic environmental features as the rest of the blessed planet. No sign of life.

We just can't seem to get an exploratory crew to return to give us the go-ahead on settlement expansion.'

'Send in a bigger crew—armed,' Cal suggests.

Moro gives an exaggerated nod. 'Jem's crew numbered fifteen and they took a hundred armed droids.'

This unsettles us. Cal is silenced. We try to imagine what could have prevented such a squadron from returning, or at least making contact.

'I thought Nattalia was the most liveable planet in the universe?' I put to him.

'Yes, my fresh intern. The resort-style human settlement and its surrounds are the utopian world promised with the perfect safety record. It just isn't an all-planet state of being.'

'Your induction will start shortly. Would you like me to escort you to the chamber?' Beck asks me in the courteous, amiable tone typical of synthetics.

'Yes. That would be very helpful.'

Moro raises a brow. 'I thought a psychic like you would know your way around a ship like this in no time.' His chuckle forms low in his chest.

It's the last crack at my expense that I can let pass. I lift my chin. 'Seems to me there's a certain contingent of people at EASA who are threatened by the whole idea of a psychic. They just love to poke fun at the notion whenever they can. Put them in their place. Why would that be? Got something to hide, Commander? Something you don't want me to see?'

If anything, he's amused at my attempt to stand up for myself. 'Me? No, not me. Too old and beat up to bother with hiding anything. Maybe they just think your science is a bit of a rort, you know, just an excuse to skip the hard training.'

'So that's it? Don't think our training is tough enough? What do you exactly know of our training? That we sit around guessing at playing cards?'

'Now, now,' Cal cuts in. 'Where's this all coming from? We all know the psychic department is responsible for locating habitable planets and guided the building of all the Hatches. We attribute to them the finding of rare minerals and cures for diseases. No one is saying—'

'Sure, sure. They've had their use,' Moro says, no longer grinning. 'I look forward to seeing what you'll contribute, Tate. More than your brother, I hope.'

He turns his back. I'm dismissed.

My anger rears on his last remark and I want to call him out on it. Cal doesn't let me. He takes my elbow in his grip and walks me away, saying, 'Don't take the bait. He respected Jem. Trust me. He's just worked up about him going missing. It doesn't add up and Moro senses something isn't right about it. Yes, senses. His intuition isn't bad.'

'Then why's he always giving me a hard time?'

'If I had to guess, I think it's because he likes you. Stop smiling. Come on, you're late for induction. Beck's waiting to take you down.'

I walk into a round room where there are large, soft balls leaning against a curved wall. I see Dad and Neath straight away. My eyes are drawn to them. They have saved me a ball. I sit, sinking deep.

Once the room is full, the lights dim and a three-dimensional projection fills the centre of the room. The words 'What to expect during your journey' loom large across a background image of space.

We are shown the usual Nattalia advertisements of a wonderful setting, rich in flora and non-aggressive fauna. They mention that the other side of the planet is yet to be developed and best avoided due to the lack of facilities there.

The scenes that follow explain that I have boarded a Hyper-vessel, powered by fusion energy created from minerals sourced from Nattalia.

We will travel almost at the speed of light. After launch, we will all be put into hibernation and will not be woken until we have gone through the first Hatch; the first being the closest to Earth and in a series of twelve, inordinately expensive man-made gateways developed by Centory Limited.

The next scenes are dedicated to explaining the mechanics of the Hatch, something I find fascinating. The voiceover states in a smooth, easy-listening tone that the Hatch relies on the unique conditions created in a binary system; that of two super massive suns in close orbit around each other. These two massive stellar objects have a common rotational centre in free space, known as the 'still point'.

Here, a line is drawn from the centre of each sun and a cross is marked on it to identify the location of the point of orbit. A graphic labelling it the 'still point' comes up beside it.

So far, I'm following...

The voiceover continues to explain: *Huge magnetic fields are created by the violent exchange of materials, atomic and subatomic, between the close-orbiting suns.*

Now circles with arrows are drawn to show each sun's magnetosphere and how they are interacting with each other.

The magnetic lines of force are gigantic at the still point. At this point, the Hatch is placed.

The Hatch appears; a huge, long cylindrical shape, rotating at right angles to the suns, the ends pointing out toward open space.

The Hatch is a hollow, cylindrical structure, five hundred and fifty metres long and twenty-five metres in diameter. The outside surface is covered in robust super-hardened solar cells used to spin the structure at phenomenal revolutions.

The inside wall consists of tens of thousands of super-conductive rods, three millimetres in diameter, running back and forth along the length of the Hatch. This amounts to some thirty thousand kilometres of superconductors cutting the massive magnetic field.

The display zooms in to show a section of conductive rods

cutting the magnetic lines of force, generating electrical currents within each of them.

The voice, sounding more excited now, says: *Thousands of megawatts of power is produced, which is stored in batteries along the entire length of the Hatch, all connected to a circular focal array like a large convex mirror.*

To facilitate deep space travel, purpose-built spacecraft approach the Hatch at sub-light speed.

We see a craft, similar to our Hypervessel, appear on the projection, flying toward the Hatch.

The Hatch detects the craft and, at a timing down to the millisecond, the stored energy is released into the convex array, focusing a thick beam of highly charged particles, known as the Hadron, at the ship.

We see the Hatch firing a beam straight at the approaching ship.

I feel my father flinch beside me.

The voiceover is quick to assure us that the ship is not disintegrated by the Hadron beam. *The ship fires back. It has a proton gun on its nose with the capability of firing just one proton beam. It has one shot. Ships have neither the storage space or energy production to generate much more. But it only needs one shot. This one proton beam will collide with one of the millions of proton beams produced by the Hatch.*

The combined collision of these particles, at perhaps super-light speed in the vacuum of space, creates a virtual event horizon, or a black hole, just for a nano-second.

We now watch a collision between the spaceship's thin beam and the Hatch's thick beam; we see an explosion of sorts and a black tear in space. The spacecraft then flies into the black tear and is gone. The tear vanishes with it and we are left looking at the peaceful rotation of the Hatch and the watchful suns.

The voiceover concludes: *So, where has the spacecraft gone? Wherever it wants. Before flying into the event horizon, the ship sets predetermined coordinates. This allows it to be instantaneously winked to the desired locale in space. Of course, that location is usually within close proximity to one of our eighteen human settlements, all of which exist on planets located within binary systems, allowing for access to another nearby Hatch and return travel. Four of our settlements make use of the same Hatch and share the same binary system.*

Hatch travel is very safe and the sole reason humans have been able to populate further afield, exploring new planets and benefiting from new resources, allowing for incredible technological advancements and wondrous discoveries.

It is the future of human space exploration and colonisation; the nature of which our ancestors couldn't even dream about. Lie back, sleep well, and enjoy your dream journey. For Centory is the maker of futuristic dreams.

I sense Dad cringing at the marketing spiel.

The projection fades out. The lights brighten.

Beck walks to the centre of the room and faces her class members. 'Any questions?'

Many hands go up, Neath's included, and I know he's wanting to ask about power supply for Ray-Ray and his other devices as well as communication capabilities in terms of hologramming friends on other spacecrafts.

'I might go lie down,' I say to Dad, finding the room too stuffy. I figure Dad and Neath will fill me in on any interesting information relayed during the question-and-answer session.

As I make my way to the door, I hear Beck call out. 'Miss Tate?'

I turn. Beck is looking at me and soon the rest of the class is peering my way too.

'You don't have any questions? Not a single one?' Beck sounds disappointed in me.

I search my mind, then open my thoughts for a question to form.

My lips part and I ask, 'How accurate is the Hatch? I mean, what's the chance it screws up our coordinates and plants us a few thousand light years off course? Ever had errors like that?'

She smiles. She loves the question. It fits well with her programmed lecture.

'This spaceship has extraordinary navigation and universal mapping tools, but what's more, it has an automatic locking system built to latch on to our nearest Hatch,' she says in an overly animated fashion. 'If we are off course, our ship will send out a signal in the hope of it being received by a Hatch. If received by a Hatch, it will ping back at us, allowing us to lock on to its location and be directed there.'

I can see she is proud of this feature, but I don't think it will work in all circumstances. 'What if we are flung too far from a Hatch and don't have the supplies or fuel to get to it?'

'Then, Miss Tate, we are truly lost in space. It did happen in the early implementation of Hatch technology. We had a few anomalies, a few mishaps. Ships were lost, never recovered. Who knows what happened to their crews. But I assure you, these days such mishaps are extremely rare. The margin for error is minuscule. Hatch travel is very safe.'

'Yes. It is the journey of futuristic dreams.'

'Correct. Any other questions?'

I don't stay to hear them. I take my leave. My thoughts are on their usual track of late, casting back to Jem. Could he have had a Hatch mishap? Could he have been delivered too far out in some dark spot in the outer reaches of space? If so, he would never be able to return. He would be lost in space. It would account for scanners being unable to find him and his inability to make contact. While such accidents are supposedly very rare, they are still possible. Is that why he was apologising to me, telling me he was 'gone'. Was he just wanting me to let him go so I wouldn't try to go after him? Any rescue attempt would be futile. If he did survive the droid attack, is he out there now, in hibernation, waiting for his supplies to run out?

Just my imagination again? Dad would be laughing at me

right now for thinking such wild thoughts. Yet, I still can't help wondering if there's any truth to them. The image of Jem lying in hibernation feels right. I find room forty-nine and don't open the sliding door. Instead, I stare at the number etched into the door's side panelling. Forty-nine. What do you mean? You mean something. I meditate, there, alone in the quiet of the corridor. But nothing comes. I just see the dark without the whispers. Just dark. Nothing. I have nothing.

I see Moro's smile. What kind of psychic are you?

CHAPTER SEVEN

Selected interns are to be in the front cabin for launch. I've been chosen as one of them. I leave Dad and Neath in an upper side compartment and make my way to the front. Once there, we are seated on the lower deck, before a wide viewing screen. After strapping in, we are taken through a safety drill, in which we are shown what to do in case of issues during or after launch. I find it hard to listen to the android and my mind drifts, or maybe I just know I won't be needing any of the safety instructions and just choose to conserve my mind. The lecture winds up and we are told to wait for launch.

I'm surprised and pleased when Cal suddenly sits in the vacant seat next to me.

'Nervous?' he asks.

'No. I feel it will go well.' I'm wearing white flowing pants and a lime green sparkly top with two white stripes down the sides. 'If nervous I'd be wearing darker tones.'

He smiles. 'So, if I ever see you wearing black, I should be concerned?'

'I don't own any black.'

'I like an optimist.'

'Do you?' I ask this a little flirtatiously. He doesn't buy in.

'Your father and Neath okay about going?'

'Neath is. Dad, not so much. How about your carer family?'

Cal pretends not to have heard my question. He swipes at the screen on the back of the seat in front of him and reads the weather conditions outside. As usual, it says it's hot.

As is my way, I question him further. 'Are they leaving Earth?'

'What? My carers? I don't keep in touch with them. I do have parents. They're on Nattalia. They moved there when I was twelve.'

'Twelve? Just a kid. You didn't go with them?' The words tumble out before I can stop them, even though I see they are being received like kicks to the stomach.

Taking a breath, he says, 'They thought I'd get a better education on Earth. That's why I had to board with a carer family.'

Screens light up around us and a message flashes on one: *Prepare for launch. Final checks.*

'Carer families... Wasn't there some kind of scandal?' I begin.

'All true. Carer families were taking in kids for financial gain and neglecting them. My carer family was the same, used me, and I was nearly starved to death in the meantime.'

'Were your parents aware of it?'

'We're close to launch. It's about to get rough.' Cal adjusts his straps, obviously grateful to have something else to do other than answer my question. I take the hint and drop it.

'How many times have you been in space?' I ask.

'Third time. Though I've never been through a Hatch.'

Speakers ping on and Commander Moro announces, 'Counting down to launch.'

I count to eight in my mind and then we are being thrust back as our bulky craft roars with its reach for the skies. I close my eyes and continue my counting to ten, twenty, thirty, forty... I lose my place and I can't remember why I'm grabbing at numbers. Forty-nine, forty-nine, forty-nine. Of course, my mind won't go beyond that magic number.

I feel ill. Oh no. I'm going to throw up. Please no. I work to suppress it.

The next clear thought I have is that it is quiet. The acceleration has ceased. There is no more pressure. My legs and arms are floating up away from my body. I look around.

'Activate centripetal forces,' Moro says.

My arms flop by my sides.

Cal turns to me. 'Okay?'

I nod, too nauseas to speak.

He smiles. 'It will pass. Here.' He hands me something hard and tiny in a white wrapper.

'Drugs?'

'No. Ginger and mint candy. Good for your stomach.'

'Thanks.' I smile back at him. He watches my lips as I slide the orange candy into my mouth. Our eyes stay with each other's. I can see why Jem adopted him as a friend. There's much genuine kindness in his eyes.

'All right, interns.' Moro's voice easily fills the cabin. He's addressing us without the use of the amplification. 'Now you have work to do. Go with Beck to level four. You are to be briefed on Hibernation Assist.'

* * *

The low-lit level four compartment of the Aquila Forty-nine holds aisle after aisle of vertical hibernation capsules. As interns, it is our role to assist in putting all the civilians on board to sleep before we ourselves are put under.

About twenty interns form a huddled semi-circle in front of Beck, awaiting her instruction.

Standing in front of one of the capsules, she opens its transparent dome by pressing her thumb to a side panel. 'This will be your chilly home for about four years,' she says.

'Seems like a long time to stand up,' I remark, then feel silly. It was a dumb thing to say.

Beck disregards my comment and continues, 'Its outer casing acts as a radiation shield. There's padding inside for comfort and firm straps to hold you in place. As you can see, several tubes are thread through this gap in the top: one for oxygen, one for nutrient-enriched IV fluids, two for monitoring your vitals, two for toileting—these you will not have to insert. We have enough droids to install these once you are in your coma-like state.'

I want to express my gratitude regarding the toileting installations but hold my tongue.

'While electric shocks will be applied to help stimulate your muscles, we will also program an exercise routine, which will move your limbs. See how this can move your legs, simulating a bicycle and this moves your arms like you are marching?'

She demonstrates the workings of the capsule's inner mechanics with wires and pulleys, lifting and pulling. I feel like we will be turned into sleeping marionettes.

'Looks fun,' I mutter and am surprised when Beck computes my sarcasm.

'Got a problem with it?'

'No. Just not used to exercising while sleeping,' I finish softly.

'You won't remember it,' she says.

I want to explain that I don't like doing things I can't remember, but I don't get a chance. At that moment Cal walks in with Garth, sporting his uniform of badges, and the athletically endowed Tilly.

'All going well?' Cal asks. 'Moro's keen to get our passengers into cryosleep.'

'We need a few more minutes,' Beck asserts. 'These trainees learned about hibernation at EASA, but it was only in theory. Practical application is a little different for each different model of sleeper. Cal, why don't you climb in? I want to demonstrate how to hook up a human in one of these.'

'I don't—'

'It would help.'

'Go on,' says Tilly. 'Be our test dummy.'

Cal looks embarrassed. 'All right. All right.' He steps in.

Beck takes us through the procedure and finishes by closing and locking the dome. Cal closes his eyes, playing the part. I am surprised at how peaceful and relaxed he looks and it strikes me that his usual state of wakefulness is quite tense.

'Have you really put him to sleep?' Garth asks. 'He's sure knows how to play that part.'

Cal opens his eyes. 'What did you say?'

'You're good at something—sleeping,' Garth says louder.

'Thanks. Yes, it comes naturally to me,' Cal shouts back.

'Well, you're about to get plenty of it,' Tilly says. 'Glad they've added the exercises. I can't imagine going four years without moving.'

'That concludes the demonstration,' Beck says. 'Any questions?'

The interns are silent. I have a question, but I'm hesitating in asking it.

'Britta? Question?' Beck always expects more from me.

I lower my voice. 'Can a person astral travel in a state of hibernation?' I'm suddenly worried that once put to sleep, I'll lift out of myself and spend four years travelling the universe—a prospect that does not appeal at all. Not to mention, if I leave my body without much in the way of control, I might not have the ability to come back in. I don't want to get stuck in hibernation, unable to wake up.

'What is she talking about?' Tilly asks. She looks confused.

'I don't recommend it,' Beck replies. 'Your body temperature will be lowered and slowed. Your vibrational levels will be altered. If you astral travel in this state, you could easily become confused, find it hard to return.'

'I see. I'll take that on board.'

'If there are no more questions, let's get started. We'll call the first passengers in. There are many to assist. Don't worry if you do something wrong. We've got a team of androids onboard who will check and continue to monitor each capsule. By this time tomorrow, every human on board will be in hibernation and we will all see each other again in four years and three months—on the other side of the Hatch.'

Cal steps out of the capsule and comes to stand by my side. The other interns begin to chatter amongst themselves.

'I suppose this is good night. I might not see you again for a while,' Cal says, his breath warm against my ear.

'I hope all goes well.'

'Don't you think it will?' He darts me a look of concern.

'I'm sure it will. It's just, I keep wondering if perhaps Jem had an accident going through the Hatch. Could he have ended up too far out to come back? It would explain his lack of contact and disappearance.'

Cal considers my idea, weighs it carefully. 'It's possible but unlikely. Our technologies have been refined. I'd like to think you're wrong and yet... I don't know what else could've happened. Let's not think too much on it now. Just focus on getting everyone settled in. We can talk, well, later.'

'Sure. Much, much later.'

'It won't feel that way. Sweet dreams.'

Cal leaves me and strolls over to Garth and Tilly and the three of them depart, just as the first passengers come pouring in for Hibernation Assist.

CHAPTER EIGHT

I SLEEP. AND THEN I AM AWAKE.

We must have travelled at almost the speed of light for just over four years, gone through the Hatch, and been winked to a patch of space within easy reach of Nattalia.

Hopefully.

I see Beck, syringe in hand. She looks calm, businesslike. Though even if we had been subjected to a mishap, some catastrophic wrong turn and cast beyond reach of a Hatch, she probably wouldn't show it. I can read people, not androids.

'Vitals are strong. Slowly come aware. Nice deep breaths,' she says to me.

I'm surprised how aware I am. Straight away, I'm aware of my higher self, my personality, my ego, and my intellect. My emotions are yet to register. They are numb and I'm in no hurry to rub life into them.

I force myself to focus on the physical now; the pressure of air rushing up my nostrils. I marvel at how I enjoy the sensation. Groggily, I lower my eyes. I look to my arms. They are like thin stalks, but firm. I've lost some weight but been well maintained. I'm clean. The scent of lemon is in my nostrils.

'Drink this,' Beck instructs, handing me a tube of liquid with a straw.

Amazingly, my memory resurrects Tilly's advice not to drink too quickly. I resist the urge to do just that, as my throat is parched, and I sip tentatively. The highly salted, bitter drink immediately makes me gag. I'm glad I didn't gulp.

I gaze around and see other interns; some are still sleeping upright, some are sitting in the aisle, their heads between their knees. Beck moves to the capsule on my right and unlocks the dome cover to awaken another. 'Drink this.'

Soon after, I hear vomiting and see clear fluids hitting the floor.

My head aches, my gut feels tight, as though it's been twisted, and my lower back is so sore, it must be bruised. Free to climb out, I do so slowly, testing my limbs and strength. I don't get far. Like the other interns, I'm soon sitting, taking deep breaths. I don't know how long I rest my head on my knees. My headache is easing when I hear Beck's voice over the speakers in the compartment.

'Once strong enough, please make your way to the hygiene jets, then you may return to your rooms where you can be reunited with any family or friends on board. In five hours, be ready to receive news and updates via holograms to be transmitted to every compartment on board. The all-passenger messaging is of high importance and you must ensure full attendance. Thank you.'

I wonder why we have to wait so long. I want to be updated straight away and I ache to ask her where we are, what's been happening on Earth for the past four years... does Earth still exist? But Beck has left, moving to another compartment of hibernation capsules. I'll just have to wait for the updates, like everyone else.

Nervousness. Perhaps that's the first emotion that registers with me. Anxiety, restlessness, fear. With these emotions, all born from uncertainty, comes a strong desire to go find Dad and Neath.

I do as Beck instructed. I get cleaned up and change my clothes, choosing a red floral vest with tan pants. They help to ground me.

I find Dad and Neath sitting in our room. They look pale and, ironically, tired.

'Sleep well?' Neath puts to me, rising to greet me.

'Soundly,' I reply, and we hug warmly. He smells of home.

Dad, too, wraps his long, lanky arms around me and I stand on my toes to kiss his cheek.

'Happy birthdays everyone,' Dad says. 'We've all missed a few.'

'Perhaps we shouldn't count them given we haven't aged,' I say. 'Let's just pretend that time didn't happen.'

Neath grins and says flippantly, 'No such thing as time anyway.'

'Except the time spent without Jem and your mother.' Dad can't help but think of them at such a loving family moment. I have to agree. The time passing without them is painfully long, and I fall silent with Dad and Neath as we reflect on the years.

'And there is a time we can't miss. Time for the updates,' I say, bringing us back to the present. 'I can't wait to get news.'

'Let's go see if there's any real food about,' Neath suggests. 'My throat feels like someone has been scraping tubes down it. Then we can go to the communication together.'

'Good idea,' Dad says. 'My stomach's tight but I'd like to put something in it.'

'Before we go, I want to power up Ray-Ray,' Neath says. 'Help me out?'

I bend down to the animatronic. 'Sure. We'll have him back up in no time.'

The battery inserted, Ray-Ray is soon kicking his legs and bouncing on all fours, his eyes shining with happiness. If only we could all be programmed to explode with such instant joy and abundant radiance. The tail-wagging, ear-flapping pet is ready to perform and makes me smile. I'm glad we brought him along.

'Come on, Ray. Let's go find food.'

We are not the only ones feeling parched and famished on waking. The main dining area is crowded, and we wait a long while before it is our turn to sit at the bar where sloppy grain is being squirted from mobile jets into circular indents. I wait for the indent in front of me to be filled and am surprised at how appetising the mushy serving looks. As soon as the jet moves on, I begin to slurp the sop through a tube. My tongue gets out of the way and I swallow in gulps.

'Easy, Britta. Your system won't be used to it. Nice and slow now.'

'Yes, doctor,' I say in return, smiling fondly at Dad. He's right as always. I take a moment to breathe, then recommence at a more considered pace.

We walk off the meal, strolling the corridors and talking with passengers who have become familiar to us. Everyone seems to be coping relatively well with the post hibernation symptoms. We swap stories of headaches, blocked sinuses, queasy stomachs, and sore throats. It feels good to share these travel stories and establish a sense of what's normal.

The beeping starts later in the afternoon. Passengers teem the halls, heading for the hologram chambers, desperate for news.

We are in the compartment in which we undertook induction. Sitting against the wall with Ray-Ray panting noiselessly beside me, I become aware of escalating tension in my body. Black birds are in my mind's eye, their eyes are darting side to side, flashing warnings, while their wings are pulled in tight, feathers pointing down. Not a good sign...

The hologram delivers a grim-faced Commander Moro and there is an instant hush.

'Good awakening day to everyone. The date on Earth is 6 June 2383. We have passed through the Hatch and been cast into the binary system of Theta-Sirius 14, placing us only a short hyper-speed flight from Nattalia. News, stored by our super computer and withheld from us, has just been released. I've read through these four-year-old news reports...' Now he stops. I sense his throat tightening.

'Please be prepared,' he begins. He clears his tight throat, then informs, 'It appears, before we departed Earth, EASA had detected an asteroid on a direct collision course with our home planet.' He pauses, knowing what effect this information will be having throughout the ship and I hear it in the gasps around me. While I had expected a threat to Earth, given Meela's prediction and Jem's warning to me, I'm still stunned on receiving the news. It sounds definite, so final, so catastrophic. An asteroid. Scientists over the centuries had predicted that would be our end. I just can't believe it's going to happen in my lifetime. As a psychic, I don't want to see it. I don't want to look forward—not to that.

'Examining the data, there is no chance of a near miss,' he continues. 'Earth will be hit and most life-forms will cease to exist.' He swallows. 'Asteroid size is two hundred and eighty kilometres in diameter. Predicted time of impact... four months from now.'

Four months? Suddenly time has real meaning.

'Obviously, EASA did not want us to know this until now as they didn't want to cause mass panic amongst us. At the time of our departure, the number of people who had booked the free flights to leave in the pro-development campaign numbered just two billion. Eight billion remained behind.' Moro has the dignity to pause and lower his eyes. 'Every available ship was booked. Since then, the people of Earth have been advised of the asteroid's path and more ships have been built. A lottery system was introduced. I believe they will continue to build more ships and evacuate more people for as long as they can,' he says.

I struggle to take it in; the horror of it.

'The reports stated that EASA had known about the asteroid for some time, but had been confident that we had the technologies to knock it off course. They did attempt to do this. Those attempts failed. At the time of our departure, all methods of destroying the asteroid had been exhausted and there was no hope of the asteroid being rerouted.'

Moro takes a breath then tries to sound reassuring. 'We will push on to Nattalia. We will seek refuge there. Our futures will be in their hands. I have no doubt you have many questions. We will do what we can to answer them. Please log-in to the screens along the back wall of your hologram compartments and key in your queries and requests and we will work through them. As for all EASA personnel, your nano-bands will still be functioning for intra-ship communications, so please keep checking them for updates. You will note you have lost connection to Earth. As we approach Nattalia, your bands will pick up the planet's signal and reactivate.

'Please everyone, understand, like you, I believed we would have an Earth to return to and I am sorry to be the bearer of this most catastrophic of news. May all our thoughts be with the peoples of Earth...'

The hologram shuts down, sucking his image away.

I'm left trying not to tune in to the panic and fear on Earth, but I can feel it too acutely and I wipe at fast sliding tears. As I clear my eyes, I see people in my compartment gathering around me.

'Is the asteroid really going to hit?' The question is posed by a large woman with wild eyes and stringy hair. I can tell she's a mother and in my mind I see an image of her grown children still on Earth. Love gave her the courage to ask. The others are staring at me.

'You're a seer,' one of them says. 'You must know.'

'Just tell us,' a tall, dull man demands.

I cross my arms, not sure how to respond.

Suddenly, Neath steps in front of me. 'Really, you'd ask that of her?'

'Her reputation for sensing the future is well known. We have a right to know what outcome she sees,' a grey-haired man says, his voice deep and gravelly.

'You're asking a bit much of her, aren't you?' Neath asserts. 'Asking her to determine Earth's fate! I mean, what a thing to look ahead to. Would you if you could?'

'We need to know,' the mother says.

On hearing her desperation, I uncross my arms. 'I could try to...'

'You don't have to,' says Neath, turning to me. 'If you see Earth being slammed by an asteroid... if you see mass death, mass suffering... you don't have to look, you don't have to tell... it's a lot to have to tell, isn't it?' Neath looks back to the gathering. 'And what would that feel like... to lose all hope, to know we can never go back.'

'She might see differently,' the woman says.

'And there it is.' Neath's voice rises. 'Hope. You're still hoping she'll see differently. Why don't you just hold on to that and go back to your rooms?'

'Because false hope is no good,' the old man states. 'We want the truth, from her, as she sees it.'

'What if I see wrong?' I say. My face is apologetic.

'From what we know, you're not often wrong,' the tall man, who's looking less dull, puts in.

My father steps forward. 'It's Britta's choice. Let her decide. If she chooses not to see, you all have to respect that.'

I feel all eyes look to me for my decision, willing me to peek forward. Their uncertainty is driving them to despair.

'It's okay, Dad and Neath,' I say, giving them both a grateful look. 'I'll see and I'll decide. I won't be shown anything I can't handle. And I think the people are right. We need to know as much as we can glean.'

'Thank you, dear,' the mother says.

I close my eyes and breathe out my fear. This is hard to do, and I breathe for a long time. At last, I feel a shift in my mind and try to feel forward, yet strangely, my thoughts go back.

I'm a child.

My mother is departing on one last quest. She doesn't want to leave us. She cries into our hair as she kisses us goodbye. She tears herself away from us, and finally I see why. My mother saw this day coming, a day when Earth would face its final hours and she had known, right back then, that there was a way to stop it.

My mind rolls further back. I see my mother lying on a table, her beautiful hair has been cut off, her hands are strapped in, wires attached. She wakes and there's two droids standing over her. 'Where did you go... what did you see?'

'I saw a planet with three moons. There's a species on this planet. They have the weapon we seek.'

'Are you sure the weapon will be strong enough? It can knock an asteroid off course?'

'Yes. They told me. They are willing to trade for it.'

'Trade what?'

'They want me to come to Nattalia. They have much to explain. I think they need our help.'

My mind rolls, in what direction, forward or back, I don't know, but the next image I see is of darkness and I hear whispers. 'Help us. Help us.'

My eyes open.

'Well?' the old man asks.

I can't speak. I don't know what to say. So many thoughts are flowing from the images I've just been given.

'You can tell us,' the old man adds, puffing up his fragile chest. 'We can hear it.'

'I think there's a chance Earth can still be saved. How much of a chance, I don't know. What I was shown... suggests... hope.'

'What were you shown?' the mother almost shouts.

'Now, now, good people,' Dad says. 'She's done her best and told us what she can. Let's go back to our rooms and hope she's right.'

'Hope! If EASA had been honest with everyone as soon as they discovered the asteroid, more people would have hope right now! Perhaps evacuations could have started sooner and we could have crammed more people on the ships. More could have been saved. My adult children... their applications weren't accepted! Why not? Weren't their lives good enough to save? I only left because I thought I could return to them. Why weren't we trusted with the truth until now?'

'To prevent panic,' I say meekly.

'Better to panic than to be left in the dark, not knowing what's coming, and therefore unable to save yourself or your family, or at least to choose to die with them.'

I look at the woman, her face etched in sorrow and regret. 'I agree,' I say. 'They should have trusted us with the truth from the beginning.'

Dad then guides me through the gathering, Neath and Ray-Ray following behind.

When we reach our room, they don't ask. But I know they want to know more.

'I saw Mum,' I say.

They look at me, waiting without breathing.

'She went to Nattalia for a weapon; a weapon that could divert an asteroid.'

Dad's face looks pained. 'She never made it back, with or without a weapon. It could have been the weapon that blew up her ship.'

'Jem went to Nattalia... Maybe he went there in search of the weapon too,' Neath says.

'Why search?' Dad asks. 'If the settlers on Nattalia have a weapon, why haven't they just handed it over?'

'Not the settlers,' I say.

Dad's confusion turns to exasperation. 'There's no other species with intelligence on the planet. It is known for—'

'What it is known for,' I say, cutting him off, equally as exasperated, 'is its tranquil colonies on one side of the planet—one side. I'm referring to the other side.'

Dad absorbs this and his expression clouds over. 'It doesn't really matter why they went there. Your mother... and Jem. It's time we... I don't know what you're hoping for. There's no point to any of this. To be honest, I wish I'd stayed behind on Earth. I didn't know losing it would feel this way. I wish... I'm going for a walk.' He heads for the door.

'Dad, they were trying to save Earth.' I feel proud as I say this.

But Dad can't share the sentiment. It cuts too deep. 'And they failed.'

He leaves the room.

CHAPTER NINE

I'M AFRAID TO GO TO SLEEP; AFRAID OF WHAT I MIGHT DREAM, what I might see. Too many terrors are forecast and I anticipate at least nightmares.

Eventually, tiredness dictates that I must shut my eyes. I have to sleep. I ask for kindness, to be shielded, to just sleep soundly.

When sleep comes, it is not nightmares that flood my mind, but a picture of myself lying still in sleep, wrapped in silvery sheets. It is not just an image. I'm out of my body, looking down. There's no electrical current aiding my travel and yet I've done it again, lifted out of myself. Eager to make use of the opportunity, I think of Nattalia, will myself there.

It happens. In the twilight sky sit three pinkish moons; three discs of pastel light.

Tearing my eyes from their beauty, I scan the planet's landscape. I don't see people, houses, bridges, boats, or traffic of any kind.

I'm on the other side, where I want to be. Here, the trees are spectacular. Thick, gnarly trunks hold up vast canopies of wide, green leaves and large cup-like flowers; the orange cups face skyward to catch whatever rain falls. Flowering vines string from tree to tree and are covered in small blooms. They are yellow with red marks, shaped like kisses—so many of them. The ground is covered in leaves and curled petals; a colourful collage of soft, warm offcuts from the trees. I have the sensation of lying down upon this dense carpet, joining it. For a while, I just see colour. My vibration is high now, higher than usual. I pulse with creativity yet feel so peaceful, so loved. Love. Mum and Jem. Earth.

My eyes refocus. I gaze at the dark, fungal-wrapped trunks and I search for Jem's crew, for an intelligent species, for an Earth-saving weapon.

Scanning the forest, I suddenly catch movement. There. Low in the underbrush. What are they? Beings; elongated, light beings with radiant skins as delicate as butterfly wings and as intricately patterned. Bristles run the length of their bodies, the tips of which giving off a yellow glow. Their narrow faces have eyes that taper down into a tear-like shape. They have two arms, two legs, hands, fingers, all of which are long and spindly.

'Do you need help?' I don't know why I think this question, but I know they've heard it. Sweeping bristles blink over their eyes before they leap away in such slow bounds; they appear to be floating. It is like watching long jellyfish propelling themselves through water.

I am about to walk over to where I had seen them when I see a large leaf lean to the side. The leaf remains on an odd angle, its shape compressed. Something or someone is still there.

Instinctively, my sight goes slack, my vision softens, blurs. I lift my vibration and see it: a being. One remains. It is taller and even more translucent than the others. Its bristles glow stronger. It is older. I know it.

A message arrives in my mind and I know it has come from this extraordinary creature. 'We can help you if you can help us. We can trade.'

'You knew my mother and brother.' For some reason this thought matters more to me than all others.

'Yes.'

'You didn't help them.'

'We can help you.'

'Is Jem still on the physical plane?'

'Yes.'

I breathe through this, needing to stay calm to hold the connection, though my inner smile has escalated my vibration.

'He needs help. We can help you,' the being says.

'Is he in trouble? Injured? How can you help?'

'We will meet on Nattalia. Here. You will come.'

'Do you have a name?' I think this at the same time as its name arrives in my mind and I'm not sure which came first, the question or the answer.

'Your brother gave me a name. Tasma.'

'Tasma,' I repeat.

Help. Find Tasma. So that's what Jem had meant in that long-ago whisper to me. He wanted me to find this being. Jem had named it Tasma, after our old animatronic. He must have liked and trusted it to give it that name.

'Come here. We help you, you help us.'

My visit to Nattalia is over.

I wake up. All that's in my ears is the urgent buzzing of my nano-band.

I want to go back to sleep and travel again, but my nano-band won't stop buzzing and I'm trembling in a cold sweat. My fingertips are red raw as though I was pulling in static from the air. I feel dazed, fatigued, and shaky.

Dad and Neath are not in the room. Ray-Ray is lying by my side, his tail wagging gently to indicate it has sensed my attention. He watches me, waiting for a command.

A knock on the door startles me.

'Come in.'

Ray-Ray sits up and his eyes turn to the door protectively. I'm in a sparkly blue night shirt with thin straps. My hair, long and no longer green after four years without reprinting, is its lacklustre chestnut colour. The smile I'm wearing is broad and ecstatic.

'Hibernation suits you then?' Cal comments, his face at the door. 'We're preparing for our hyper-flight to Nattalia. You're meant to be on the flight deck. All interns have been called. Your nano-band...'

'It's buzzing.'

'Yes, for at least twenty minutes.'

'It has been?' I'm impressed that I could still astral travel while that irritating thing was vibrating at my wrist.

'Britta? Are you okay?'

I want to tell him. I should. I hesitate, wanting to be absolutely sure, though I know what I heard, what Tasma said. Can I trust its word?

'Need help getting up?'

'No. I'm right. I'm good. I'll come.'

'Did you... see Jem again?' Cal looks hopeful.

'No. But I think he might be still with us.' The happiness in my voice is contagious and Cal starts grinning too.

'Why don't you get dressed? I'll wait outside and walk you to the deck. You can tell me on the way.'

I tell Cal about my earlier vision of Mum and her quest to find a weapon, as well as my trip to the other side of Nattalia and the beings that are there.

'Jem is okay.' Cal is joyfully relieved on this point.

'Still lost and in need of help, but yes. He's alive.'

'And you think these beings have a weapon to trade? That's why Jem went there?'

'It's possible.'

'But you say they are not of the physical world. That you lifted to a higher plane to see them.'

'No. I saw the small ones. They were definitely standing there. The taller one, I had to use my higher sight.'

'I suppose you plan to astral travel there again and ask more questions?'

'Yes, of course. Jem wanted me to find this Tasma. It can help.'

'Just... just be careful.' We stop walking and Cal looks at me intently. 'If they are astral beings, we don't know what they're capable of. If your brother and mother interacted with them and then... you know. I don't want you taking any risks. Promise me you won't.'

Warmth flows from him and wraps around me. I'm surprised by it.

'I'll stay safe,' I say. 'And thanks. Thanks for caring.'

I look at him then, really look at him. Coming out of hibernation, he seems a little flushed and slightly leaner, but mostly unchanged, yet I'm more aware of him in relation to me. For instance, I'd never noticed before how if I were to lean in and lower my head, my face would rest neatly against his upper chest and tuck in beneath his chin. If I were to tilt my head up, I would, at a stretch, manage to prop my chin upon his shoulder. We are the perfect heights for each other and all the angles are right. We seem to be made for each other... we fit.

'Of course I care. Your Jem's sister.'

The reference to Jem stings a little. I want him to care for me, not just because of my relationship to his friend. I'm jolted by how much I want this. I smile, trying to hide the tinge of sadness my longing is creating. After all, he is not just Jem's friend to me. For a long time, I've felt we are meant to walk together and perhaps have walked together before, hand in hand, soul to soul. Can't he feel it too?

These thoughts torment me as we resume our walk, shoulder to shoulder. Last to arrive on the flight deck, we are handed weighted vests, steel mesh caps, and anti-nausea tablets. Cal straps in beside me, and while his presence is a comfort, he soon lapses into a troubled silence.

'You okay?' I ask just before the countdown to hyper-speed.

'Not really.'

'Your parents?' I guess.

He nods. 'I'm not looking forward to being reunited with them after sixteen years of abandonment. You could say I'm not exactly anticipating a welcome home party or anything.'

Ten, nine, eight...

The ship starts to tremble. A computer beeps and Moro slams forward a lever, thrusting us into hyper-drive.

I'm shoved back and struggle to breathe against the sudden pressure on my chest. Every inch of my body tightens, clenches, and shakes apart. My brain rattles. Squinting through half-open lids, I look to the front and see we are shooting through space, lights streaking around us. I close my eyes, blocking out the disorientating assault. If it weren't for the anti-gravity buffers, we would be flattened like pancakes under the immense G-forces. It seems a full hour goes by until, at last, the jolting and rumbling settles and, after a long while, peters out.

My senses feel fried and my muscles are exhausted from pushing back on the pressure.

'Now what?' I manage to ask, finding my voice.

'Now we cruise at high speed for a couple of days. We're free to walk around. We'll strap back in for deceleration. Next time your nano-band buzzes, get up here, all right? Excuse me a moment.'

Cal leaves me all too quickly and joins the immaculately dressed Garth and the elastic Tilly, who is in that moment showcasing her flexibility by holding her ankle with her hand in a high leg stretch. Tilly swing-drops her leg on his approach and the trio comfortably launch into rapid conversation. I wonder what he has to share with them so intensely and I can't help wondering if he's telling them about the weapon and Jem and, for some reason, hope that he isn't. I've told him those things in confidence, though I didn't tell him to keep it secret. Surely, he knows that information isn't for open discussion? Tilly laughs and Garth snorts with amusement. I relax. They couldn't possibly be talking about asteroid-blasting weapons. What then? I feel excluded. Stupid. I'm not part of their group and can't expect to be after such a short time among them. Cal will invite me to join him when he feels like it, I think, and I try to catch his eye, as though this is a likely eventuality. But the three move off and leave the deck together. Cal doesn't look back at me. He's dismissed me and it hurts. It shouldn't. Come on, I tell myself. He's got a lot to think about. We've all got a lot to think about.

* * *

I drag my busy mind and somewhat injured heart around with me over the next couple of days. I avoid Dad and Neath. I'm not ready to tell them about my almost certain belief that Jem is alive. Almost certain isn't enough and I'm afraid of giving them false hope. Avoiding them turns out to be easy. Dad has patients on board to tend to—many passengers didn't cope with the shift in acceleration and the droids have given him permission to administer anti-nausea medication. As for Neath, he's proven himself popular among the girls and is constantly in the company of one or several.

It isn't just Neath or Dad that I avoid. Future uncertainty means I'm hounded by people wanting to know their fate. People stop me wherever I am, asking for advice. I shake my head at them and scurry away. I don't want to tune into them. I could, and maybe I should, but I'm scared. Seeing is easy. Telling is hard. I've never been good at the telling. Good news is fine. It's the bad news—not that I'm expecting to see bad news for everyone. I just don't know what I'll see.

I thought Cal and I were a fit, but his dismissal of me doesn't make sense, and if I can't make sense of my own life and emotions, I don't feel qualified to be reading others.

Self-doubt, so much of it. I guess getting older means everything starts to seem more complicated and less clear. I don't like it. I want to shut down my thoughts and emotions and just listen to the tune of the universe. I want to hum with its chords and see the ebb and flow of negative and positive. I want to be a clear channel, pick up messages, and help everyone around me. But all I feel is lousy and frightened and useless.

Come now, I hear my mother's voice. These are troubled times and fear has become an ocean around you. You must learn to stay afloat without getting wet. My mother would say that. I wish I could float. I close my eyes to practise it, when my nanoband starts to buzz.

Time to decelerate. Nattalia is near.

I hurry to the flight deck, not just to be punctual, but because I haven't seen Cal for at least forty-eight hours and I'm keen to be with him again.

As I find my seat, Ray-Ray comes bounding in and slides over to me, his paws skidding on the recently polished floor.

'What are you doing here? You're not allowed up front.' I stand and reach for a handful of fur to guide him out.

'Too late to get him back.' I peer up and see Cal. His watchful gaze is on me, taking in my grey dress and silver leggings. His eyes come to rest on my face, which must show signs of stress and fatigue. He, too, appears tired and uptight, but his tone is kind. 'Just power him down and put him in the box under your seat. It's there for personal items.'

'Thanks. Good idea. Ray-Ray is a personal item of sorts,' I say, a little too quickly. Cal's presence is making me nervous. I bend and curse at my shaking fingers as I work to stow away my amiable pet. When I stand, I lock my hands behind my back and take a steadying breath.

'Need help with your vest?' Cal asks. Before I can reply, he holds it out and I find myself extending my arms to be dressed like a young child. His proximity is causing me internal havoc. How is he keeping his hands so still as he ties up my weighted vest? Oh yeah, his fingers are synthetic. They never shake, never give away nerves... Next, he puts on my cap, his hands brushing against my ears.

'Here.' He hands me medication. I chew it obediently. 'Let's strap in.'

Cal sits beside me. I'm pleased. He seems to want to be there. Without thinking, I tune into him. Lightning. I see an image of lightning cracking stone. A shock. He's got a shock coming to him. I look at him, wondering if I should say something.

He meets my troubled stare. 'What is it?'

'Nothing.' I don't want to tell him. I don't have to, do I? I look down and mutter, 'Just anxious.'

'Understandable, with Moro at the controls.' His quip at the commander's expense makes me smile and he smiles with me. My nerves relax a little.

Oblivious to our smiles, Moro counts us down and the ship is thrown into deceleration. I close my eyes through the merciless turbulence and become impatient for it to end. I start thinking of all the unpleasant experiences I'd prefer to endure than to go through this for another minute. My tolerance evaporates many times. I'm not coping, just suffering from the long, enforced exposure to high G-forces. At last, the shuddering stills. In the calm, all I can feel is my head throbbing and my neck aching. I reach behind to massage my sore muscles and glimpse beside me.

Cal's eyes are wide and searching, waiting for a clear view out the window. Artificial gravity gives it to us and, as space comes into focus, my eyes light up on the planet that my father describes as cursed: our family's black hole.

Nattalia.

It is a wondrous blue sphere surrounded by a light blue haze. A thick, perfect band of purple light rests against the blue: a planetary shield.

But it is not the shield or its three dazzling moons that has us transfixed.

The planet is orbited by unexpected objects. Spaceships, tens of thousands of them, of all shapes and sizes, stretching as far as the eye can see, all seemingly parked in space, waiting to land. The panoramic abnormality is both staggering and inherently disturbing.

'Earth ships. What are they doing? Why haven't they landed?' Moro blurts out.

The sight is as peculiar to him as it is to us.

No one responds.

'Some of these ships departed before us, at least five years ago,' Moro observes, using a magnifier to zoom in on the craft's names stencilled on their sides.

There is a series of beeps alerting the Aqulia crew to incoming messages. Long ago sent, we are only now receiving them as our ship comes within range of Nattalia's communication satellites. Moro swipes at a screen and a mini hologram rises from it.

It is the leader of the World Council, Mandon Allic.

His synthetic eyes are cold and hard within his angular, tattooed face. I sense the tattoos were meant to draw attention away from the red, unnatural eyes, but they have not achieved this.

Beep.

'If you are receiving this message, you have just arrived at Nattalia from Earth. On behalf of the World Council, I am alerting all ships that Nattalia has issued a no-landing policy. It will shoot down any that defy this order. We are trying to find out what's behind this preposterous hostile stance.'

Beep.

The hologram fades, then reloads.

'This is the World Council. We've learned that Nattalia's sudden opposition to incoming peoples from Earth is the result of a leadership change brought about by a violent coup. The new leader, Odell Granton, is an extremist with a history of political ambitions. We are holding an urgent meeting to discuss our response.'

Cal tenses. I glance sideways. Lightning; a shock.

Beep. It fades and reloads again.

'An update on the status at Nattalia. Thousands of Earth's refugee ships are running low on supplies. Most were not equipped for a long standoff. Many are reporting critically low levels of oxygen and water. We will begin transferring those at risk to the better equipped hyperdormal ships, but that is not a sustainable solution. We are considering our options. War is among them. To the crew of the Aquila Forty-nine, as soon as you receive our communications, make contact. We've learned that the son of Nattalia's new leader is a member of your crew. We request his counsel at once.'

All eyes turn to Cal, who has been looking increasingly uncomfortable. My heart lurches in sympathy for him. This is the lightning. This is the shock.

The hologram fades out and stays out.

'Cal Granton,' Moro bellows. 'It appears your father has given himself quite the promotion. Seems he's now the new and somewhat hostile leader of Nattalia. What's your relationship with your father? Any chance you can talk him into some peaceful concessions such as letting thousands of ships land? War is not an option that I favour.'

'You heard the Council. My father is an extremist. He can't be reasoned with. We don't have a relationship.'

'In that case, we could be up for a battle that none of us are ready for.'

'Oh, trust me. My father is ready,' Cal replies.

I try to rest my hand on his arm, but he moves away abruptly. Unstrapping and flinging down his weighted vest and cap, he flees the many watchful eyes, his almost tangible shame and embarrassment trailing behind.

'You are all dismissed. I'll contact the World Council and let you know the outcome later,' Moro says. I hear tiredness in his voice.

Although I have an urge to chase after Cal to see if he's okay, I decide I'm better off learning what the World Council wants of him. I wait until most have left the deck, then make my way over to our commander.

'Excuse me, sir, if it's all right with you, I'd like to stay. Cal's been good to me and he's a friend of my brother's. I'd like to hear what the Council has to say.'

Moro glances at me. 'Are you not in your mind, intern? No way. Dismissed means everyone. Go.'

Annoyed, I turn to leave, then remember Ray-Ray. He can listen for me. I hurry back to my seat and bend down, opening the storage box. Quickly, I turn his audio recorder on, being careful to press 'new record' so I don't delete the stored one of Mum's voice. I leave Ray-Ray in sleep mode and slam the box lid shut.

Moro glances my way. I shove my hand in my waist belt as though I've just retrieved a personal item from the box and make a slow show of taking off my weighted vest and cap. Impatient, he snaps, 'Dismissed is a command that has immediacy to it.'

I don't retort but scurry out, feeling satisfied that the commander is unaware of Ray-Ray's presence. I wait just beyond the cabin. It is a long wait, but at last Commander Moro exits and I can gain access.

Nervously, I enter and hurry to the box. I flick Ray-Ray's switch at the back of his neck. He pants into life.

'Come on, boy. Let's go.'

He follows me out, trotting at my feet. I return to our room and make the black and white pet sit and look at me. I can't help but give him a cuddle before turning on the recording device.

'Let's hear what you've got there, boy.'

'Commander Moro reporting in. Aquila Forty-nine is in Nattalia's orbit. We've received your communications and are dismayed to learn of the current state of affairs. Cal Granton is among us and has been informed of his father's new status.'

'Good. An escort will be dispatched to collect him. We require him here.' I recognise the voice that blasts from the speaker. It is Mandon Allic himself.

'I believe the father and son have been estranged for some time. Of what use do you think he'll be?'

'That is for us to decide. But I don't mind telling you that we believe he'll be very useful when we send him to Nattalia to meet with his father and initiate peace talks. We expect he'll be granted passage through the planet's security shield. If nothing else, we hope he'll be able to establish his father's motives and, perhaps, some terms.'

'And if his father doesn't give him passage?'

'Then we know there's no chance of negotiation and we go to war.'

'We are not equipped for battle. We came here on a pro-development mission. We are civilian ships,' Moro points out.

'EASA's officers and interns are well represented amongst us, and we have thousands of droids and over a hundred fighter ships ready to be deployed. If it's war he wants, we'll give him war.'

I feel my blood run cold. War.

'And the planetary shield? How successful will our assault be against such a defence?'

'We're working on a way to dismantle it. Your young Granton might be useful in that regard when he gets down there.'

'If he gets down there.'

'Our psycho-assessments say Odell Granton will let his son land.'

'You won't send him down alone.' There is concern in Moro's voice and I'm touched by it. He cares.

'I'd rather he had company. The more eyes we can get down there, the better. I'm sure we can convince Odell that his son needs the assistance of others to land his craft.'

'He has a squad here; one he trained with. Would you consider them for the mission?'

There is a prolonged silence before Mandon responds crisply, 'Certainly. I trust your recommendation better than anyone's. Tell Granton and this squad to pack light. We're on our way to collect them.'

The hologram monitor beeps and I know the call has been terminated.

* * *

I order Ray-Ray to return to our room and I go in search of Cal. I need to tell him what I've learned so he can prepare to be dispatched as a peace negotiator to Nattalia. I ride the glass tube from level to level, asking people if they've seen him, but they brush me off. They are hurrying to catch the latest news coming through the hologram communicators. As I walk the corridors, I see through open doors, people gathering around Moro, appearing as a grim-faced three-dimensional projection. I catch enough keywords to know that he's informing the passengers of our predicament. I hear groans, curses, even a few sobs.

Reeling from the news of the asteroid, they were hoping Nattalia would provide a safe-haven; a place of comfort to help deal with the devastating loss of Earth. Now that we can't land, our own situation has become dire. Fear fills the halls, flows out, engulfs everyone, and before Moro has finished, whispers of war can be heard.

I quicken my steps. Where's Cal gone? I message him through my nano-band, telling him I need to see him urgently, but he doesn't respond. I message him a few times, stressing that I have information he needs to hear. He doesn't come back to me. Obviously, he's shutting me out. After covering most of the ship, I give up the search and turn my focus to packing. I'm going with him. I don't know at what point I made that decision, but I know I have to go. I have to be part of the squad accompanying him. He'll need me.

I visit the storage area, enter my password, and begin to pull out my clothes and some practical boots. In my haste, my childhood doll falls out and lands at my feet. I can't help but take a moment to marvel that it has stayed with me for so many years. I pick it up and turn it over, remembering being small and playing with it. By swiping its belly, I could make the doll laugh... such a bubbly, contagious laugh. I would swipe it over and over and over, just revelling in the joyous sound. It's been a long time since I heard the doll laugh, myself laugh, Mum and Jem... I miss the sound and the sensation of it. I pine for it.

But the doll is broken. Everything feels broken. *The darkness is broken*, I say in my mind.

I hold this thought for a long time.

Many minutes later, I shake off the self-indulgent melancholy that has descended over me and, putting the doll back in the box, decide that there's nothing wrong with being serious given the current circumstances.

Carrying my things, I make my way back to our room, only to walk in on an argument.

'You can't stop me,' Neath is shouting at Dad. I've never seen him so worked up.

'Stop you from what?' I ask. Ray-Ray bounds over and I pat him absently, my eyes taking in Neath's livid expression.

Dad raises a brow at him. 'Not going to answer your sister?'

Neath is breathing hard, like a bull snorting air before a ramming charge.

Dad shakes his head. 'You're more scared of her reaction than mine.'

'I'll tell her,' Neath fumes. 'I want to sign up.' He is not looking at me now.

'Sign up...?'

'He means—' Dad starts.

'I'll tell her. Moro told us about Nattalia. How we can't land. He said the World Council already has an army prepared. They are asking us to put our name down to join it, in case of war. The ship's droids will soon go door to door.'

I am stunned at how quickly they are mobilising to conscript fighters. They sure don't like to waste time. We've not had a chance to process our situation and yet already they are planning to send the droids to prepare a roll of walking dead. Neath wants to be on that roll. He wants to fight. This jolts me. A protective surge pours from my heart. Stay calm, I think. Stay calm. Opposition will only make him more determined.

How to respond? I do the first thing that comes to mind.

I laugh. A mirthless, ugly laugh—more like a hysterical chuckle.

Completely taken aback, Neath glares at me. 'Are you laughing right now?'

'Trying to.'

'Why?'

'Because I'm tired of not laughing and this war will only drag out our misery. You can't do this to us, Neath.'

'I'm not doing it to you, but for you.'

'Are you? For us? Odd way of looking at it.'

'They need to start training people for battle. They say the World Council is going to try to negotiate peace terms, and if that fails we have to be ready.'

'They have enough droids to wage battle,' I state.

'Droids can pilot the ships but they need people to deploy the weapons, to fight on the ground.'

I grind my teeth in frustration. 'There's a planetary shield! You won't get on the ground.'

'Why would you want to do that?' Dad asks, looking sadly bewildered.

'Why do you think?' Neath shouts. 'Didn't you hear Moro? We have limited supplies. Earth is about to be destroyed. Other space colonies are already full and refusing to take more. We have nowhere to go but to Nattalia and some sociopathic new leader won't let us land! They are just going to stay down there in paradise and leave us up here to die. Who does that?'

I know precisely who, but don't say it.

'Britta, tell him not to do this,' Dad says, appealing to me.

I take a deep breath, force myself to stay calm, and gaze softly at Neath. My sight softens and I am shocked to see an image of him surrounded by flames. No. An explosion flashes between us and I feel heat. When the image fades, I hear Neath ranting.

'After Moro's news, I talked to an EASA officer. If we try to land, the Nattalians will shoot us down. There are neutron particle guns on standby. They are all around the planet's capital and across the settlements and there's a planetary shield. If we can just shut down that shield we could get close enough to pound those guns. Our ships have missiles, bombs, gamma photon guns. We thought we'd need them in case of alien encounters, but if we have no choice, we can annihilate the Nattalian capital in a few days. And I say let's give it to the selfish pigs.'

I'm thrown by Neath's anger. The red in his cheeks has spread to his neck and his lips are moist with fury's spittle.

'Calm now, son,' Dad says. 'When has war ever settled anything? We come here in peace. Those are our people on that planet and there will be support on the ground for our cause. We just have to hope our supporters can overthrow this self-appointed leader.'

'Has history taught you nothing? Did you not study the Deadly War? Waiting is the worst thing we can do. Besides, the Nattalians would never revolt. Who do you think lives on Nattalia? These are the families of the rich. The kind that has had everything served up to them all their lives. There's not a fighter or rebel amongst them. They are the takers, the entitled. They are the system! If you're relying on them, we're dead.'

'Nattalia was settled through a lottery,' I say. 'They were just lucky enough to win the right—'

'Britta, please! It was the most rigged lottery in our history. Ever looked at the demographic of the winners?'

I shake my head. I knew there was some rigging, but there had to be some real winners, weren't there?

Dad exhales tiredly. 'Rigged or not. Entitled or not. They don't deserve to be bombed. Don't forget, it's in our interest to keep Nattalia in one piece.'

Neath crosses his arms defensively. 'So, what do you propose? We just wait here until we die?'

Dad and I don't answer. It is then that Neath notices the bundle of clothes and boots in my arms.

'What are those for, Britta? Going somewhere?'

It's my turn to squirm. My turn to defend my actions. 'I'm going with Cal to the ship of the World Council.'

Dad pales. I didn't know he still had more colour to lose. 'You can't leave us now,' he says, his voice high with panic.

'They want Cal and a squad to go to Nattalia to begin peace talks with the rogue leader.'

Dad looks slapped. 'You... Peace talks?'

'Yes.'

'No.' Dad looms over me and grabs my hand. 'You stay. You both stay. I didn't come all this way to watch you both die. If you want to die so much, we should have stayed on Earth.'

'There's still a chance for Earth, maybe even still a chance for Jem, if I go to Nattalia,' I say. I meet his eyes, wanting my words to sink in.

'What's this about Jem?' Then harsher, 'Are you saying you're going after the weapon? Are you crazy? It's too late.'

'So everyone keeps saying,' I say, plunking down my clothes. 'Can't you please just trust me and believe in me and... let me go.'

'I let your mother go. And Jem.' Dad's voice breaks, tears gather.

Guilt lowers my gaze.

'Let her go,' Neath says, suddenly passionate. 'We know her gifts. If there's any hope she can find Jem or reach a peace deal, we should not stand in her way. If she brings peace, I won't have to fight.'

Dad releases my hand and turns his back. He's upset.

'I don't want Neath to fight,' I say. 'Neath, I've seen—'

'Stop,' he says, holding up a hand. 'I don't want to hear it.'

'You need to hear—'

'No.' Neath is adamant. 'You and Jem and Mum all had gifts. Dad's a healer. What am I? Nothing. This is my turn to do something real, to count for something. Let me have a heroic moment. Just one.'

Quiet descends as we consider our fates. The love between us only adds momentum to our fear.

When Dad speaks, it is with stern conviction. 'I don't want you to go, Britta. If you go, it's against my wishes. Same goes for you, Neath. No son of mine will be a soldier of war. You both know how I feel.' Dad looks to Ray-Ray. 'Come. Let's walk,' he says to our pet. When Ray-Ray leaps to his feet and joins him at the door, Dad glances back at us. 'At least someone in this family listens to me.'

The door shuts with a thud as he leaves.

Neath looks at me. 'If you don't stop the war, I will join the battle.'

I know there will be war. I've seen it. Neath's fate is sealed. 'You join it. You die,' I say. I was determined to tell him. As much as I don't like to deliver bad news, this is different. I don't want to lose him. Yet I can't help but feel sorry and guilty as shock widens his eyes. He recovers too soon. The desire to be usefully heroic fires up his courage. 'An honourable death then,' he puts to me. 'Goodbye, Britta.'

He walks to the door and it opens. My chest heaves with pain. Is this it? Is it really goodbye for us? 'Neath, you have to listen to me. You fight, you die.'

'Nice try. And we always thought Jem was the protective one. Love you too.'

'I'm not...'

He slips out and the door shuts. I'm in a confused state. I'm overwhelmed by sadness as though I'm already remembering his death, feeling the grief. And there's nothing I can do about it. I just have to know it, carry it, and fight against a future I've already seen. Surely, it's a battle I can't win?

I don't run after him. He has heard me, been warned. He knows I speak the truth. Surely, he knows I wouldn't make that up just to protect him?

I reach for my tube and start packing it.

CHAPTER TEN

I'm the first to arrive at the docking bay. The World Council carrier is there, waiting to pick up Cal and his squad.

Commander Moro strides from the elevator, taking me in. 'Didn't you get the message? No one's going to Nattalia.'

'Except for Cal and a selected few.'

'Did your boyfriend tell you that or are you finally using your gifts?'

'He's not my... it doesn't matter how I know. I'm going. You will accept my application to join them.'

'Must be one of your less accurate predictions. You're not going, intern. You're too fresh.'

His arrogance gives me pause, but I suck up what courage I can and push on. 'I'll tell you why I'm going. I know there's a species on the unsettled side of Nattalia with a weapon powerful enough to blow an asteroid off course. You need me to go down there to get it. Earth needs me to go down there to get it.'

'A weapon?' I've got his interest. I see his mind digesting the information, mulling it over. 'How would you know? Even if there was... it's too late...'

'No, it's not.'

'The asteroid is due to slam Earth in four months.'

'We have use of the Hatch.' I throw this at him without knowing where the idea has come from.

'What? The Hatch? Are you insane? Do you not understand... the Hatch is a transporter! It facilitates jumps in space by tearing a hole in it and we make use of it without fully understanding how we're even doing it. You really want to put an alien weapon through that? What if it explodes while going through the tear? What could that do to the fabric of our universe? You know nothing of science. Just give up. It's too late. Accept it. I have. We're stuck out here, with nowhere to go except to war.'

'A pessimistic view.'

'I'm a realist.'

'Well, I'm a visionary and it's not how I see it. I'm going down there.'

Moro stares, his frustration evident. 'That side is not safe. I strongly advise—'

'I know. It's good advice. But with eight billion lives at risk, why should you care about a risk to mine?'

Moro doesn't have a response to that. Cal walks into the bay, flanked by Garth and Tilly.

I catch my breath. He looks striking. Anger has given him a harder edge, a stronger gait.

He gazes at me without the same spike in admiration. His expression is one of guarded bafflement that rapidly switches to displeased annoyance. 'What are you doing here with that pack?'

Moro glances between us. 'So, he didn't tell you. How then?'

'I'm a psychic intern,' I remind him smartly. 'And I'm going, aren't I, Commander?'

Moro issues a definitive nod. 'Yes, she is. She's got a point. Her life isn't that important in the scheme of things.'

'What?' Cal is shocked. 'She's not coming with us. Her life does matter and I won't have it put at risk.'

His words fly at me, lifting my spirits. He cares. He just said as much!

'You're being kind,' I say, trying to keep the adoration out of my eyes. 'But it's my life and I'll risk it how I like.'

'Commander?' Cal says appealingly, wanting to bring the feud to an end.

'You two can argue about it on board. The World Council is waiting.'

Five tall, human-like droids decked out in red armour are standing by the carrier. They have the symbol of the World Council, the blue and green sphere, tattooed on the back of their bald heads.

'Board now,' one of them says.

Furiously, Cal follows their command and walks up the ramp into the carrier. Garth and Tilly struggle to keep up with him.

I look at Moro. His eyes lock with mine and I feel him willing me to succeed.

'Good luck, Tate. Give it all you have. Sadly, you're all Earth's got going for it. I'd rather an army backed by a scientific solution, but who knows, hey?'

* * *

Seated on the carrier, Cal refuses to look at me.

I understand his anger. It is not really intended for me. He is concerned that I'm joining them, but not furious. His fury is for his father and for the shame his father's actions are bringing on him and that much anger and angst must go somewhere. Right now, I'm an easy target. I don't mind. Better for him to scowl at me than to implode.

Looking out a side window, I watch the steady approach of a mammoth ship shaped like a pyramid—the little Egypt of space.

Cal leans forward. 'This is as far as you'll go. You'll stay on that ship,' he whispers urgently, pleadingly. 'I know what you're thinking, that I'm your ride to getting down to Nattalia and that you'll go around to the other side to find those aliens and talk trade; but it was too dangerous for Jem and your mother so it's too risky for you. It's too late. You have to accept it and give up.'

I don't say anything. I don't want to feed an argument.

* * *

A couple of hours later, we skirt the base of the pyramid and roar in to a wide landing bay. A few more minutes and we put down. We are met by dozens of red-armoured droids and led through sterile corridors to a compartment. It is mostly a room of round silver cushions on a tatami mat. It smells fresh, like clean straw and lemon.

A large, buxom woman is leaning by a far window and straightens as we enter. I know her. I recognise her from our encounter on my first day at EASA. Treesa Breenswick.

'Welcome, come in. Be seated and at ease,' she says in greeting. 'Best you wait at the door, outside,' she says to the droids, which stride back out on her command. She has an animatronic with her. It's a large bird, as large as an owl, though slightly slimmer, with a pure white face and body, and black wings that contrast startling with its snowy feathers. Its eyes are half black, half blue and it has a sharp, pointed beak and fierce talons. The magnificent pet is perched on the window ledge.

I do as our host requests and sit on a cushion between Tilly and Garth, though it is hard to be at ease in the circumstances.

'Nice to have you along, Miss Tate. I did not expect you,' Treesa says.

Being sensitive to the fact that Cal doesn't share her view, I respond simply by giving her a cordial smile. Cal, who is yet to take a seat, rubs his fist over his chin.

Treesa senses his irritation and puts to him, 'You'd rather she not be here?'

I'm impressed at her perception and bluntness.

'I prefer she wasn't,' he's quick to confirm.

Treesa weighs up the tension between us and decides it needs addressing. 'All right. Let's hear from both of you. State your case and I'll decide the matter here and now and that will be the end of it. Understood?'

I nod, in awe of her power.

'Yes. Understood,' Cal replies respectfully.

'Cal, you begin.'

'All right, I will. Miss Tate is just an intern. Her brother was a friend of mine, Jem Tate, the officer who's gone missing.'

'Yes. I know of him,' Treesa says, staring at Cal with absolute absorption.

'I believe her reason for going to Nattalia is to investigate her brother's disappearance. She's…' He hesitates. I see the direction of his thoughts and know he's about to reveal what I've told him in confidence; at least he hesitates. 'She's astral travelled to the other side and is aware of a species there, one that could have a weapon; a weapon powerful enough to knock an asteroid off course.'

Tilly and Garth frown. They are not sure what to make of it. I see they're struggling with Cal's acceptance of my intelligence obtained by paranormal means.

In deep, Cal pushes on. 'Britta thinks Jem was drawn to this species to negotiate a trade for the weapon and his disappearance is associated with that. So, the last thing I want is for an intern to head into territories she knows nothing about and go down the same fated path as her brother. She's not interested in talking peace with my father. She just wants to put her life at risk to go after her brother. I propose that once we deal with my father, I be put in charge of a mission of going after Jem Tate.'

'Your friend. Yes,' Treesa says absently before eagerly switching her focus to me.

'All right, Miss Tate. Your case.'

I am indignant that Cal has revealed all that I told him without my permission. He may have done it to protect me, but I wasn't ready to inform EASA about my knowledge of the weapon.

'Britta?' Treesa prompts, searching my eyes with an urgent thirst for knowledge.

'Cal is wrong. I want to go to Nattalia to help protect him, to talk peace so that my younger brother won't have to go to war on the frontline and die, so that my father won't perish on a ship when it runs out of supplies. Do I want to secure a weapon to save Earth? Do I want to find my brother? Of course I do. But I don't want either of those missions to fail.'

Treesa is watching me closely. 'You want to protect your loved ones, of course. But a weapon, if there is one on that planet, could save billions of loved ones. Getting the weapon ought to be your priority. Are you in talks with these beings?'

I gaze into her eyes and float into her memories. When I emerge, I feel let down. 'You've been waiting a long time for me to make contact with them, haven't you? That's been it? That's what you trained me for.'

'I couldn't tell you,' she says. 'You don't understand. There are ears on every ceiling, around every corner, in every droid. Not everyone is on our side, not everyone can be trusted. By not telling you, I've kept you safe.'

I think of Jem and the droid that had turned on him on his ship, a droid he had trusted. Not everyone is on our side...

'Safe!' Cal shouts. 'You're going to send her down there, aren't you? An intern! You're going to send her to her death.'

'Talk of this can't leave this room.' Treesa suddenly slips a rod from her belt and points it at two drones attached to the ceiling. With two quick beeps the drones start to disintegrate and the acrid stench of burning chemicals fills our nostrils. The bird darts into the air, flapping its extensive wings, and collects one of the drones with its efficient beak. Treesa swipes at her nano-band a couple of times and a floor tile peels back revealing a yawning hole. The bird drops the drone into the chute and repeats the process with the other drone.

The tile slides back into place and the bird returns to its perch.

None of us say a word. Destruction of drones is a criminal offence attracting a harsh life-long prison sentence. I can hear Garth and Tilly breathing hard next to me. The fact that the head of EASA is believing every word I say has them questioning everything they know and believe.

Treesa turns to Cal. 'I understand your concerns, but you will be with her down there, able to guide and protect her, and you must confess that her gifts might prove useful in your talks with your father. She would be an asset to your team.'

Facing all of us, she continues, 'Council droids will assist with your launch. The Red Vipers, I call them. Be careful as to what you say in their presence. As I've said, it's impossible to know who to trust and too much is at stake as you know.'

Her eyes fall to me. 'Britta, what will these species trade for the weapon?'

I cast a sidelong glance at Cal. His eyes are dark with rage. He sees that by sharing the information, he has not stopped me from going to Nattalia but assured my passage down there.

'I don't know yet. They want to meet me on Nattalia. They want to help.'

I see her hopes rising. 'You will meet them. Do what you can to finish your brother's and mother's mission.'

'How's she meant to do that?' Cal asks.

'With your help.'

'If my father doesn't kill us first.'

'You need to make sure he doesn't.'

'I can't...'

'You have no choice,' Treesa says, cutting him off. 'You have your mission. Yes, it's risky, but Britta is now our only chance and I'm going to do everything in my power to see she has a shot at it. I expect you to support her in that. Do I have your word that you'll have her back?'

Cal's face is impassive. He nods.

'Good. Now, I'd like to speak to you alone. The rest of you go to your rooms, freshen up, eat some nutritional bars, and get a few hours' sleep.' Treesa fixes Cal an intent look. 'We need to know everything you can remember about your father.'

Cal goes rigid. It is not a task he will enjoy. I feel for him.

The door slides open and the Red Vipers appear.

'Escort our guests to their rooms and see to their needs. I'll be speaking with Cal Granton alone.'

'Take care,' Garth says to Cal as we pass.

'Be strong,' Tilly adds.

Cal looks at me, sees my concern for him. 'Looks like you'll be joining us,' he murmurs.

I nod, feeling uncomfortable, wanting to say something apologetic.

He leans closer to me. 'I'm glad.'

Glad? Have I heard correctly? I search his eyes and see his expression is sincere. What's made him change his mind?

'I'm glad you're glad,' I mumble and give him a grateful look. 'Good luck with it.'

'Thanks. I'm going to need it.'

We leave and the door closes, leaving Cal to an interrogation of his childhood that he can't avoid.

* * *

Maybe it's because Cal accepted my placement on his squad, or maybe it's because I feel I'm getting closer to uncovering what happened to Jem and to helping him, or most likely a combination of all those things... but as soon as I close my eyes to grab a few hours' sleep, there is enough peace in my mind to be free of clutter, allowing my spirit to elevate out of my body and into the wild forests of Nattalia.

Orange and red leaves and tiny yellow flowers dance and swirl across the floor of the forest.

I hear a roaring, like a rolling sea, high above me. I peer up. The treetops are swaying, thrashing against each other; each flay spraying forth a shower of leaves, flowers, and crimson pods, which flutter down to join the vigorous wind-blown waltzes below. Some land and stick to my hair, eyelashes, and clothes. I close my eyes and feel light brushings against my cheeks.

Tasma. I call for it. I'm summoning the older one. I know it will come.

It quietens. The wind stops playing with branches, and the fluttering settles.

I blink my eyes open, relax my gaze as before, and wait. Tasma looms into view. It emerges from seemingly nothing, though in that moment it is not hard to imagine it has opened a door just a hairline crack and slipped out into ours from another secret world. The being, as delicate and beautiful as a paper lantern, hovers merely a stone's throw away. As well as the glow of its bristles, little balls of light are moving up and down its limbs as though it has swallowed dozens of glow flies, each one darting here and there in chaotic fashion, perhaps seeking doorways of their own.

I feel it waiting for me to ask and yet I'm sure it knows my question. In the end, I don't know who asks and answers first, but I hear, 'We will trade the weapon for a long-range ship and a droid.'

'The weapon is strong enough to break up an asteroid?'

'Yes. It will save your Earth.'

'Isn't it too late?'

'No.'

I let this information settle over me and enjoy the hope it brings.

'It won't be easy for me to travel to you. There could be war.'
I think this slowly and clearly and I watch the lights in Tasma's limbs fade to a low orange smoulder.

'War? What is it?'

A surge of shame floods through me as I realise I'm dealing with a species of peace that does not know of conflict.

In response, I don't think words. I think pictures of guns, explosives, radiation, plumes of chemical-laced smoke. I remember the historic images of the Deadly War; the shocking, wasteful, atrocities… Such cruel, undiscriminating acts, wreaking damage upon millions of people. My mind fills with fires, broken bodies, burning flesh, and screams.

When I stop, I see Tasma's tear-shaped eyes are sorrowful.

'Why war?'

I don't know how to reply. I remember Neath. I use his words to explain. We have to fight or die, he had said. I replay our conversation in my mind.

'Fight or die? Die fighting,' Tasma thinks.

'Yes. Many will.'

'Not you. You must come and trade. Help Jem. Help your planet.'

'Yes,' I say. 'I will. Somehow I will.'

'I will help you come. You will be safe.'

'Thank you.'

The lights within the being shine brighter until I am blinded by them. I close my eyes.

My lashes flick up. I'm in the confines of a capsule on the ship of the World Council and someone is saying my name. It's Cal.

'Britta, sorry to wake you. We have to attend a briefing. They want to send us straight down to Nattalia.'

I sit up and press fingers to my forehead. Ouch. I examine my fingertips. They look scraped and close to bleeding. As before, I've been drawing in higher energy through them. I edge out of the capsule and slide to the floor, coming face to face with Cal.

He looks imposing in his immaculate uniform, the black sheen of the fabric accentuating the darkness of his eyes. While his face is heavy with tiredness, he is buzzing with nerves. Like a sponge, I absorb his highly charged anxiety until I think it must be my own, and rapidly shake off my drowsiness.

Immediately self-conscious, I become aware of my clothes: olive green leggings, slim-lined boots, and a long, dusky mesh top. It's not a uniform but they're practical and comfortable. I run my fingers through my tangled hair.

'Ouch.'

'You're hurt?'

'Just sore hands,' I say, turning my palms inward against my sides, dismissing them. 'How did you go with Treesa?'

He reaches out and lifts one of my hands, turning it over in his large, synthetic palm. He notes the burn-like marks on the pads of my fingertips and looks at me inquiringly. My chest is rising and falling a little too obviously. His touch has affected me.

'It's nothing.' I slip my hand from his gentle grasp.

'You've been astral? To Nattalia?'

I hold his gaze, reluctant to speak of my latest encounter with Tasma.

An amused smile appears. 'You don't trust me. I get that. You know, your brother used to get sore fingers too.'

'He did?' I'm glad to hear it. It's normal for us then, I think.

'I was just trying to protect you,' he says. 'That's why I told Treesa. You know that, right?'

'I know.' I'm not angry. I understand. Still, I don't want to tell him about my burgeoning hope. I need to process it; feel forward on it. No point spreading hope without some sense of certainty.

He sees that I choose to hold my silence and exhales. 'Yet the trust is gone.' He is downcast. He rubs his palms to his cheeks in frustration. 'Britta, I didn't want you to come with us because... well, facing my parents is not going to be easy. I'm going to be distracted by it. It's going to mess with my head and in that state, I don't know if I can give you the protection you're going to need. I know what you're going to say. That you don't need it, and I get that. But what you don't know is that when Jem used to take me to his home on our pass days out, and you would follow us around, Jem would see my interest in you. And he told me...' Cal stops, looks uncomfortable and, breathing into cupped hands, holds my gaze and pushes on.

'He told me not to think of you like that, that I'm not meant for you. He saw you getting hurt and it happens with me at your side. He didn't want you near anything or anyone connected to EASA. He made that very clear. What I'm trying to say is, your psychic brother, my closest friend, told me to stay clear of you. And I... care too much, I... I've always cared too much. You're Jem's little sister and the girl who used to look at me and see me, like no one had before. I wanted to help you find Jem, of course I did. Your family was so good to me back then. Now the way things are going, I'm starting to get a sense of what Jem saw. You are getting in too deep into something you know nothing about and that can't be good. If your search for Jem gets you killed, I know for certain that Jem wouldn't want that. And I can't live with that, especially if it ends up being my fault.'

I can't move. His words are punching images and thoughts in my head and holes in my heart. Jem told him to stay away from me for my protection! That I can believe and it makes me furious. Just because he had a vision of something bad happening while Cal is with me doesn't mean it won't still happen if Cal is apart from me. Jem would know that. Some things are set in stone. What about my feelings? What about the fact that Cal and I had felt something for each other all those years ago! How could he do this? Interfering and using his insight to scare Cal away from me!

Cal cares! He said he cared about me and always has. That realisation trumps all else.

Encouraged, I decide to fight for us to be together, to be allowed to explore what could develop. I take a deep breath and launch, 'Cal. What Jem saw can't affect the choices we make. I could get hurt whichever way I turn, if pain is what I'm meant to experience. If I die, it will be because my time is up and that will happen regardless of who I'm with or where I am. It will happen anyway. Every choice I make is because it feels right to me at the time and I can't live my life any other way.' Breathless, I pause and inhale again. Trying hard not to let my voice shake, I state effusively, 'I don't want you to stay clear of me.'

Footsteps behind us quickly grow louder, then Garth and Tilly are in the room and bearing down on us. 'Come on. We're about to be briefed. Now.'

Cal and I are locked in an emotional maelstrom and Garth's words take a few seconds to penetrate.

Clearing his throat, Cal blinks his head clear and says softly to me, 'We've got to go.' He rests his hand to the small of my back. 'We'll talk later.'

I nod, desperately wanting that.

Struggling to get our heads back on our mission, we lag well behind Garth and Tilly, trailing them down a maze of corridors. Cal frequently glances sideways, and when I finally give him a smile, he is quick to return it.

'I've got your back,' he says.

The statement says a lot. It means he's not going to let Jem's prophecy dictate our future together. He's going to stay by my side and make sure I don't get hurt. I want to offer him the same support.

'You won't be facing your father alone. I'll be right there, you know.'

'Thanks, but he's going to see I'm not the kid he left behind.'

'We are meant to be engaging in peace talks,' I remind him.

He smiles impishly, and my heart leaps in response.

His hand lifts and squeezes my elbow. 'You know, Treesa was right when she said you were better off with me, where I can keep an eye on you. There's not a chance I'm leaving you here with droids coined the Red Vipers. I mean, I can see where she got the name.'

I'm laughing on the inside, when we take the corner and see Tilly and Garth waiting for us at a shiny steel door.

'Let's go in together,' Tilly says.

She puts her hand on it and it slides across. We enter. Inside the high-ceilinged white room are several Red Vipers.

We keep the door close behind us, standing as far from the Vipers as we can. We barely have time to gather our thoughts when Mandon Allic sweeps in from a rear entrance.

I'm stunned by his height and wonder if his legs as well as his eyes and hands are synthetic. Unnaturally tall, he fills the room easily, casting an air of intimidation. There's a coldness to him. His energy is dim, dark and insular. He is dressed in a similar fashion to the Vipers, only there is bulkier armour at his chest.

'Cal Granton,' he says, looking at him directly. 'Your father has, as we anticipated, given permission for you to land. However, he has stipulated you must land in Jucca, the planet's only capital city, and that your mode of transport must be a Sub-Scouter.'

I remember from my training that a Sub-Scouter is a slow cruiser. Its design resembles that of the first scuba diving helmets: bulky and round with thick shells. They are sluggish and awkward to navigate but useful for sightseeing in space.

'We'll be a dawdling target in that tourist contraption,' Cal says with apparent bitterness. His father continues to embarrass him.

'You are allowed a few people of your choosing to accompany you, but no droids. Odell was quite adamant on that point.'

'What should we do once we land?' I ask. I'm not comfortable addressing the head of the World Council and fight the urge to shrink beneath his fierce gaze.

'You will be met by Odell Granton's droid soldiers. It seems he was able to reprogram the city army to do his bidding. That's how he managed his coup. I don't know how this was even possible,' he says, his voice a low growl. 'But when you are delivered to him, you must find out what it will take to get him to shut down that shield and lower his guns so we can land.'

'What if his terms are not acceptable?' This question is posed bravely by Tilly and her face remains impassive as she becomes the focus of the leader's glare.

'If you stop asking questions, I will tell you,' he says. Each word is ground out like sandpaper swiping over stone. 'You will deliver his terms to us. We will decide if they can be met. If they can't be met, we will go to war.'

'While we are down there?' Garth asks, drawing the hideous gaze his way.

'Yes. If you can make your way back to your Sub-Scouter, you will have some protection from the bombing in that.'

'Bombs won't get...' Cal begins.

'I know,' Mandon shouts, spittle flying in every direction. 'I know the bombs won't get through the Nattalian shield. You,' he stabs his steel finger against Cal's chest, 'will find out the shield's power source and shut it down.'

Cal does not flinch, but my anger flares protectively. Mandon has no right to talk to Cal or any of us like this. He is full of demands, yet how does he expect us to achieve such an impossible mission? Before I have a chance to pose this question to him, he delivers the answer.

'You will have a concealed weapon. This.' Mandon holds up a small red chip between his long, plier-like fingers. 'Insert this into any of his droids, into their main computer, which you can access at their back of their necks. You will see a green chip in there.

You replace the green one with this. Then you will have control over the droid. You will have it show you how to shut down the shield, to help you gain access to it, and then you will command it to protect you while you do so. This you will do as soon as you can. Even before the peace talks. You do this at the first opportunity. Understood? You will have a chip each. You will all attempt to win over one droid. That way we'll have four chances of success. Got it? Green chip out. This one in. Shut down the shield. One of you... one of you has to get this job done.'

'Even before the peace talks,' I echo. 'So, no matter what the terms, you will bomb the city.'

Incensed by my highbrow tone, he aggressively closes the distance between us, standing so close now that our noses are almost touching.

I peer at his boring eyes quizzically as though his proximity is interesting rather than threatening, and I see him become unsettled. It is not what he expects. He expects me to cower.

'We will do what's necessary to protect millions of people.'

'By bombing millions of people.'

He stares at my throat. It feels so fragile, so vulnerable beneath that murderous glare. Then suddenly his red eyes lift. There's a change in his stance. 'You're Amelia Tate's daughter and Jem Tate's sister. You are one of the most psychically gifted EASA has ever trained. True?'

'I've been well trained.'

'Not well enough. You don't wear the uniform.'

'It didn't suit me.'

Mandon smiles on the inside. I feel it. It's more menacing than his glare.

'So Miss Tate, do we win the war?' He can't help but ask. He needs to know. I practically smile too, enjoying being in a position of power over him. I have something he wants: the outcome. And I know it. I've seen it. War. It's happened. All I'm doing now is remembering it. He sees that I know, sees that I see.

'Well?'

His impatience amuses me, but the future holds much sorrow. I pull myself upright. 'Many will die,' I begin, wanting to school him in the consequences of war. I feel a need to, yet he doesn't want to hear any of it.

'Do we win the war?' He shouts so loudly his breath hurts my eyes.

Concerned, Cal starts toward me though stops when I toss him a pleading look not to intervene.

Mandon's eyes zoom out, taking me in fully. 'Answer...'

'Yes. You will win this war. You will land on Nattalia.'

Those eyes can't display emotion, but I sense elation radiating from somewhere deep within. The self-satisfied leader turns away, barking at his obedient Red Vipers. 'See that they collect their things and take them to their craft. They are ready to depart.'

'Mr Allic, sir?' I say. I take a deep breath, for now I want something from him. He stands still but doesn't look my way. I push on. 'Do you know the whereabouts of my brother?'

I've taken him off guard. He hesitates, confused, then I sense his disgust. I don't think he's used to such audacity. He leaves me waiting for a few seconds, then dismissively says coldly over his shoulder, 'If you don't know, how are we supposed to know?'

He strides out, the door closes behind him, and the Red Vipers urge us to get moving.

CHAPTER ELEVEN

'So you really believe our mission will be a success, or did you just say that stuff to get Mandon off your back?' Tilly asks as we strap into the dark and dingy Sub-Scouter.

'It's not really a success if there's war,' I say and want to sigh. I know what the success will cost. I fear for Neath and my father and my crew. Strangely, I don't fear for myself. I remember Tasma saying I will be safe. Perhaps I'm believing in that.

'You believe the things you see really do happen? How can you be sure? I mean, how does it work?'

I can tell from Tilly's curiosity that she wants to believe, yet it is still a step for her. I don't regard her as a doubter. She's more in the camp of the undecided, waiting for something empirical to happen to convince her fully.

Cal, deep in concentration, suddenly gives us an insight into his thoughts. 'If my father managed his coup by reprogramming the droid army, it suggests a central control point. I say we win over one droid to help us gain command of the whole lot of them.'

'We don't need an army,' Garth says, sounding irritable. 'Let's just keep it simple. Get one to help us shut down the shield.'

Garth's dark eyes are bloodshot from lack of sleep. He seems overwhelmed.

'You all right?' Cal asks him.

He doesn't answer at first and Cal leans forward, forcing him to meet his eyes.

Garth regards Cal for a long time before saying, 'It's just... we can't fail.'

'We won't.'

'I know. That's what worries me. I don't want war.'

'Nobody does.'

'But we'll let down the shield and start the war. We will be responsible for all the fatalities that follow.'

'Responsible? Not personally,' Cal says, recalling his training. 'We have orders. If anyone is to blame for all this, it's my father.'

I want to say something to them, to help them prepare for what's ahead, and yet there are no words to offer. Can anyone truly prepare for war?

In the silence that ensues, I refocus my own thoughts. Getting the weapon ought to be my priority, Treesa had said. It suddenly seems the easier mission. All the higher species wants for it is a long-range ship and a droid; a simple, easy trade. Too easy? Why didn't Jem just return with it then? Where did he go? Perhaps the ship and droid are just part of a quest. Will they want me to fly that ship somewhere... like Jem did? My thoughts tumble around. I have to be cautious. Mum and Jem weren't. I have to learn from their mistakes. Make their actions count.

'We're approaching the shield,' Tilly says, sitting up. There's fear in her voice.

I look up. The shield is a bright band of light, purplish at its rim. I respect its power, its ability to disintegrate our craft and all our lives in seconds.

'Shouldn't it have turned off by now?' she asks, her anxiety escalating.

'My father's not going to take any chances of a fighter ship

THE HATCH

trying to slip in ahead or behind us,' Cal says. 'He's going to make this window real small. After all, a mistake will only cost him his son's life.'

We watch our ship edge closer to the shield. Its light fills our ship and we shield our eyes.

'Shut down,' Tilly says. 'Shut down.'

I take comfort in Tasma's promise to keep me safe. If I'm safe, my accompanying crew must be too. Still, I'm holding my breath.

'Come on,' I hear Garth mutter.

'It's not going to...' Tilly ducks her head and braces. Light washes us, blinds us.

'No,' I shout as the nose of our ship nudges the outer rim of the shield.

At that precise moment, the light evaporates.

Cal, keeping his head, reaches for the controls and slams on our thrusters, pushing our antiquated transporter to its limit. 'Go, go,' he mutters.

It feels like only seconds later, the light snaps back.

Tilly jolts against her straps with the fright of its sudden reappearance and exhales loudly as she realises we're through. We look at each other, our eyes wide, our chests still heaving with our lack of faith.

'That was tight,' Garth says, his hand trembling a little.

Cal curses under his breath. Irritated, he keeps himself busy and checks our position. 'Won't be long now before entry. This old bucket is pushing its limits. She's a little warm, holding though.'

I tighten my straps and adjust my weighted cap.

'Will your father... will he even meet with us, do you think?' Tilly asks, starting to wonder how our arrival will play out.

Cal shrugs. He's not sure. He doesn't know where he stands with his father after all these years.

As I consider his qualms, and the hurt behind them, I focus

on the meeting to come and let my thoughts drift. They seek out an image and usher it into my mind. While I'm not sure what I expected of the reunion between father and son, the image of Cal shaking hands with a man, a man of similar physical traits, is contrary to every other expectation I had. The handshake suggests a deal is being done.

The image is so clear and sudden, I'm startled by it and I shift in my seat.

'What is it?' Cal asks.

I don't know whether to tell him. Is he ready to consider such a pact is possible? That the talks could end in an accord?

'Britta, I know that look.'

'Let me guess... Jem used to get the same look?'

'Yes, he did. So? What have you seen?'

He wants me to trust him, his eyes are imploring me.

'Are you sure you want to know?' I say, trying to prepare him.

'Not really, but go on.'

'Okay. I've seen a handshake; an agreement with your father. You will reach a compromise with him.'

'Compromise! There can't be. He either turns off the shield and lets the ships land, or we do.'

He's angry; his muscles tense. I don't retort. There's no point. I'm used to people arguing against my insights. The future can appear stranger than anything they can imagine and what is strange can be frightening.

'I can't believe I'll agree to anything he proposes. He only thinks of himself. I'd never support him in shoring up his own power.'

I look out the side window and wait for him to let off steam. He rants for a few more minutes and I do not respond to any of it. After a long while, he exhales heavily.

'I'm sorry. You can't help it if that's what you saw. Are you sure?'

I face him, wondering again how to respond and decide just to give him a simple nod.

'Compromise. Him and me. Who'd have thought?' He's trying to accept it, trying to be open to the notion, and I see he is not entirely unhappy at the prospect.

'You can't actually be considering that's possible, just because she said she saw it?' Garth asks. His incredulous tone can't be missed.

Cal doesn't reply.

Garth and Tilly exchange a look. They are both not sure what to believe and are surprised that Cal is not being more sceptical, especially given the long, ongoing bitterness that exists between him and his parents.

I peer at Cal, wondering if he will come to my defence, whether he will at least try to convince his unit that my prophetic foresight is worth trusting. He remains quiet. Their opinions appear to matter to him. I guess they've known each other a while, shared a lot, and formed a friendship.

Still, I bow my head, disappointed.

Eventually, we enter the planet's atmosphere and before long we are hovering a few metres above uneven ground. Our awkward craft roars and descends, lifts, grumbles, descends. It does this throughout several false starts to land, dropping, then rising; a see-sawing of sudden motions. I feel queasy.

'Sorry,' Cal says, struggling to put down. 'Of all the transporters! All okay?'

'Been better,' I say.

There is a thud and my head jolts forward. I savour the stillness for a few minutes, while Cal and Garth check the craft's readings. 'All looks good.'

A round opening at the rear of our craft hisses open.

We're all eager to put a sky above us. I flick off my tight straps and roll my sweat covered shoulders, savouring the freedom of movement in my upper body. Swiftly, rising to my feet, I follow the others in a hurried shuffle and am the last to leap out, Cal holding out a supportive hand as I do.

Oxygen. I breathe it in hungrily. It's so sweet and fresh and plentiful.

'That's some nice air,' Cal comments, his voice soft and throaty against my ear. 'Not getting dizzy?'

'No.'

My eyes drink in our surrounds; we're in wonderland.

'Got your chip?'

Cal is keeping to the practical. Is he not affected by this beauty-draped environment? Are his nerves really blocking out such splendour? I can hardly breathe from astonishment.

'Britta, the chip?'

'Yes, I have it,' I mumble. It's tucked beneath my nano-band. I can feel it there, sharp and firm. I hope I won't need it. I want Cal's father to shut the shield down willingly.

'Well, we're here,' Tilly says, ogling our surrounds with such fascination that she can only manage to state the obvious.

We've put down in what looks like a field. Thick-bladed grass of pineapple yellow is pointing straight up like a spread of upright needles, yet it appears soft. The grassy opening is circled by trees—and what trees! Their black trunks lean against each other, reminding me of a crowd of people, all resting their arms on the shoulder of the person next to them. Their leaves are red and gold, and they are also covered in vine-like plants that creep across the canopies and drape in curtains of purple flowers. I guess they are flowers. They are pretty and round and decorate the vines like vibrant baubles.

'Have you ever...?' Tilly says breathlessly.

'This way.' Garth has quickly found his bearings, using his nano-band for geo-data, and leads the way. As we begin our trek through the grasses, the blades part, bending to allow our passage to avoid being trampled. I learned about it in my studies, though right now I can't recall if they sense motion or flex on first touch. It's stunning to behold this parting of the grasses and I find myself smiling delightedly.

'Over there. The trees aren't as close. Could be the entrance to a path,' Cal points out.

We go through the natural opening and seem to be upon a path, where branches are arching in the fashion of an alley. It's as though the trees have lifted their arms for a tall animal to pass. We walk in single file for a long while, content to breathe in air laced with sweet scents and a hint of salt, to feel the warmth of mild humidity and the sweeping of red and gold leaves beneath our boots.

We emerge from the hugging trees and halt.

'Zinga! Would you look at that!' Tilly cries.

We are on the sandy shore of a vast harbour, two suns shining down upon it. Bright orange arches traverse the waters; a spectacular bridge of amazing design. In fact, there are two bridges in our view—one above and one mirrored on clear waters. What is apparent on second glance is the weaponry affixed to the bridge's top arches: seca guns and box cannons that could be used to protect the city from air raids coming in over the sea.

Below the bridge are a series of jetties, long winding pathways that have been constructed in the shape of a fish. Silver and gold boats are tied to them.

Facing the harbour are green hills, dotted with little white stone houses. Each house has large round windows. The residents must wake to sea breezes and views of this beauty every morning, I think. How wonderful.

Paved paths link the dwellings and I see people walking along them. The women are dressed in long sweeping skirts of rich colours and prints. Their tops are short and show off their slender, bare waists. The men are mostly in red and orange saris, with hair tied back in ponytails. Their sun-baked arms and legs are thin and gangly, lacking tone; they are not labourers. Among them are philosophers, artists, academics, intellectuals—that is what the population of Jucca is known for.

The men and women converse casually with each other. I see laughter, a lightness of step. These people are happy and, abnormally, all beautiful. Of course, they are. Nattalia is renowned for providing its residents with free designer surgery, placing a high value on beauty. This charming population is well crafted and educated and catered for.

'They are like dolls, so pretty,' Tilly observes.

'And breakable,' Garth says, referring to their obvious lack of strength.

Tilly glances at him. 'But don't you think their fragility makes them adorable?' She looks back at the people, her eyes shining with idolisation.

'It is so quiet,' I say, lifting my eyes skyward. There's no air traffic here. How do the city folk get around? As soon as I pose this question, I see the answer. Green carriages are floating up and down the hills via cables, like the cable cars of old. They blend into the trees, coasting along silently. Other people are riding vehicles—four seats encased in a soft green shell on wheels. From what I can tell, they appear to be running on pedal power, and given the ease with which they are travelling uphill, I assume they are also tapping into solar power. No noise accompanies them, no pollution.

I breathe in the air and take pleasure in its salty scent.

The peaceful, sensory moment on that shore comes to an end all too quickly. Droids approach. They are genderless and without recognisable cultural traits. Their hairless faces have fine lines and feminine eyes but strong jaws and firm, straight lips. They have small, solid mounds for breasts above hard stomachs, straight hips and muscled arms and shoulders. Their skins are bronzed, their eyes almond-shaped, and their heads are bald and capped with domed helmets. Their uniform is of silver fabric. It stretches across their bodies like vinyl, though I assume it is tougher; hard to penetrate or burn.

'The city seems less fragile now,' Cal states, assessing this rigid army of manufactured force.

'Come with us.' A droid in the second row on the right has addressed us, indicating there is no apparent leader among them. When they turn as one to lead the way, we examine their necks; uncovered and exposed. If we manage to bring one down, we should easily be able to flick open whatever casing exists to insert a controlling chip.

I glance at Cal and see he is thinking the same. It won't be hard. All we need is an opportunity. Should we do it now?

Cal reads my expression and shakes his head. 'Too many,' he whispers.

We walk away from the harbour and along the streets of the pretty and clean city. The wide streets are tree-lined and beneath the trees are outdoor eateries. People are sitting at small tables covered in woven cloth and are sipping at tall drinks of various colours. They are chatting with lively eyes. What do they talk about with such animation? Men and women and even children —all ages, sitting around, eating and drinking. The food is unrecognisable, but the aromas stir my appetite. I long to try those soft parcels swimming in white sauces, those crispy looking flakes, those edible floral arrangements.

'Government House,' Garth says as we take a corner.

Before us is a hard sand path cutting through a field of shimmering white stones, leading up to a large, sprawling building of gleaming white rock and black-tinted glass. Its roof is covered in solar panels, battery packs, and steel communication studs.

Keeping watch are hundreds of droids. They stand side by side around the building's grounds. So still and erect are they that I imagine that from a distance the circle of guards could be mistaken for a silver fence.

We walk up the path and a huge iron door is pushed open to let us in.

My boots tread lightly over shiny floors. Above us are arched ceilings and solid beams and high beaded windows letting in natural light. We walk across the room, admiring mounted statues of animals and birds that are native to the planet. My studies had covered such creatures and I'm pleased to remind myself that despite their intimidatingly pointy long teeth, curved claws, or sharp beaks, they are relatively harmless to humans.

I admire the largest statue: a ghoron. I'm impressed I can recall its name. It's part horse, part dog. From memory, they run wild on the planet, though there are plans to try to domesticate the creature. Ride it for sport more than industry. I wonder what its silky fur would feel like.

After a long stroll, we pass through another door.

'The Great Stone Hall,' a droid announces.

The hall is at least ten times the size of the foyer we just walked through. It is predominantly empty and lowly lit, giving it a cool, unnerving ambiance. Its floor appears to be made of white marble impregnated by orange and silver stones placed in concentric circles. There are many narrow, rectangle windows along one wall, though the dark glass dulls the light.

A huge hologram is glowing in the hall's centre. Our eyes are drawn to it, mesmerised. It presents an image of Nattalia and the surrounding Earth ships. So many of them!

The shield is clearly present; a purplish glow around the planet, locking the ships out.

'Good morning. Welcome.'

I turn in the direction of the nasally voice. A man in a long blue coat of muslin-type material is strolling toward us. It's Odell, Cal's father; the man from my vision. Yes, father and son have the same dark eyes, the same width apart. Odell's white hair is in three ponytails, one on top of the other, a style usually reserved for heads of corporations or army generals or leaders of state. Yet he is not regal, nor arrogant, and I don't regard him as particularly power-hungry. Clearly, he has not partaken of an appointment with a designer surgeon. His natural gnome-like face appears better suited to geology or research than leading droid armies into war.

'Welcome?' Cal bellows and takes two strides toward him. 'That's not what the ships of Earth have been led to believe.'

I am surprised at how quickly Cal has opened fire. He's not even bothered to return his father's greeting. Garth, Tilly, and I stay behind him, understanding his need to lead the charge on the so-called peace talks.

His father looks startled by his son's remarks and stammers, 'I mean that you are welcome. You, my son. Not the ships. They should just go.' He waves his hand to indicate an about face.

'Just go?' Cal looks at him as though his father is mad. 'They can't. Earth is as good as gone and their supplies are low. You must know this.'

'They can go to the settlement on Colmono. I can courier supplies to those who need them. Anything to see them on their way.'

'Colmono? It's full, like all the other space colonies.'

'They can take more.'

'Not without becoming unsustainable. Nattalia is the most capable of resettling the people of Earth. It can accept all those ships up there and more.'

'It can't. It can't and won't.'

'Then our talks are done. We will go and I will die with those you have refused to help.'

Odell bristles and sputters. 'But we have much to catch up on. Your mother—'

'Doesn't care. Couldn't possibly. You haven't communicated with me in all this time.'

Looking pained, Odell shakes his head. 'I wanted to. I wanted to call for you. I couldn't. There's much to tell you.'

'Father, I'm not here for me. I'm here to ask on behalf of the people of Earth. Let them land. You must take them in! Surely—'

'I can't, and I won't. It will be the death of Nattalia.'

'How so?' I ask, keeping my voice calm, so calm I could have been inquiring about the weather.

Odell glances at me. 'And you are...?'

'Does it matter who she is? She's from Earth, advocating on behalf of humanity.'

'Britta Tate,' I say.

'Tate? Tate! Any relation to Jem?' He looks hopeful.

'Yes. I'm his sister. You know of my brother?'

'Yes. Yes.' Odell's eyes are boring into me. 'Jem. I was sorry when he vanished. Without a word to anyone. He was helping, you see. Trying to save our Earth, like your mother. I was hopeful... It would have solved much. If only all these ships could just go back to Earth.'

'You knew my mother?'

Odell doesn't have a chance to respond. Irate, Cal asserts, 'The ships can't go back. They are looking to you to save them.'

'I wasn't the one who brought them here.'

'No. The threat to Earth brought them here. Other colonies took them in. Why can't you?'

'You're ashamed of me.' Odell states this, weighs this knowledge, and his eyes cloud. 'You think me capable of mass murder? That I'll be responsible?'

'What else can I think?'

'Think? I don't want you to think. I want you to understand. But you won't even listen to me, give me a chance to explain.'

'Perhaps then he will listen to me?' The voice has come from across the room.

I turn and see a woman striding toward us, head high, determined. Her dark hair is long and wound in a dense tail that hangs down one side of her chest. Her sari-styled dress is grey, dull as smog, and without adornment. Her natural face, with its expansive forehead, thick eyebrows, and generous mouth, holds intelligence and exhibits much sensitivity. She is not what Cal has led me to expect.

As she approaches, her gaze finds Cal and her expression becomes complicated. She wants to reach out to him and yet her guilt, pain, and sorrow hold her back. Hope eases the strain in her eyes. 'Hello, my son.'

Cal remains silent. Although he has a need to lash out at her for all the years of hurt and separation, the love now emanating from her has him completely disarmed.

'I've longed for this day,' she says, stepping forward to press a disciplined, small kiss to his cheek. Her touch ignites his anger.

'You both think I have come here for you? For a family reunion? For explanations? I haven't. I've come because I want you to turn off that shield. I want you to do the right thing by these millions of people who have come here seeking refuge.'

'We can't,' his mother replies and takes her husband's hand.

'All right,' Cal says. He exhales slowly. 'Why not? Explain it, if you can.'

'We should sit. Be at ease.' She indicates a large cushioned pit fashioned in emerald green coverings off to the side of the room. 'You can introduce your friends.'

'This is Britta Tate, Jem's sister,' Cal says crisply and I nod in greeting. 'Tilly Marshallite and Garth Reng—members of my unit.' He turns to us. 'This, as you've gathered, is my father Odell Granton and my mother Cillian, virtual strangers though I believe we are related.'

Cillian's face hardens. 'Strangers? Yes. Unfortunate for all of us. A terrible wrenching for a mother to part from her son. You come to us without knowledge and plenty of judgement. It is disappointing. Hear us out. Hear me, then judge.'

Her words shake Cal. The air is loaded with tension.

'I think this talk is long overdue,' I say, taking Cal's arm. 'Let's sit.'

We move to the pit and step into its cushioned arena, plopping down with a soft bounce.

Once we are all seated, Cillian brushes her hand along her husband's arm. 'You tell it,' she urges.

'All right. There's a lot to go through, so please hear me out. The first thing you need to know is that I worked at EASA.' He looks at me pointedly. 'Yes, I knew your mother.'

I am surprised and terribly intrigued.

'Your mother had certain gifts. She could astral travel. You know, visit planets in her spiritual form and see things that our technologies couldn't. One day, she saw an asteroid and knew without any science to prove it that the hurtling rock was on a collision course with Earth. She saw it all those years ago, and not only that—she saw a way to stop it.'

I feel chills cross my upper back. His words support my vision. What I had seen of my mother did happen.

'Of course, EASA supported her in putting together a crew. I was to be part of it. We were to come here to Nattalia to trade with an alien species for a weapon—a weapon that could stop the asteroid. Such hope we had, such high expectations. We really thought we could save our planet. I know this may be hard to believe—'

'We know,' Cal cuts him short. 'We know about the weapon. What does this have to do—'

'Let him finish,' his mother pleads.

Odell looks confused. He's lost his place and his mind struggles to regather his thoughts.

'You came to Nattalia in search of a weapon,' I prompt.

'Yes, the weapon. Of course, you know about the weapon. You are her daughter. You must see things too, like Amelia and Jem. Anyway, where was I? Oh yes. I joined your mother's crew and we came to Nattalia. Cillian stayed behind.' Odell looks at his son. 'She stayed to look after you. You were only a young boy then.'

'But she didn't stay,' Cal says flatly, bitterly.

I know how he feels in this moment. I'm remembering the same thing. My mother leaving us to go on the mission; our tears, our pleas. I'm struggling to stay calm.

Cillian lifts her chin. 'I wanted to stay and care for you. But I had to go when I found out the truth.'

'Truth?' Tilly presses.

Cillian nods. 'I discovered the most terrible thing. I learned that EASA's mission to find the weapon was not going to be allowed to succeed. The World Council was going to do all it could to see it fail. Mandon and his councillors don't want Earth to be saved. They didn't want it back then and they don't want it now.'

'Oh,' Tilly says on a sharp inhale.

I'm staggered by the claim. Mandon is cold and calculating to be sure, but this... wanting the destruction of Earth? Why? I recall Treesa's mistrust of the World Council and their Red Vipers. Does she know something of this?

'Do you have proof of this?' Garth asks.

'Yes, how did you learn about it?' Cal adds.

We all look to Cillian, needing and yet fearing her explanation. No one wants to believe in an evil that potent.

She squares her shoulders. 'I stayed with Cal on Earth. But I was still working at EASA. There was a project to build a massive, fuel-loaded rocket capable of nudging the asteroid off course. A lot of people were working on it. There was so much enthusiasm for it. Everyone believed it could be done and that the asteroid threat would soon be eradicated.

'Then suddenly, without warning, the majority of the team were redeployed, only a core few were kept on the project. No one could understand why. Many of the team members complained, demanding they be reinstated, but their access codes were changed and they were literally locked out.

'I was friends with one of the few still on the project. I won't tell you his name, but one afternoon, I came across him in the refuelling bay. We were alone. He was sitting down and seemed to be suffering from some kind of shock. I asked him what was wrong. At first he wouldn't tell me but I kept on at him. Eventually, he told me that he had been ordered to reduce the dimensions of the rocket. He was very distressed by this. He said it was as though they were being told to build the rocket to fail. He said he was going to raise his concerns internally with his superiors. I encouraged him to do this.' Cillian lowers her eyes to hide her pain. 'He was found dead the next day.'

There is a grim silence as we appreciate what her story implies.

'I was upset and nervous. I became convinced that people knew he had talked to me and that my life was at risk. There are ears everywhere at EASA. I didn't know who to trust, then I thought I should go right to the top, to Treesa. She seemed set on saving Earth. So, I asked for a private audience with her. Thankfully, she agreed to see me and I told her what happened.

'She didn't seem surprised. That was the strange thing—how quickly she believed me. Odell had not long left with a unit for Nattalia and she advised that I should follow them and warn my husband and Amelia about what I had uncovered. She said she needed them to be alerted to possible internal sabotage, perhaps even a spy among them, and to take greater care. There was a cargo shuttle about to be deployed. She wanted me on it. Treesa said she couldn't use any other channel of communication.'

Her eyes soften as she looks to her son. 'Cal, I had to go. I had to leave you. It was too dangerous to bring you with me, knowing what I knew. You were only a young child. I had to give you up to keep you safe.'

My thoughts are whirling, trying to sense for the truth. Is it true? I'm feeling green, seeing green. Confirmation. Truth.

'Why?' Garth asks. Disbelief is in his tone. 'What would the World Council gain by having Earth destroyed?'

'What do you know of Nattalia?' Odell counters.

We look among ourselves. We know a bit, enough.

Cal shrugs. 'We know what everyone knows. It's the most liveable planet in the universe. It's rich in resources, food, beauty...'

Odell nods. 'Yes, yes, and who owns it?'

We don't answer. We don't know. Our briefings were more science based. We were informed of Nattalia's atmospheric composition, its moons, terrain, gravity, water content, and so on.

Odell straightens. 'Go on, have a guess.'

'The government?' I ask.

'Which government?'

'Earth's World Council?'

'That's right. They own the land. Think about what a massive influx of people would do for them? I don't mean in land sales. Rents—astronomically high rents.'

'They wouldn't destroy Earth just to capitalise on rentals,' Garth says.

'You have a good heart,' Odell says. 'I see that in you and that's why this is so hard for you to accept.' He raises his voice slightly, trying to sound more convincing. 'Believe me, we let those Earth ships land and their passengers will become slaves to those greed-driven councillors. They bought up Nattalia's land as soon as they learned about the asteroid, using hidden proxies to secure the sales. They planned a marketing campaign to ensure the majority of those leaving Earth came here. Now, they have every intention of leasing the land to reap high rents. They will then exploit these dependent, new arrivals as cheap labour to mine and rape the planet of its natural resources; resources such as the highly sought after mineral zillet, and they will sell it off to other human settlements for their own personal and profitable gain. That is why they want Earth gone.'

There is silence. We are aghast. Could it be true? Could

Mandon on learning about the asteroid only have seen opportunity? A chance to guide mass migration to a planet where he and his councillors could fiscally benefit?

'You believe this?' Cal asks of his father.

'Yes,' Odell says vehemently. 'And that's why the shield can't come down.'

Cal turns to me. 'Is he telling the truth?'

'I sense truth in it. I know he believes it.'

'What proof do you have of these land sales?' Garth demands to know.

'Jem Tate knew. He had seen it in one of his travel dreams. He told me he had heard conversations between the World Councillors talking about the sales and the rents and their prospects in trade. He learned that Nattalia was previously owned by NESCA, an interplanetary high-tech company. The World Council paid them over several instalments for ownership and landlord rights of Nattalia. He had seen the electronic receipts.'

'You mean,' Garth begins loudly, 'that you've based your coup and this planetary lockdown on psychic intelligence alone! No hard evidence whatsoever?'

'Jem Tate's word is all the evidence I need.'

'With all due respect, you have to drop that shield and let them in. There are so many...'

'That's what I'm afraid of,' Odell argues. 'Too many. And with them comes all kinds of problems. Nattalia is beautiful. I want to keep it that way. We damaged Earth's environment beyond repair—our capitalist natures, our consumerism, our carelessness and apathy.'

'It was the war that did the most damage. War. And if you don't let those ships land, Mandon will go to war with Nattalia. Surely, you don't want that? Britta has seen it. You believe in foresight. Britta, tell him... tell him that you've seen war.'

On Garth's insistence, I meet Odell's eyes and what he sees in mine elicits a protest from him. 'No, please no.'

'I'm sorry. I have seen it. Death, bombs, fighter ships...' I stop. Odell has become visibly upset. He believes me.

'We love these lands,' Cillian says, as though she needs to explain her husband's expressive reaction.

'We do,' he readily agrees. 'Surely our shield will ward off any offensive?'

His question exasperates Garth even further. 'Oh, I get it. It's all right for you to live here, behind that shield, enjoying the planet's resources, but not others. Ever thought about that? What gives you the right to all this privilege and to decide that other women and children hoping to start a new life on a beautiful planet, just like you have done, are not permitted to come here?'

A red flush crawls up Odell's neck and spreads across his face. 'It's not for my comforts. How dare you imply... The shield stays in place.' His final declaration holds a note of hostility. 'I won't hear another word.'

There, the heated exchange ends. We are all left to our distressing thoughts, which hang on a long silence.

Cal's head is bent and I observe his inner struggle. He does not know which way to turn. He is searching for a solution, a compromise that could work.

'There is something we can do,' I offer. 'I believe there is another weapon.'

'No,' Cal says loudly, swiftly.

'Let her speak,' Odell says.

'The species are still willing to trade. I want to go to them. You must let me give them what my mother promised: a long-range ship and a droid.'

'That is right. That's what they wanted for the weapon. You know! You really think it's not too late? They are still willing to trade with us after all that has happened?' Odell asks.

'I believe there's still time.'

'How could that, any of that, even be possible?' Garth mutters.

Odell ignores him. He is nodding. 'Of course! Why didn't you say so straight away? What are you waiting for? I will give you what you ask. If Earth can be saved and these people sent home...'

Cal rests his hand on my shoulder. 'Britta, you can't do this,' he says. 'It's too—'

'You come with me,' I say. 'Help me do this.' Then more forcefully, 'What choice do we have?'

He rubs his eyes and drags on his cheeks. 'What about what Jem saw? What if my going with you puts you at greater risk?'

'Tasma has promised me protection. I believe in it. And I want you with me.'

My last words sway him. 'All right.' Cal fixes his father a steadfast look and grounds out, 'We'll do our best to save Earth, but if we fail, you have to let the people land. You can't really want all those deaths on your hands!'

'Of course, I don't want it.' Odell stands and steps out of the cushioned pit. He begins walking up and down the length of the Great Stone Hall, working up a sweat. 'Of course, I don't.' He stops and gazes upon the hologram of Nattalia and the vast number of ships sitting outside of its protective shield. 'All right. Deal. Tell Mandon, when Earth is destroyed, I will take down the shield, but only then, only when these people have nowhere else to go.'

'My love, are you sure?' Cillian cries.

'I have to put trust in something—it might as well be in our son, and in Amelia's daughter. She says there's another weapon...' Odell's eyes plead with his wife to understand.

Cillian gives a slight nod. 'Yes, you are right.' She gazes lovingly at Cal. 'We trust in you and in what the Tates have foretold,' she affirms.

Cal's cheeks twitch. He's touched. 'You will be placed under arrest as soon as they land.' He says this to warn them, to be kind.

'Your mother and I will take a pod and leave in the confusion of their arrival. There are many places we can hide on this planet.'

Cillian rises and joins her husband, pressing a kiss to his cheek. She casts her eyes over her shoulder to look at Cal. 'But if we hand Nattalia over to them, it will be the end of this magnificent planet. You have no idea of its natural wonders and what will be lost. It will become the greatest tragedy ever to be inflicted by humans.'

'And if they don't land, it will be one of the greatest human tragedies in space,' Garth says. He bounds out of the pit and faces the couple. 'That asteroid is about four months from striking. You're saying that those people have to wait four months before you will let them land. Four months is a long time in cramped conditions, with low supplies of food and oxygen.'

'Oh, we'll send up supplies. We're not monsters. But just to be clear, we don't expect they'll be landing here. Earth will be saved, and they will go back to it,' Cillian says.

Garth's mouth is a thin line and he is struggling to curb his temper. 'The faster you can send up supplies, the better. But I'd rather not have this long wait over an attempt to secure a nonexistent weapon.'

Irritated, Cal is up, striding over, speaking curtly as he does so. 'While I respect your concern for the passengers on those ships, Officer, I don't like your complete lack of regard for what I'm trying to do. I'm in charge of this mission and I don't like the way you're referring to it.'

'You're in charge of these talks. This other... really, you want to call it a mission?' Garth's face is ugly with derision. He waves his hand in my direction. 'She says she's talking to a higher being of some kind that has a weapon powerful enough to take out an asteroid, which is, and this is the best part, hurtling across space some thousands of light years away, only four months from Earth, and it is not too late to stop it. Are you really going to make us wait for this? Can you see Mandon being okay with this?'

Cal is clearly becoming irate. Garth has never spoken to him in this manner before. No one has ever questioned his call, ridiculed it, in fact. 'You're telling me that years of predictions by EASA's psychic department, ninety percent of which did come to pass...'

'And right there is another argument to back me up. Ninety percent came to pass. What if this prediction falls in that ten percent? How detailed were the department's predictions anyway? Weren't most of them a bunch of symbols, open to interpretation? Didn't researchers read more into them after the events to suit their own predetermined agenda?'

I keep my voice soft and calm to help him hear his own agitation. 'Garth, you don't have to believe there is a weapon. You just have to know that I believe there is one and that I'm going to try to get it.'

'Britta, you are free to do what you want. I don't care what you do. What does concern me is what you do, Cal. You with her?' Garth glares at his reporting officer.

Cal swallows. He looks at his parents, his unit, and then me. And he makes a choice. His eyes take on a determined gleam. 'I promised Jem Tate, Treesa Breenswick, and even Commander Moro that I would protect Britta Tate. I believed in her brother. He was at the top of that psychic department. He knew things, things about me I hadn't told him, things that were about to happen—and they did. And I believe in his sister.' He casts troubled eyes to his parents. 'As you've heard, I don't have the support of my crew on this one. I ask that you accommodate them and make them comfortable. I will go with Britta.'

He returns his gaze to me and gives me a look of such conviction that my heart soars. Something significant, a shift of sorts, passes between us.

Keeping quiet all this time, it's Tilly's turn to chime in. 'You're not going with her because you believe in her,' she says tartly. 'You're in love with her! You're not thinking straight. This isn't like you. You can't really be serious. Cal?'

'I've made up my mind. War should always be a last resort.'

'You don't think I know that? You think I've just been arguing for war?' Garth throws up his hands. He's furious. 'I'm done with this.' He struts away, taking hurried steps to cross the vast floor to the door. Tilly decides to leave with him and breaks into a trot to keep up.

A trio of city droids follow the fast departing pair.

'See them to their rooms,' Odell tells the droids.

They exit and I feel a wave of calm flow in. My mind is still clinging to what Tilly had said, playing it over and over in my mind. *You're in love with her*, she had said. While I think it somewhat of an overstatement, I can't help feeling a twinge of euphoria. For if Tilly thinks that, it's possible there's some inkling of truth to it and nothing would make me happier.

'I'm sorry,' Odell says, referring to the split in the crew. He pulls on his blue coat, wrapping it tighter around him.

'Don't be. I thank you for talking with us, with me.' Cal gives me a knowing glance before extending his oversized hand to his father. 'To turning things around.'

A smile spreads across Odell's lips and he doesn't hesitate in reaching out and shaking his son's hand.

'I'm so happy you're here,' Cillian says to her son. 'You've made the right decision. I'm not gifted in my senses, but something feels right about it.'

Cal gazes deeply into my eyes and sees my inner calm. 'I agree,' he says. 'Besides, I don't feel like there was any other choice.'

CHAPTER TWELVE

ODELL GRANTON WASTES NO TIME COMMUNICATING OUR PACT to Mandon Allic. He fires up the hologram and puts the offer to him.

'When Earth is gone, you may enter under official refugee status. Adequate supplies will be sent to the larger ships for distributing to sustain four months of waiting. If, by chance, the asteroid does not destroy Earth, they will have to turn around and go home.'

Mandon is incensed. He claims there is no possibility of the asteroid missing. Computers have been modelling the asteroid's path thousands of times, accounting for a range of variables based on the precise data available, and not once does the asteroid pass Earth by. He demands the shield be shut down instantly. He threatens war.

Odell doesn't shift and negotiations end badly.

The next communication, only a short time later, presents a more subdued Mandon. He agrees to the terms, reluctantly. 'Send up those supplies. We'll see you in four months to thank you for them in person.'

Afterward, Odell is in good spirits. It has given him much

pleasure to gain ground with the World Council by forcing them to agree to a postponement and to cease all mention of war. With enthusiasm, he helps us make plans to undertake our quest at first light the next day and asks Cal to accompany him to the Jucca Space Station to see about a long-range ship and a suitable droid for our trade.

'You all right to stay here?' Cal asks me.

'Of course she is,' Cillian answers for me, linking her arm through mine. 'We should have a special dinner tonight, a fitting send-off for you both. How about we start by finding you something fresh to wear, something nice?'

'I think Britta would like that,' he says. 'She's not one for standard uniform.'

'Perhaps because she's not standard,' Cillian says. 'Come. This you may find of interest.'

Cillian takes me beyond the hall and through a maze of glowing passageways that rise and fall. After a while, we enter a section where the walls are covered in purple flowers. On inspection, I see they are growing there, inside damp alleys inserted into the walls.

'Oh my, they're beautiful,' I breathe, running my fingertips along their petals.

'Beautiful, and their scent aids in sleep. These are the sleeping quarters and through this door is the clothing chamber. I have to assume the former leader had an interest in fashion.'

'The former leader? Where?'

'Safe and sound and being looked after. Our coup was not particularly violent. Once we took over the droids, the people followed our lead. They are a very content population and as long as they can keep going about their idyllic lives, they don't care very much as to who presides over them.'

'I see.' I wonder at it. Imagine living in such bliss that your ruling government means so little—as long as your conditions remain delightfully the same.

We walk into a vast circular chamber with a curved ceiling. 'Look.' Cillian dims the lights and swipes at a central pad. 'Stand on the cross.'

A cross is glowing on the floor. Curiously, I wander over and stand upon it. A scanner passes a light across my body, taking my measurements. I wait patiently while she presses a few keys.

'Now. How about this?' Cillian swipes at the pad and next to me forms a three-dimensional hologram of myself in an off-the-shoulder blue dress, studded in tiny pearls. My hologram turns so I can see my form in the dress from every angle. 'Like it?'

I'm smiling. I can't help it. 'Can I see it in musky pink, with a light sleeve, and no pearls?'

Cillian smiles. 'I knew the minute I saw you that you would find this amusing. I'm not one for pretty clothes and things. I find them distracting, but I admire the joy it brings others, and thought after all you've been through, you know, losing your mother...' Her voice drops away and her eyes find mine. Her sympathy is sincere and touching.

So, I think, it's my mother she wants to talk about. That's why she's brought me here.

Of course, I want to accommodate her. 'You knew my mother. What was she like?'

'Strong, and intuitive. She had a way of knowing things and acting in perfect timing. I was quite the admirer. She had many.'

'You tried to warn her not to trust anyone,' I say, remembering Cillian came to Nattalia to do just that. 'Did she already know there were those seeking to oppose her mission?'

'I'm afraid I didn't get here in time.' She is troubled by this. 'I failed her and Earth. She had left before I got here. They say her ship exploded. I can only assume the World Council planted a device on her ship or something like that. If only I had told her...'

'Your guilt is not warranted. Everything happens as it should in the timing that it should. Every event is part of a pattern, a dance of sorts, and must happen when it does to direct the next step.'

Cillian searches my face. 'I would like to believe that. I don't understand when terrible things happen why they should or how they... fit in. I just wish she had succeeded in getting that weapon back to Earth.'

'Your husband didn't go with them?'

'He stayed behind on Nattalia to complete the trade. He was to give the higher species a ship and a droid. He was meant to leave it for them in the forest. But...'

'He didn't.'

'No. When I got here, the World Council was seeking his arrest. He found me as soon as I arrived, and we went into hiding.'

'In the hills.'

'Yes.'

Her energy calms as she remembers her time in hiding; a time when she was in peace in nature. I can see joy in these reflections. It was during this time that she fell in love with Nattalia and its lands, a period of immense wonderment, though I sense longing too, a constant, all-consuming longing. She was yearning for her son to be with her.

'Thank you for telling me this.' I smile gently and she returns it.

'You are a lot like her, your mother. Strong and wise and attractive. I think Cal thinks so too.'

Cal? I'm taken off guard and I think I blush. My cheeks heat up.

'You like him. That's good.' She swipes her hand and the hologram of myself is dressed in pink. 'Like it?'

I stare. I hardly recognise myself. Do I really look like that? There's a womanly confidence in my stance, with my arched back and angled hip, that I don't feel I possess. Do I really look... desirable? I'm trying to see myself through Cal's eyes.

How does he see me? Still just Jem's awkward little sister. I look again at my face; it seems less elfish, more feline. My eyes are shining with promise, wakefulness, and sensuality.

'Can I see it with silver straps? Thin straps?'

'Ah, yes, that will suit very well.'

* * *

Later that evening, I arrive to the dinner in musky pink with silver straps across the fabric at the chest, waist, and hips. The sheer garment clings to my slight build. Cillian's talk has made me more conscious of my feelings for her son. Is my affection for Cal so obvious? Affection? Is that all it is? I smile at myself. I am falling in love and the pink is helping me to feel it.

I look for him as soon as I walk into the dining area and am pleasantly surprised to see him out of uniform. He has adopted the dress of the city, wearing loose trousers and a long flowing mustard shirt. It makes him look younger, sunnier.

Tilly is still in EASA's black, even though she was also offered a choice of dresses. Garth, too, keeps to the uniform, unable to shed his duty-bound skin.

'This is alcoholic nectar and of a kind you've never tasted before,' Odell says, entering from a noisy kitchen area. He has changed into a long green coat for the occasion. As he passes through the door, it slides shut, sealing out the sounds of sizzling hotplates. 'Just a small taste. It requires a tolerance to drink in bulk.'

Cillian, clothed in light grey, heads the table. She holds up her tube-shaped glass as her husband scurries around the table pouring the golden liquid into them.

Tilly and Garth place hands over their glasses. 'Not for me,' Garth says. 'I'm fine with water. Is it safe to drink?'

'Yes. Everything here is safe to consume,' Cillian says. 'Especially the alcohol. This bottle is of aged nectar. Forty-nine years it's been waiting for us.'

Forty-nine! I'm the only one, leaning back in my chair, in surprise. What is it with that number? I wish I knew.

'Come on, Miss Tate. I know you'll try it,' Odell says.

I let him fill my glass and tilt it politely toward my hosts before taking a sip. Velvet warmth slips down my throat and leaves a light citrus aftertaste upon my tongue. The heat reaches my chest and climbs to my head, prompting psychic images to start presenting, demanding my attention, like children trying to clamber on my lap. Not now. I push them back. Leave me, I think.

Trying to control my focus, I concentrate on my surrounds. It is just the six of us seated at a round table in a dining room built to seat at least four hundred. Overhead the curved ceiling serves as a screen for a projection of the night sky. Nattalia's three peach-tinged moons are the main feature. It is dazzling. The tiles on the floor are chequered, yet have a strange three-dimensional effect. Sometimes the black on the white appears like a step, descending or ascending, depending on the angle of view. I learned when I came in that it was best to walk without looking down. The artworks on the walls are of landscape scenes. The artist has captured scenes of Nattalia as perfectly as a recording. They, too, have a three-dimensional quality. I feel I can walk into the works, be there. One scene of a thundering waterfall and lake surrounded by lush greenery and cup-like flowers holds my attention. It must be the most beautiful place I've seen. Does it really exist?

'I see you like the art?' Odell says, patting my hand. 'Nattalia has a most vivid creative culture. Art, music, dance. In fact, I've got some entertainment planned for you. I want tonight to be special. Who knows what will happen after... well... It's always good to live in the moment, don't you think?'

'I was just thinking the same thing,' I say, making the old man beam.

Droids stroll in, carrying covered plates. A dish is set before each of us and our emotionless waiting staff lift the lids on them.

Shells, larger than walnuts and the colour of aubergines, have been prised open and lie splayed, swimming in succulent juices upon a bed of red leaves. An aromatic steam rises from it all.

'You must try these,' Odell cries, tipping the contents of a shell down his mouth. 'My wonderness. Try them.'

'Are they shells of the sea?' I inquire.

'No. Fresh water. They are exquisite and plentiful here.'

I copy my host and tip a shell against my lips. A morsel of tender fish-like meat rolls into my mouth. I taste cream, herbs, and an explosion of rich flavour as the white flesh breaks apart. After nothing more than vitamin-based food bars and pills, this beautifully steamed concoction is simply 'wonderness'.

Cal is yet to try one. I sense he's overwhelmed by the opulence of the room and the exotic display of food and drink. I recall his carer family had come close to starving him through neglect. I can appreciate how difficult it must be for him to come to terms with his parents leaving him without proper care in place while they were here, treating themselves to the comforts of Nattalia.

'Try one, Cal,' his mother urges. 'I've always wanted this for you, you know. I've wanted us to be together for so, so long.'

He stares at the shells, working through a range of emotions.

Garth and Tilly are also yet to touch their plates.

'If you're not going to eat them...?' Odell says, indicating Garth should hand over his plate to him.

Garth does. Watching Odell tuck in to his second serving, he snipes, 'It's not right to feast while the people up there...'

Odell dismisses his comment with a wave of his hand, his low hanging sleeve almost knocking his nectar. 'We're sending up food. I'm a leader of my word; not many of those around. Stores are being loaded on to ships as we dine.'

'Please, put more in your stomachs than this misplaced guilt,' Cillian says sweetly. 'Indulge in roast meat of old traditions.' On cue, a droid enters holding a tray, a plump baked bird atop it. Another droid follows close behind with an even bigger tray of green, purple, and orange vegetables. The next droid carries a deep dish of fresh, warm bread and tubes of spreads.

The droid cuts the large bird at the table. Mesmerised, we take in the sound of crispy skin being torn and watch clear juices dribble down the thickly sliced pieces of meat. I have not seen anything so robust, so appealing, so generous in all my years on Earth. This one tantalising meal is a sign of what bounties Nattalia promises.

'Are these birds plentiful too?' Cal asks.

'They are everywhere,' Odell enthuses. 'Children can catch them. No one goes hungry here.' He turns to Garth. 'And we want to keep it that way. Would you like a piece?'

Garth's eyes are reproachful. Still, the aroma alone is irresistible and he holds up his plate, grudgingly accepting slices of meat, bread, and a scoop of vegetables.

The meal is the best we've had. The food served to us during our time at EASA was not worthy of the label. It was nutrients, not food. Though people of Earth outside of EASA were not faring much better given the scarcity of meats, harvests, and fresh water. Seafood had become compromised with polluted seas and needed treatment before consuming, making it too expensive for most.

As I chew on my third piece of bird, I start to feel guilty too. It's not so misplaced. No other settlement in our universe would have people eating so well. It doesn't seem right to be indulging while billions can't.

It makes me start wondering. If Earth's refugees arrive, how will they cope, learning how much better off these people are and have been for years. Not just the food, I think, recalling outside cafes, colourful clothes, enhanced looks, easy laughter and conversation that doesn't have to focus on topics of survival or dreary necessities. Their way of life is so much simpler and richer. I start to see that it will require considerable adjustment on behalf of the new arrivals to forgo their habit of struggle. Perhaps they will accept Mandon's terms of high rents and labour, for it's what they know. They will accept their lot and go to work and work hard. No doubt Mandon is counting on that.

'More bread?' Odell asks.

'No thank you,' I say. 'I've eaten more than I'm used to and more than I really need.'

The others are done too. Indulgence is not our custom. With the meal completed, the table is lowered into a cavity, taking away our plates and glasses for cleaning, and the promised entertainment is introduced. We turn our chairs to face arriving performers.

Androids, a choir of them, all featuring young, smooth faces, slender figures, and luscious, moistureless lips. They sing perfectly, not a note out of place, and the song is beautiful, haunting. A group of them dances. Not a step wrong. Timing perfect. Agility extreme and choreography impressive. Yet, I feel nothing. There is nothing to sense. What is it? I ponder. Then I realise—there's no soul. The show lacks the imperfection that makes art interesting. It lacks the emotional storytelling, the creative spark of an improvised addition. A human may have spontaneously performed an extra spin for the moment called for it, for it was so inspired to do so. These androids add no sudden nuances. Everything that was programmed to happen, happens, and I don't expect any surprises, any exchanges between them, any nerves or memory lapses or stumbles or a moment that was exceptionally better tonight than any other night. The show we see is the same that anyone will see on any occasion. It is beautiful, so lovely, so precise that I find it dull.

As they depart, we turn our seats to sit back in a circle. Lights dim, making the stars in the projection overhead even brighter. A droid pushes a ball into the centre of our circle and turns it on. It glows warmly, giving the impression that we are sitting outside around a fire. Except there are no breezes, no outside sounds or fragrances or shooting stars.

'What did you think of them?' Odell asks. 'Entertaining?'

'Do you not have human performers?' I counter. 'You mentioned the planet had a culture of creativity.'

'Yes. Humans perform. But not for me,' Odell says wearily. 'I've taken this city by force by reprogramming these droids. I took a few at first and had them reprogram others. Before I knew it, they were reprogramming dozens, then hundreds. I have no human followers. The only way I could get humans to perform for me would be under threat and then it wouldn't be very entertaining.'

'You have no followers?' Garth asks.

Odell shakes his head.

'But the people don't rise against you? Not even in protest?'

'No. They've had it so good so long, that if nothing changes or affects them directly, they are not too fussed as to who sits in this hall. Yet, if you were to ask them for their preferred leader, they would say Mandon Allic.'

I'm surprised. 'Why?' I ask.

Odell smiles sadly. 'They know what he stands for. Trade. Commerce. He has promised to make Nattalia rich by bringing Earth's people here to labour—to mine and harvest the planet of its resources, ensuring them more luxuries, more free theme parks, gaming, entertainment. You have no idea the promises... The people want the shield to come down, but not enough to fight the droids for it. They are too lethargic to do anything much. Like I said, they've had it too good. Why fight? They believe Mandon will get here. He's worshipped like a god. They believe he can do anything and his coming is just a matter of time. I'd like to say the people see me as a peculiar delay, but they don't really see me.'

'You don't paint a very nice picture of the Nattalian people,' Cal says. 'Self-interested, greedy, and lazy.'

'It is the human picture though, isn't it?' his mother queries. 'It's what ruined Earth.'

'I don't share your negative sentiment,' I say.

Cillian's tone is crisp. 'You don't?'

I smile, trying to convey the depth of my optimism. 'I like to think the people of Earth have learned from that destruction. Things have been hard. We've gone without. We've hurt. Suffered. We've choked on the air we polluted and starved when our environment no longer supported growth of our food or provided for our water supplies. Artificial everything has left us weak and sick. But we have learned. We value what we've lost. It is through loss that we've learned how to protect and nourish. Our technologies are now focused on sustaining life, saving it, restoring it. Besides, look at the residents of Nattalia. They are living sustainably. It can be done.'

'You have an inflated opinion of our residents,' Odell says. 'The people here have not had hard lessons in their lifetime. They will consume more if more is offered. The Earth people will be used to increase that supply.'

'They may be pampered, but don't they have hearts?' I query. 'Won't they want to share their lifestyle with these people who have had no choice but to come here?'

'That's not Mandon's plan. They will believe what he tells them because it will suit them very well.'

'They don't fear these new arrivals may rise against them?' Cal asks. 'It's happened in history before. When masses are suppressed and used for a minority's gain.'

'That's what the droids are for,' Cillian replies. 'Imagine, an army without a conscience, under Mandon's control.'

Odell stands and looks into my eyes. 'If you don't find a

weapon and billions of people on Earth die, and its refugees come here... this settlement, this last bastion of peace and beauty, will fall to greed and corruption. I wish you were right. I wish people could learn. I've seen so few examples of it. Good night, all of you. Goodnight, son.'

Cillian rises too. 'Goodnight.' She kisses Cal's cheek and he stands and embraces her. It is a touching moment and I look away, wanting them to have it to themselves.

Our hosts leave, their heels clicking on the floor as they go.

Cal scans his silent crew members. 'I know you want the asteroid stopped just as much as we do.'

'Of course,' Tilly says. 'But it's impossible. We have to deal with the issue at hand and that is the people up there want and need to land. We have to help them. Our mission is to help them.'

'You don't think there's any truth in what Odell is saying? That Mandon wants this? That the people will be exploited?'

'What's the alternative?' Garth wants to know.

'We help them by stopping the asteroid,' Cal insists.

'Even if you save Earth, has it occurred to you they may not want to go back? They've come all this way. They are on the threshold of paradise. How could you send them away now?'

They lock gazes, their thoughts are grim.

'I'm not so naïve as to think a planet like this wouldn't be sought after by an ambitious leader like Mandon,' Garth concedes. 'I can see there could be truth to Odell's claims. But let's fight one battle at a time. Let the people land, we take stock, and see if Treesa can't work something out for the masses.'

Cal also adopts a conciliatory tone. 'Okay. That sounds reasonable. Yet, Mandon has agreed to wait four months. We have four months to think on it. Let's talk again on our return.' He stands and looks to me. 'Can I walk you to your room?'

'Of course.' I come to my feet.

Tilly stands suddenly. 'Cal...'

'Yes, Tilly.'

She bites her lip, her hands fidget nervously, and her eyes are troubled. 'Good luck.'

* * *

'You okay?' Cal asks when we reach the corridor just beyond the hall. Two droids have fallen into step behind us, watching and listening. Our feet are taking us back to our sleeping quarters at the corridor's far end.

'Not really,' I say. 'It's a lot to take in.'

'I know. Must be even harder for you. You see it. You see war.'

'Yes.'

'So, either Mandon doesn't keep his word to wait or Odell doesn't keep his word to let them in.'

'Or we go to the trouble of saving Earth, but the ships don't want to turn around. Garth could be right there. Why wouldn't they want to come to the most liveable planet in the universe when they are so close to it!'

Cal stops walking and I stop with him. 'Britta, say we do trade for a weapon. What then? How do we launch it from here?'

'Through the Hatch.'

His breath catches. 'That's your plan?'

'Tasma can help us.'

'Using the Hatch to deploy a weapon... it's never been done.'

'I know.'

'You think it could work?'

'Yes. If we can get the exact coordinates. Tasma should be able to help with that. It is inter-dimensional.'

'How do you even think of these things?'

I shrug, embarrassed. 'I can't take credit for ideas. They float around for anyone to tap into, really.'

He stares at me; his expression is one of bafflement. I feel my feet shuffling. I'm not sure what he's thinking. His thoughts are going down a path I don't seem to be able to follow.

'Your dress is... very you.'

He's thinking about my dress? I'm thrown by the change in his focus, pleased by it too. I become overly conscious of my attire and want to readjust the strap, yet I hold still, except for the quickening rise and fall of my chest.

'Jem didn't want this,' he says softly.

'Want what?'

His gaze lowers, fixes on my lips. 'Oh.' It seems he is accepting my appeal not to stay away. He's so very close. I feel the silent invitation, to connect, to touch and how I want him to do that, to kiss me! The essence of him, the serious intensity of his intent, is overpowering all my senses. I wait. I think I part my lips slightly.

'We should get some sleep,' he says abruptly, withdrawing, pulling himself up to full height. 'There's a lot riding on our mission,' he throws out. 'We're going to need clear heads.'

'Sure, sure.' Somehow, I manage a weak smile. 'That's very true and also very responsible.'

'I know.' He casts his eyes down and mutters, 'I hate myself for it.'

My smile gains a little more strength and I offer, 'But I love you for it.' With that, I cut the energy and walk away, knowing he watches me walk the length of that well-lit, sparkling clean corridor until I reach my room and disappear into it.

I think I hear him quietly cursing. I like to think he is, because I know I am.

CHAPTER THIRTEEN

ODELL AND CILLIAN WAKE EARLY TO SEE US OFF.

Cal embraces them both. They are too tired and anxious and overcome for words, but I see much love and regret pass between them. So little time together, so much to digest and far too much to process.

'Good fortune,' they say, and I feel them willing it upon us.

Our packs are loaded with fresh food as well as EASA-distributed nutrition bars, clothes, blankets, and water. We haul the gear into the cabin of a Hiberdernian. The ship holds six hibernation capsules, a two-seat short haul pod, and one of the city's genderless droids. It is yet to be activated. The Hiberdernian ship and droid will be part of our trade. The pod will allow our return to Jucca.

Cal and I, under advice from his parents, are wearing armoured vest plates along with loose tan coloured clothes, utility belts, and boots that mould against our feet and ankles.

Given my heightened stress, the colour serves to ground rather than excite my already highly charged nerves.

As the ship erupts into life, Cal glances at me. He seems ready, psyched.

'All okay,' he says, wanting to check in with me.

I nod.

We lift off and blast across the city and I'm sure there'd be a few residents wondering at our odd flight path.

We know from our studies that, like Earth, a large proportion of the planet is dedicated to seawater while the lands are divided by mountain ranges and deeply etched river systems. The windscreen gives us a good view and we are impressed at the sheer natural beauty of the terrain. We pass over a pink lake covered in white birds and I long to be down there, exploring. I imagine Cal's parents hiding out in such lands and envy them anew. The planet truly is a paradise worthy of love and protection.

'Minerals,' Cal says.

I gaze down and see a rocky ridge lined with orange streaks. 'Zillet?' I ask.

He nods. The mineral is precious. Most our ships make use of it for hyperdrive capacity and a lot of our weapons rely upon it too.

As my eyes follow the ridge, I discover it is home to an array of small birds. There are animals too, scampering up and down its slopes; long rabbit-like creatures with striped tails. I don't want to imagine Mandon's mining blasters moving in to smash this habitat to rubble for the facilitation of zillet extraction.

Mandon... Just thinking about him, my head starts to ache. I try to think of something else, though the pain only develops and becomes sharper, like splinters digging in.

'What's wrong?' Cal asks, noting my discomfort.

'I'm not sure. I've got a headache. It's come out of nowhere.'

'We have a painkiller pump in our pack if you need it.'

I shake my head. 'No. They make me drowsy.'

'Why don't you go in the back and lie down? I'll wake you once we're over the equator.'

I don't want to miss seeing more of the wondrous planet, but my head is pounding and I know I will need my energy once we get to our destination.

'All right. I will.'

I lie in the back in one of the capsule beds and start tossing around images of war and destruction. I try to look forward, beyond them, though I can't seem to get off that track.

I try to contact Tasma, who promised to keep me safe. There is no response.

'Jem, Mum, what is it? Why do I feel this way? Why the pain?' I wish they would talk back to me. I wish I could settle enough to breathe in answers.

At last, I go back out front and Cal hands me a food bar.

'I was about to call you. We've just flown over the Dianella Ocean. Forests now as far as the eye can see. If anything looks familiar, let me know. You get a feeling about when we should stop, just tell me.'

My eyes take in canopies covered in the flowering vines, displaying the cherry reds and yellows of my dreams. I savour the natural wonders, tuning into them, and open my mind, lifting my vibration. It helps to ease the tension in my head.

It isn't long before I get an urge to stop. 'Here. Land here.'

With nothing else to go on, Cal takes my advice and we put down in the first clearing available. We alight, packs swinging from pinched shoulders and water containers hooked to our belts, and waste no time in scouting the terrain. Golden grasses come up to our shins. They part for us as we tread into dense forest. We weave in between trees, stepping over fallen logs, pushing through low-lying foliage that is sometimes so thick it is like trudging through hedges.

We welcome the next clearing, pleased to be back in the light. Long-legged and pretty-winged insects hum and buzz above flowers as large as our torsos. Air, sweet and dry, rushes up my nasal passages and down my dry throat. On my tongue, I weigh oils, pollens, and citrus fragrances.

I've seen these sights in my astral travelling, but it doesn't come close to the physical experience of it. I'm delighting in the joy of all my senses.

'What do we do? Summon them?' Cal puts to me.

'Yes.' I sit on a flat rock that's perfectly cubed, disturbing a tiny purple reptile that was sunbaking upon it.

Cal grows anxious. 'Good. I'll stand watch.' He rests his hands on his waist belt where he wishes he had a weapon stored. I had told him not to pack one. I didn't want to risk scaring away the species.

'They are peaceful,' I assure him.

'I'll be the judge of that. What are you going to do?'

'Call them.'

'Right.'

I sit, breathe deeply and evenly, and quieten my mind. I close my eyes and call for Tasma. It isn't long before Cal's tight voice interrupts my drifting.

'Ah, Britta. Little ones.'

My lids flick up and I see the beings—about a dozen of them. They are no taller than our hips. This time I have a clearer view for they are in bright light. They stand like lupus flowers; soft, vertical banners with a gentle sway.

'You see them too?' I ask Cal.

'Yes.'

'They seem young. It's not just their size. There's a dependent feel to them,' I explain.

'If you say so. They look sad for kids.'

'I think they are. I'll try to call the older one. It knows about the weapon. These ones are shy.'

'It's kind of weird how they're just staring at us.'

'They're curious.' I close my eyes again. 'Tasma?'

I wait until I sense another presence. I open my eyes and see it standing among the young.

'I came,' I say, though that is obvious. 'I have the ship and a droid. Can you still help us?'

'Who are you talking to?' Cal asks.

'The tall one.'

'Not seeing it.'

'Please help us,' I say to Tasma.

I hear its response in my mind. 'Yes.'

'Do you have the weapon for me?'

'It is not here.'

'Where is it?' I hear the panic in my voice. Here comes the trap, I think. Here comes the part where I have to travel to get the weapon and never come back.

'Your mother has it.'

I shake my head. 'I know you gave it to her. But she lost it. Her ship exploded. She was killed.'

'She's not dead.'

I put my hand to my mouth to steady my breathing. I'm glad I'm sitting down. I know I've gone pale. It's as though my blood is pooling in my feet. What is it saying? Of course, she's dead. She died when her ship exploded.

'You okay?' Cal asks, concerned. 'Is it doing something to you?'

Tasma shimmers in the light. I'm afraid it will disappear.

'Tasma?'

'She's out there, sleeping in hibernation. Jem went after her. He's there too.'

'Where?'

'On the edge of darkness. Send the droid for them. The droid goes in the long-range ship and brings them and the weapon back.'

'Jem and my mother and the weapon?' I hold my chest, which is rising and falling erratically.

'What's it saying?' Cal asks. 'What about them?'

'It says they are alive, both of them. The droid can get them. They have the weapon. They have it.'

Cal is struggling to process it too. 'The droid can get them? How will it know where they are?'

'Tasma knows. Oh Cal, I don't know what to believe. I want this too much. I don't want to hope in case...' Tears are burning in my eyes.

'Take a breath. Okay, this is good. This Tasma can locate them. We should go with the droid.'

Grateful that Cal is keeping me on track, I pose the notion. 'Tasma, I want to go to them. Can you take us to them with the droid?'

'It is not necessary. I can do this, if you help me in return.'

'You want something from us?'

'Yes, your help. You, Britta Tate.'

'My help?'

'Yes.'

'What kind of help?'

'Your help.'

'What is it saying?' Cal asks.

'It wants my help in return.'

'What does that mean?' His cynicism is as thick as my own. Have we really lost our ability to trust?

'Okay, I'll help you,' I find myself promising.

'Now hold on,' Cal warns.

I don't want to hear it. 'Please take the ship and the droid and go get them.'

'All right. You're doing the trade. What about the shield?' Cal asks. 'How will the ship come and go with the planetary shield up? We'll need to talk to my father and arrange...'

'No need,' Tasma says to me. 'The shield is down. You know this.'

Its words free my mind from the splinters that have been stabbing at my thoughts. The pain is released as clarity flows. I turn to Cal. 'Garth and Tilly never had any intention of waiting the four months. They've done it. They've won over a droid with a chip and got it to take down the shield.'

'What?' Cal shouts incredulously. His expression is one of denial. 'They wouldn't... We had an agreement with Mandon. No. I don't believe it. Why would they...?'

His exasperated question prompts a picture of Garth to come into my mind. I see him in the arms of a woman with slender arms as dark as night.

'Because he has family up there, a wife. You should have told me!'

Cal simply stares at me for a long moment until understanding dawns. He nods slowly. 'Yes. A wife, a child, parents, nephews, nieces, even a grandparent.'

'Tilly too?'

'Yes. Sisters and parents.'

'They are doing it for them, to give them a better life.'

A low growl is heard in the distance, which quickly escalates into a roar. The shield is down and the fighter ships are through, streaking through skies high above us on their way to Jucca, the capital. Does this mean war? Now? Cal's father will order his Nattalian droids to fight back, to shoot down the ships.

Neath. Is he among them? Knowing Neath, he'd be up the front. No.

'Tasma.' I gaze at its soft lights. 'Can you keep Neath safe? My brother?'

'I will if I can, but some things must happen.' I see the image of a chain and realise it is telling me to understand that events link together, each one leading to the next. The image only serves to increase my anxiety.

'I don't want...'

'I know.'

'You can change it.'

Tasma doesn't answer. I feel it withdrawing, and I know it can't do anything.

I breathe in sharply and put out my hands, trying to push back on a wall of grief that is starting to build around me.

'You okay?' Cal asks, kneeling beside me. 'Neath?'

I shake my head and feel a single tear wet my cheek.

'What? Did Tasma say Neath will die fighting?'

'No.'

'Then... he'll be okay. He's a survivor if ever I saw one.'

'He is, isn't he?' I want to believe it so much.

Cal rubs a hand against my back. 'We can't do anything about the war, but we can still save Earth,' he says, trying to keep me focused. It is hard to concentrate with the fighter ships still roaring above us.

'Come on. Neath's okay. You have to think of Jem and your mother.'

A picture of Jem fills my mind. Cal's right. I can't dwell on what might happen but what is happening. 'Tasma, where are they?'

'Close your eyes.'

As soon as I shut them, I see space. It is an odd sensation having an image thrust into your mind not of your own creation.

'Here's Nattalia.' I see the hazy blue planet with the three moons. We zoom out quickly to take in our galaxy, which contains Earth as well. 'Here's Jem.' I am flying across the universe at impossible astronomical speeds, my eyes taking in thousands and thousands of light years of space. It spins rapidly by—thousands of galaxies and their stars, suns, planets—all blurring, all seemingly turning, rotating, round and round. I hear the words: forty-five billion light years away. The sheer incomprehensible distance makes me feel alone, fearful, and sick. I'm disorientated and giddy.

My eyes fly open. 'So far! How... Was it an accident through the Hatch?'

'No accident. Close your eyes again. I will show.'

It takes a little while for me to resettle, for my mind to open to the images that are hovering at its fringes. Given I want to see them and am practised at clearing my thoughts, it is not long before they start to stream in unimpeded.

I'm on the flight deck of a ship. The view from the broad screen over the ship's nose shows a Hatch. Its magnificence at this proximity is something to behold. The crew are seated, heavily restrained, except for one woman who has just released herself.

She holds herself well. Her highly attuned physique supports a posture and movement that is smooth, deliberate, and confident. Several ropes of her hair have been twisted and clipped on top with a clip-blade, the clip doubling as a hairpiece and a small knife. Without it, her hair would comb her shoulders with waves of luscious caramel. Mum.

Her crew eyes her quizzically.

Bending down, swift and sure, she drags out a weapon and starts an assault on the droids at the controls. The droids are World Council issue. I can tell by the Earth tattoo on the backs of their bald heads. Mum knew. Mum knew they would never let her ship return to Earth with the weapon. Pride wells.

What follows is the crew's scramble to get away somewhere out of reach of World Council security. I see her courageously authorising coordinates that would send them further than anyone has ever dared travel, flinging herself and her terrified crew into the deep unknown.

Now they are on the edge of a void. I watch their frantic struggle to drive their ship away from it. I see that moment of realisation when they know they can't return. Oh, how devastating and frustrating for them, to have a weapon that could save billions of lives and no way of travelling to use it.

I see Mum contact Jem.

Now it makes sense. Jem approaching the head of EASA,

Treesa Breenswick, at the funeral and locked in such desperate conversation with her. He would have told her all he knew of Mum's plight. No wonder EASA came for him. Treesa needed to get him on the mission to get the weapon back. She would have had so few around her to trust and couldn't have just sent anyone. Jem was the safest choice and most likely to succeed given his abilities to contact our mother. It makes sense that he was sent as soon as possible away to Nattalia before the World Council could become aware of what he knew.

The awareness comforts my aching mind that has been searching for answers for so long. I refocus, hungry for more.

The images now pick up Jem's trail. I see him on Nattalia; the orange bridges spanning the harbour help to orient me. He leaves Jucca and travels with his crew, over a dozen men and a few women, on a small transporter. They put the craft down on a custom-built landing pad on the other side of the ranges to the back of the city. They alight and quickly become aware of the other spaceships stationed around them. Jem eyes one. It is new with a red sparkle in its shell, suggesting it is coated in extra layers of zillet, which would make it ideal for resisting outer magnetic influences. I can see why it appeals to him, why his eyes follow its outline, appreciating its formidable outer protection.

He gathers his crew; they huddle and converse. Soon after, Jem leaves them and wanders off into the surrounding forest. I stay with him, flitting like a bird high above to watch over him as he pushes through close-knit trees and low sweeping branches. Before long he comes to a milky waterway, and from the way he halts I can tell he has arrived at his destination. It is a pretty spot, dominated by white moss that covers the ground, rocks, shrubs, and trees. It is like a thin blanket of snow, without the cold.

Jem sits on the bank and closes his eyes. He is meditating. There is a soft yellowish glow to his aura. When he opens his eyes, I see Tasma appear. I gather they communicate telepathically. Jem seems troubled, but then calm. When he leaves the forest, Tasma goes with him and they both return to the stationary spaceships.

The halo-like glow stays with Jem, clings to him, a yellow haze around his head and body, which I soon realise renders him invisible to the human eye. I watch him walk to the impressive ship of his choice; passing security, mechanics, and engineers, EASA and World Council personnel, all without being stopped or questioned. They just don't see him.

He boards the ship, aiming to steal it. The hatch closes and the ship roars into life. I smile inwardly as I watch the space station crews erupt into panic.

Time spins forward.

Tasma is guiding Jem in piloting the ship and they skirt the void that yawns in front of them. To me their ship is like a cautious little child running on the shore of a beach, while the pounding waves of the ocean remain fixed to one side. A splash could see them pulled into the currents, yet they stay clear and dry.

I am there when they come across Mum's ship.

Ah, to see Jem's jubilation is something I'll never forget. I want to laugh and cry with him. He looks so thrilled, so triumphant. He had trusted in his images of Mum and her callings and had been prepared to go further than he knew was safe to find her.

I see it then. The droid of my nightmare. It is behind Jem, on the ship, coldly and calmly reaching for its weapon. Yes, now that Mum's ship and the weapon have been located, it can act.

It turns. The red light is on the back of Jem's head.

How has this droid come to be with them? They must have trusted it, programmed it to do their bidding. But I'm guessing the World Council were watching Jem the whole time, perhaps since the funeral. His conversation with Treesa would not have gone unnoticed. If I had thought it peculiar, others would have too. Perhaps, they had let Jem go to Nattalia and fly out, knowing they had already corrupted his trusty droid. A hidden virus in the bowels of its systems, waiting to spring and spread once the weapon was detected.

I watch, knowing in my heart that Jem will be okay. I know that Tasma is also there on the ship. I see it now; the higher being. Transparent, but its glow thickens into a denser light. It did not expect the droid to be corrupted. It had not been able to pick up on such trickery. It can now only respond to the threat at hand. It flicks Jem out of the way, like a lightning flash clipping the ground.

The droid fires. A spherical, finned, grenade-like device hurtles out and explodes against the ship's control panels. Jem is clear of it. He is unharmed. Tasma shuts down the droid with merely a thought, but damage to the ship has been done, such damage.

The device had an outer ring containing a highly flammable substance, which spills out on impact. Fire burns. It licks and taunts and spreads. I watch Jem's anguished rush to contain it. He does, eventually.

There are tears in his eyes, likely not just from the chemically laden smoke, for there's so much sorrow in them. He stands, shattered, looking out the view at Mum's ship, cruelly close enough to dock, but no longer with the controls to bring his ship in.

I slowly let my eyes flutter open. I've seen enough. I'm in a quiet stupor, shocked by all I've witnessed.

'Can't get good droids around this place,' I manage to mumble at last. My anger at them comforts my despair.

'What did you see?' Cal asks.

'A lot. I'll tell you later.' I look at Tasma. 'I gather after that, Jem went into hibernation?'

'Yes. I came back, hoping to find help for him, hoping to find you.'

I exhale in one long calming breath. It is quiet. The fighter ships have stopped flying overhead.

'Tasma, how did you get back?' As soon as I ask, I know. Tasma is astral. It can travel through time and space with ease. It can change its vibrational rate to manifest in different planes of existence including our own spatio-temporal plane. Very useful!

'We should go to them,' I say, my heart lurching with the need.

'No. Enough humans are stranded. I will go with a droid I can trust. I will show the droid where they are and guide and protect the ship while it retrieves the humans and the weapon. Jem showed me that the hibernation capsules are detachable and can be loaded on to one ship. I will get the droid to do this—load them all on to one ship and return, with the weapon.'

'But you can't do all that in time. Not in time to save Earth.'

'I have to go now.'

'Will Earth be spared? Please, I have to know. You must know.'

'I am not all-knowing. I have to go now.'

'Yes, of course. But how will you work with the droid if you're not physically present?'

Tasma takes in a breath and lowers its vibration.

'I see it,' Cal says. 'There.' He points at Tasma.

More orange than yellow this time, its bristles flex and shine along the length of its delicate, ever-changing form. There is a wave to its body that ripples back and forth, making its lights twinkle within a bright haze. Its drooping eyes are defined by an absence of light. 'I can exist on the physical and the higher planes. Your mother hasn't got much time left. Her hibernation capsule is almost out of oxygen. I will go.'

'All right,' I say, feeling flustered. 'Go, and good luck.'

It looks at me expectantly. I try to listen to its thoughts and hear, 'The chip?'

I'm confused. 'Chip?'

'To put inside the droid. It will help me trust it.'

'Oh, yes. That!'

I slide the chip out from beneath my nano-band and willingly hand it over. 'Take it.'

The chip flies from my hand and disappears within its lights. Having all it needs, Tasma floats over to our ship and passes through its outer shell. Only a few seconds later, the sturdy craft fires up.

'It's leaving right away... Hey, wait,' Cal shouts indignantly. 'We need our return pod. You can't just leave us stuck out here!' He rushes forward and I grab hold of his arm. 'Cal, no. It's too late.'

The ship shudders and we are forced to make a rapid retreat to the edge of the clearing as it begins its upward thrust. As it climbs, its roaring subsides, and at last we are left to quietly watch the vessel, a small blip high in a pale blue sky, my heart swollen with hope. So much that I love and care about rests on that ship's return and I'm trying hard not to be afraid, not to entertain the thought that it could fail.

'The little ones have gone,' I hear Cal say.

'Did all that really just happen? You did see them?'

'Well, the ship's gone, and we didn't fly it out of here.'

'It was not what I expected. I like to think I know things... don't get too many surprises. It knew I had a chip.' I'm gabbling and shivering.

'Britta...'

I can't respond. I'm numb. Too many emotions have caused an internal shutdown. I feel Cal's arm around me, trying to press warmth into my bones.

'Britta? Just breathe.' We sit and his arm stays around me.

'That was all... very strange,' I say at last.

Cal laughs. It's unnaturally thin but I'm cheered by the sound of it. I then start to tell him all that I saw under Tasma's guidance.

'Jem, of course, went after her, wanted to be the hero, and he almost was,' I say, starting to wind up. 'He got out there, found Mum. It was that droid that stopped him. Just good fortune Tasma was there to save him. But the droid's blast disabled the ship and now he's stuck out there too.'

'Stuck where? What do you mean by a void?'

I brace, knowing the impact my next words will have on him. 'They are forty-five billion light years away on the edge of a dark expanse of space.'

'Forty-five billion! What? Is that what it told you? That's impossible! No humans have ever gone that far.'

'Mum and her crew did. And Jem.'

'Britta.' Cal is shaking his head. 'Tasma will fly through Nattalia's Hatch to get there. But, seriously, it can't come back. There's no Hatch out there for a return.'

I shrug, not wanting to consider it. 'There must be a way. Tasma wouldn't suggest this if it didn't know a way back. Just because we don't know of it...'

'You think this Tasma can wink a ship back?'

'It could know of a portal or a wormhole or something. Its knowledge surpasses ours. We don't have to understand how it's going to bring them back. Just that it promised it would.'

'It promised. And it wants your help in return... to do what?'

I don't answer. I don't know.

'So, now what? We just wait out here, hoping to be found? No one knows we're here. No one. This is unknown chartered territory.'

'I didn't feel I had any other choice. Would you not have agreed?'

'I would have asked if we could unload our pod first.'

'I'm sorry! I panicked. It kept saying it had to go and that my mum's almost out of oxygen. I really felt time was of the essence, and that asteroid is not slowing down!'

Cal takes in the strain on my face. He softens. 'No. You're right. It boarded the ship and was away before we knew what was happening. Sorry. I'm just... Well, Mandon's waging war and he'll be wanting to punish my father. I really wish I could be back in the capital.'

Sympathising with his concern for his parents, I decide to put my finely attuned senses to use. I breathe in deeply a few times, emptying my thoughts, and search forward. The images come quickly. I see Odell and Cillian, dressed in padded suits and carrying stores on their backs, making their way along a narrow track within a forest of orange undergrowth.

'They got away. Feels like they are north of Jucca. Yes, I hear *north* confirmed.'

'They are?' Relief gushes from him. I know how he feels. I had the same reaction when I learned that Neath had chosen to stay out of the fighting. How we worry for our hearts and for those who are in them. 'I know they said they were ready to flee. I just didn't know how off guard they'd been taken, given it happened so soon. Remind me to kill Garth—'

'He did it for his family.'

'Yes, but their lives weren't at risk. His family would easily have coped with four more months in space. Supplies had been sent up. It's not anything like what your mum's been through. Stuck in space for years! Do you think there's really a chance... I mean, she hasn't made contact with you. You've never thought her still living? Just trapped?'

'I've felt her watching over me, you know, felt a presence, a word here and there that made me think she was around. I always assumed she had passed. It didn't occur to me she could just be astral travelling to me. But it's very possible. Jem always said she didn't want to upset me. She could have kept her distance so I wouldn't do what Jem did and take off after her. It makes sense that Jem would go by himself in the way he did. He would do anything to bring Mum home. He really missed her when she left. He was older, her firstborn. They were always close.'

Cal is quiet, considering all I've said. 'I really hope she's out there, Britta. I want her to come back to you. She would be proud of you.'

I smile to hide my awkwardness. 'I don't know about that.'

'You think Tasma can guide a droid to them? I mean, what in distant galaxies is that thing, anyway? I've studied a lot of alien forms, but nothing like that!'

'It's an inter-dimensional being.'

'What does that mean? Does it eat food, shed waste, reproduce?'

'I'm not sure, but it can function and live on different planes of existence.'

'Sounds hard to kill.'

'Cal! We don't have to fear it.' My mind scrabbles for a way to explain that he might understand. 'Look, you know the war-game exercises back at EASA? We are broken up into red team, blue team, green team, etc. Our nano-bands are set to different channels for communication purposes. Red team: channel four. Blue team: channel seven. Green team: channel nine—so each team cannot hear the other's communications.'

Cal nods, though I sense his impatience to hear my point.

'The way we operate in the universe is much the same. Humans, this whole universal plane... Let's say we are tuned to channel four. That being, named Tasma, can tune to more than one channel. When it appeared, it tuned to our channel four. It usually operates on channel seven, a higher vibration. In fact, it's not just beings like Tasma, but entire universes exist on these different channels. These beings and other universes are just floating through and around us all the time and we can't see or sense them because they are on different planes.'

This time he nods with some acceptance. 'I suppose it shouldn't be so unbelievable given we have known for some time that our universe is ninety-nine point nine, nine, nine, nine percent empty space. Something else could be there. It's strange to think that so much can coexist.'

'In the same way that light, sound, x-rays, heat, magnetism, electricity coexists without interfering with each other.'

'True,' Cal says. 'What I'm worried about is how effective this makes it. I mean, Tasma's species can move between planes, right? If we went to war with it, we'd be fighting something that could wink in and out, and am I right in guessing, it could predict our future moves and strategies? We could never set an ambush.'

I smile. 'Always war. This species doesn't even know what war is. It's peaceful. It doesn't come here to pop out on us with guns.'

'No, but it has a weapon that can smash asteroids,' Cal points out warily.

'We've called it a weapon. I don't think its original purpose was to kill life-forms. It seems to be trying to help us.'

'I hope you're right.' Cal squeezes my shoulder. He stands and looks to the sky. We are not used to skies free of air traffic. The quiet drift of clouds, shaped like parallel sandbanks, holds his gaze for some time. 'I wonder how long we have to wait for it to return.'

'Could be some time. So, what do we do now?' I ask.

'We could try to contact...' Cal looks to his nano-band and frowns. 'No signal here. I thought we'd have it.'

'The mountain ranges we flew over were high. They could be blocking it.'

'I wouldn't have thought so. Maybe, if we got higher...'

'Maybe,' I say, unsure. I release a small sigh. 'Not sure there's much to go back to anyway.'

'You'd take the alien wilderness over life under Mandon?'

I smirk. 'Let's get to know the place first, then I'll answer that. Don't worry, if needed, I can try to contact someone telepathically. Someone at EASA will have trained and achieved well enough in the psychic arts to pick up my messages and send a crew to look for us.'

We peer around, wondering what landmarks we could offer up as a means to locate us. Nothing significant presents. We need to explore and better understand our location. Currently, there's only the forest and it is beckoning our next steps.

'Best put the daylight to good use,' Cal says.

Straightening the packs on our backs, we head off. The trees quickly dwarf us. They are almost twice as high as those on Earth. Their lower branches hang down and lean on the ground, creating a challenging obstacle course. Most of the time, I can duck beneath the branches, which are adorned by large, soft, furry leaves. Sometimes, I climb over, using my strength to pull myself up before leaping down, tearing leaves as I drop. We clamber and weave and duck until the forest thins and the trees shorten. There are higher branches in this patch, allowing us to walk freely. The ground is rockier though and hard underfoot.

As we explore, I start to wonder. Even if we see berries or critters or grubs, how will we know if they're edible and not poisonous? We are facing an environment that we have only textbook knowledge about. General information, not a detailed how to survive in the Nattalian wilderness guide or anything.

Should we walk up in the hope of a better view or walk down in the hope of reaching a river?

I rely on my instincts, going on a feeling, a colour, a thought of yes or no. Cal allows me to lead, knowing I have a better chance of tuning into a higher knowledge than he, and we take a higher path that brings us to a steep incline. We climb, stopping regularly for sips of water. It's hot. The air is thick and slathers our skin with sweat.

The higher we go, the better I feel. I let this heightened state continue to egg me on, pushing us up and over larger rocks.

Soon we hear it. Rushing water.

'What's that? A river?' Cal hurries on. He reaches a large boulder and climbs it. 'Waterfall,' he announces.

He gives me a hand and pulls me up. Together, side by side, we survey a river feeding a wide, yet short waterfall, pounding into a tea-coloured lake. There are fruits on the branches of trees overhanging the water, jumping silver fish, shells on the rocks, and slow-moving birds.

We stand watching for a long while, and on the other side of the flowing waters I see small animals, like doggish cats, lapping at it. It's drinkable. It must be.

Our observations eventually reveal birds pecking at the fruit and catching the fish with their beaks. The shells could be those we ate last night. The plump, brown feathered birds with green beaks certainly look easy to catch. It is encouraging.

After a long while, Cal is the first to speak. 'Camp here the night?' Feeling confident that I will agree, he drops his heavy pack.

'It's quite the spot.' My pack joins his with a thud.

We turn, our faces are close, noses almost touching, and our eyes are mirroring each other's triumph. Survival is no longer an issue. We have more than enough right here to get by for a long while. We feel a rare surge of freedom. There's nothing else for us to do but sit back and wait and enjoy the fruits of the land, literally. Eventually, we will be found, somehow.

We look at each other and I'm drawn in by his intense gaze.

Before I realise it, my hands are in his and I absorb the affection of the act, my fingers curling around his hands' synthetic strength. I hold tightly, instantly addicted to the sense of security it offers. I don't want to let go.

'What are you thinking?' he asks. I barely hear him. His voice is just a whisper.

I'm afraid. Afraid of losing control, of falling in love with Cal so hard, I won't be able to pull back without my heart being completely shattered and I don't think I can take much more right now. I'm tired, drained and yet... when he looks at me like that! Serious and kind and loving...

We kiss.

I expected it. I know I wanted it and I don't resist, at all.

Our hands slide around each other's waists, bringing us even closer. If ever there is a moment to pause, savour, and store to memory, I think this is it. Even as it's happening, as his lips are claiming mine in long, slow kisses, I wish I could stay frozen in that moment forever; forever relinquishing my heart and hoping that the future will take care of itself. Such moments spiral high in contrast to all other moments, which tick mindlessly around in days of routines, drills, worries, loss, and loneliness. I'm giddy on the high that consumes me, that spins my emotions up and up.

'I've been wanting this since the moment we met outside the Moon Café,' he says.

'I knew you were for me the first day Jem brought you home.'

He smiles. 'Of course, you did. Look where you've brought us.' Cal turns to face the river.

'We got here together.'

He kisses my forehead and his lips lower to savour my lips again.

* * *

Two suns are in the sky and the brightest one is half set.

At some point, we had to detach ourselves to see to our preparations for night. Still holding hands though, we discovered a nearby cave to shelter in and, keeping close to each other, gathered armfuls of firewood, plucked closed shells from rocks on the side of the river, and refilled our water containers.

Now on first sunset, I sit back just inside the cave's entrance with a dawning sense of recognition. 'I have been here before.

My astral self has. I guess that explains how I could lead us to it.'

'How do you do that?' Cal finishes placing rocks in a ring around our collection of fire sticks and comes and sits next to me.

'How do I astral travel? I first did it when I was about six years old. Training at EASA really honed it though.'

'What about seeing the future?'

'That comes from trusting in what I receive.'

Cal's eyes are hooded. 'Trust? That alone is hard to do. With so much deceit. The World Council—'

'Can't be allowed to own and run this planet.'

'No. Yet you saw them winning the war.'

'Yes. That was clear.'

'You're lucky being able to see. You get warnings, time to prepare. I always envied Jem that. He always seemed ready, you know?'

I shake my head. 'It's not always good, often isn't. Besides, I still see so little. I keep trying to check on Neath, but I can't see him.'

'You'd know if something had happened to him. You'd feel it. So not knowing must be good news. How do you do it? How do you check on someone?'

'How?'

'Yeah. Any chance you can teach me? We've got plenty of time.'

I'm not sure if he's serious. I study his face and see he's intent. He really wants to know. I hesitate. I'm still a student myself and am not sure if I can teach. 'I don't know,' I blurt. 'I just use my senses.'

'Super senses!'

'Not super; same as yours. I'm just more aware of them. You have to raise your awareness.'

'I'm aware of you,' he says huskily, his eyes glazing.

I know I'm aware of him. His thoughts are loud in my mind. He wants to be closer to me. I lift my gaze to meet his and we kiss again.

'So,' he says, pulling back. 'How can I be more aware?'

'You're asking this because you want to see your parents,' I say, feeling his need to see. The desire to watch over loved ones is a powerful motivator.

'Yes, and other things.' He looks at me. 'I want to protect you. When you were talking to Tasma... I didn't like being on the outer, unable to know what it was communicating and what was happening. For a moment, I thought he was harming you and I couldn't do anything.'

'I can protect myself.'

'I knew you'd say that.'

'Psychic already?'

'Let's put it down to knowing you.'

'Ah, I see. Well, maybe you don't need to enhance your senses if you just know things.'

'Come on, teach me.' He's adamant. He takes my hand. 'Give me my first lesson.'

When he looks at me like that, it's hard to deny him anything. 'Okay. I will. As soon as I figure out where to start.' Where would Jem have begun? I muse. 'Time is not linear,' I say.

Cal settles his posture, keenly listening.

'It is curved. It is all around, happening all at once within the now. It's like I can poke my head up into it and see forward or back. For me, seeing the future is just like having a memory of the past. Right now, if I tell you to remember a moment you felt embarrassed, you can see it, feel it, still wish the moment didn't happen. When I see the future, it is the same. It has the same clarity, same sense of having happened, the same depth of feelings. It appears in my mind—not like a daydream. A daydream has an airy, made-up quality. The future comes sharper. It's more real.'

'How do you get these forward memories?'

I think for a moment. 'I use a different part of the brain. I call up an image to the front of my head, on the screen behind my eyes. I call it up using a question or a thought. Then it starts to play like a recording.'

'How do you call it up?'

I think for a moment. 'I neither push anything away or pull anything toward me, though I do seem to focus on that area of my mind and try to invite energy to come in. I watch my thoughts and let them pass. I distance myself from them and create space, emptiness. I know it helps when I'm calm. I draw the outside inside and my inside becomes outside. Does that make sense?'

'I think so, though I don't think I could do it.'

'Try.'

'Try? Me?'

'Yes. Go on.'

He looks embarrassed. 'I don't know.'

'Close your eyes. Go on, do it. Close them.'

He does.

'Calm your mind, open it. Feel the air, become it.'

'Become the air,' he says, smiling.

'Are you going to try this or not?'

'All right.' He takes a deep breath, exhales in a rush and rolls his shoulders. He is serious now, relaxed, still. Eyes closed, I can see him tuning out and bringing energy in.

'Ask a question and wait for an image. Look to the front of your mind. Accept what comes in. Don't fight it or try to change it. Just see without thinking.'

I watch his face soften. He is at ease, breathing rhythmically as if in sleep.

After a long while, he opens his eyes and frowns. 'If you see something, does it mean it will happen?'

'What did you see?'

'My father. He was on the ground, holding his leg. He's in pain. He doesn't get up. What do you think? Real?'

I ask for confirmation and see green. 'I think real,' I say carefully. 'But it's hard to say when this happens or if it has already happened. You could be picking up on the past, present, future... just one possible future.'

'Well, that's frustrating.'

'Yes, I know,' I say emphatically. 'Interpreting what you see is the hardest part.'

He looks glum. He's not pleased. 'He could be badly injured or captured... my mother alone. And we're just sitting here.' He's frustrated.

'We could find a way back. There could be ships out here. There were scouts that came to this side of the planet and never returned. Jem's crew, for instance.'

'If they have functional ships, why didn't they just fly back? And how would we find them?'

'I could try to ask Tasma or the young ones.'

'No, I don't want you communicating with them, not if we don't have to.'

'But if they can help us...'

'I don't want you more indebted to them! Who knows what kind of favour they're going to call in after all this. Tasma did say it wanted a favour in return.'

'It indicated something like that.'

He's upset. Seeing his father injured has disturbed him. I, too, share concern for the conservationist leader who had shown, if nothing else, a courageous spirit. To think he had the gumption to take over the city's army of droids and to take a stand against the World Council and its plans. I have to admire him. I had seen him fleeing with his wife, but they would be trackable...

Cal and I remain quiet with our thoughts.

'Do you think it will come back?' Cal asks. 'Tasma.'

'I don't know.'
'What about us?'
'Us?'
'Can you see our future?'

The question takes me off guard. I feel a blush creep up my neck. I've seen us being more intimate and our love deepening, but I'm not ready to share this with him. Surely, it's best just to let it happen without tabling it like a forgone conclusion. Letting it happen keeps the magic and natural flow of our young and developing relationship. I want that for us.

As for our immediate fate... if and how we get off this uninhabited side of the planet, I have no idea. Sometimes it's hard to see when I'm too scared to look. I think Cal just learned that by gaining insight into his father's woes. Knowing isn't always an advantage if you can't do anything about it.

'You don't have to answer. I feel things are going to be okay for us.' He wraps an arm around me, and I lean my head on his shoulder. I think of all that has happened to lead us to be stranded on a hillside by a life-sustaining waterfall, watching the second sun set. Each choice that got us from Earth to here. I tentatively start dreaming of a life outside of this forest; one in which our families are safe, and our lives are free to live as we please. Cal and I could be together, always together.

Dreams. That's all we have. There's nothing else we can do.

CHAPTER FOURTEEN

THE SUNS RISE AND FALL OVER AND OVER.

The light shines on our lovemaking, foraging, swimming, dreaming. They are the happiest and most anxious days I've known.

Happiest because they are spent getting closer to Cal. Every minute of our night and day is spent by each other's side. Cal doesn't let me out of his sight and I like having him nearby. The sounds, smells, and sights are new to us, yet together we have the courage to explore and make decisions without becoming overwhelmed.

Sadly, these joyful days of love and discovery are laced with anxiety. The asteroid edges closer to Earth with each passing day, and across the seas and mountain ranges a war for Nattalia is being fought. My brother will surely be in the thick of it and my father affected by it, even if they remain removed from the fighting. I wish I had news of what was going on. The isolation during such turmoil is unsettling. Of course, I should be able to use my gifts to sense what's happening, but my inner stress won't let me tune in. It's like trying to play an old, familiar song on a warped instrument. No matter how much effort I exert or how much I go over well-worn practices, everything I try just comes out muddied.

In this state of heightened tension, with the future eluding me, I look frequently to the skies and think of Tasma. Without Cal's knowledge, I try to connect with the being. I try to follow it to the edge of the void, without success.

In the back of my mind is the pressing concern that it is helping us because I have promised it aid in return. How could I possibly help such a high being? What will it comprise?

With night limiting our activity to the light of the fire, Cal and I find ourselves sitting and conversing for hours on end, sharing innermost thoughts and fears. I treasure these long exchanges that flow without interruption or argument. We talk and listen and connect. The crackle of the fire becomes the soundtrack to our secrets shared and the flames witnesses to our passion.

One night, while gazing up at the unfamiliar sky, Cal points to the brightest star, sitting just off one of the apricot moons.

'That's Kappa-Ceti forty-nine, a red super-giant. It could go nova at any time.'

Forty-nine! Of all the numbers attributed to all the stars in our view, Cal singles that one out. It's uncanny! I ponder the number and its hauntings as Cal continues. 'That star is one hundred light years away. Light has been travelling at three hundred thousand kilometres per second for one hundred years just to get to us here tonight. Can you grasp that distance?'

'I suppose. I know how much you like to measure it,' I say teasingly.

Cal holds up his artificially enhanced hand in front of the heavenly bodies. 'See the distance between my thumb and small finger?'

'Yes.'

'If my handspan represents the distance to that brightest star, then the distance to Jem and your mum is from here to there.' He points at one of the moons.

I shudder. He is right. In real terms, they are so far away. They are at a distance that the human mind struggles to grasp. No wonder I like to think of distance in terms of the astral plane. I wish I could explain it to Cal as succinctly.

'They are far and yet, their spirits could be right here with us,' I say.

'How?'

'Our spirits don't have to be limited by our physical bodies. We can go anywhere, anytime.'

'When I saw my father, did my spirit visit him?'

'In a way, yes. You opened yourself to insights by tuning in to a higher consciousness.'

'Can you explain that?'

'You do like easy questions,' I comment with a smile.

Cal strokes my hair, presses his lips to my forehead. 'I want to understand it,' he says.

'In very simple terms, the higher consciousness is the underlying fabric that binds all the universes together. It's unity and diversity. It's timeless and formless.'

Cal gives a half laugh. 'Okay. That makes my line from here to the moon look short!'

I laugh too.

'So how does this higher consciousness give you insights?'

'Well, for me, it's a case of lifting my consciousness to it, to another plane, a mental plane of thought streams. I tap into this mental plane where insights can be decoded into a language that makes sense. For instance, I often receive colours. Green for yes. Red for no. I work in colours and images. Jem tends to receive symbols from childhood fairy tales—archetypal images. If he saw a wolf, it would mean an attack or threat. Several wolves circling, would mean a pack of enemies. Some people hear words or phrases repeating over and over in their minds. Or they will hear a song that has meaning to them. It is not always easy to decipher the symbols coming through, but the more you work with them, the better you become. Without the mental plane and the symbols, it would be hard to funnel and interpret this knowledge.'

'I don't get any symbols.'

'Not even in your dreams?'

'Sometimes. Last night I dreamed we were being chased, and you're not going to believe this, given what you just said, but we were being chased by wolves!'

I shiver. I don't like it. I trace his lips with my finger, trying to stay calm. 'Did they catch us?'

'I woke up too soon to know. Do you think that dream had meaning?'

Patterns represented by coincidence always have meaning and the fact that I just spoke of wolves the night after he dreamed them is not good. Enemies...

Cal is watching my face closely. 'I won't let any harm come to you,' he says. 'We know this forest well now. If anyone or thing comes for us, we can run. We know places to hide.'

'Yes, we do,' I say, though I'm already wondering what we'll be running from.

'Remember when I told you that Jem saw us together when you...'

'Don't. Focusing on it only gives it power. I will come to no harm because I believe in that. Whatever Jem saw... just forget it. It was one image received a long time ago. He may have misinterpreted the symbols. Besides, I would do this all again. Be with you here.'

I want to go on. I want to open my heart and tell him my true feelings for him, but when I peer up, I see him swallow, his face etched in a frown. His eyes are sad and harbouring a faraway gaze. He's worrying about me.

'Stop it,' I say. 'Jem is not my keeper and he often exaggerated things because he was playing the overprotective brother. I can take care of myself. You and I are a good thing. We're good together.'

His eyes focus on me and grow even more serious. 'Yes, we are. I couldn't stay away from you now, no matter Jem said. I'll just have to keep you safe. That's my job now.'

* * *

I watch Cal fall asleep that night and try once again to contact Tasma.

'Let me see,' I call to it, feeling more desperate than usual. But as usual, I hear nothing, see nothing.

'What enemy is coming?' I try to sense forward. I seek colours, words, images. But all I feel is a tight fear in my stomach and an acute sense of time running out.

A couple of days later, on our nineteenth day of being stranded, we hear a craft.

Hope lifts my eyes. Tasma, Jem, Mum?

Isn't it too soon?

'Britta, get back in the cave.' Cal runs toward me. 'It's the World Council.'

What? How? I look down at my wrist. My nano-band is glowing. We can't use it for communication, but it can still be tracked. The World Council has traced us. If we go into the cave, it will find us there and we'll be trapped and caught.

As soon as Cal reaches me, I take him by the hand.

'We have to jump,' I say, pulling him toward the top of the waterfall.

'No. Hide.' He yanks on my hand, dragging me toward the cave.

'Our nano-bands!'

He looks and sees them glowing. Understanding dawns. Now of the same mind, we sprint toward the stream and with a quick glance to gauge our readiness, we leap into the churning current. As our bodies plunge within the force of the waterfall, our hands fly apart.

I'm alone, deep in the lake, my legs kicking hard.

On breaking the water's surface, I take a sharp breath and frantically search for Cal. His head bobs up a few seconds later near the lake's edge. He swings around and sees me, waves me over. I swim underwater and come up next to him. His hands clutch my body close to his.

'Come on, this way,' he says. Paddling further to the edge, we take cover beneath the overhanging branches of a tree. Anything flying overhead would not be able to see us.

We keep our wrists underwater, hoping that by submerging our bands, it will weaken their signals.

'What do they want with us? Why have they come?' Cal asks.

'I don't know, but our efforts to get a weapon to stop the asteroid is not in line with Mandon's plans.'

'You think Garth and Tilly told them?'

'Yes, but maybe not willingly.'

I catch a streak of red and look up. The Red Vipers are on the ridge, our packs in their hands. Their enhanced eyes scan the river and waterfall for us before looking down to the lake. We are seen within seconds.

'Go, go,' Cal shouts.

We drag our soaked bodies on to the lake's shore and run. We know the area well and our feet hurry along paths where the undergrowth is less dense. Cal is faster and runs ahead, though regularly checks to make sure I'm never far behind. We run and run, while our smart bands continue to taunt us with their persistent glowing. We can't remove them. It's impossible. They are made of an almost unbreakable substance. My chest burns with fatigue. It hurts to breathe and I am gasping.

'I can't,' I manage to mumble, but Cal doesn't hear.

'Come on.'

I hear the river on our right and realise we've been running parallel to it for some time. Perhaps we can jump back in and submerge our bands again, if only to cool down and take a break. I'm about to stop and demand that we try this when we burst into a clearing and find ourselves in front of a ring of people, mostly men, long-haired and bearded, and three women. They are all lounging around the dying embers of a fire and startle as we stumble upon them, our chests heaving, our eyes alert and wide, like those of a hunted animal.

They stare. We stare.

'Who are you?' one of the men asks and defensively comes to his feet. He looks like the leader of the odd pack. He is a product of EASA. It is easy to tell by his oversized hands and faded EASA uniform. A dark beard hides his chin, yet I can see it is strong and square, aligning perfectly with his other features. He is strikingly handsome with brilliant blue eyes contrasting against a dark complexion. A quick glance at the others and I discover their facial attributes are of equally high standards; all no doubt crafted beneath the knife of a surgical beautician and enhanced by artistic technicians. They have at some point had time to take advantage of Nattalia's complimentary services.

Cal speaks first. 'You're EASA trained. Are you the crew of Jem Tate?'

'You know us.' The man is surprised. The others sit up, their backs straight.

'We know Jem's crew were sent to this side on an exploratory mission with a small, well-armed droid army. What happened?'

A woman, with lovely green eyes and enhanced lips, poses, 'Have you come to take us back? You have a ship?'

The Red Vipers' ship can now be heard.

'Hide us, please,' I cry, shouting above the ship's intensifying roar. The crew, too stunned to react, simply look up. They don't know what to make of us or the ship hovering above the forest.

Cal grabs my hand and leads me into low-lying shrubbery where we crouch in a hopeless attempt to conceal ourselves.

'They'll know we're here,' I say, watching our nano-bands giving us away.

As if our nano-bands were not enough to draw the World Council's eye, we gain the added disadvantage of the stranded crew members actively seeking the ship's attention by shouting and waving their arms above their heads at it. 'We're down here. Help us. Here. We're here.'

I look at Cal in alarm. We're done for. The crew, seeing the ship as part of a rescue mission, are working as hard as possible to flag it down. I can't blame them. They've been stuck in this forest for over four years.

Cal squeezes my hand as fear scatters my thoughts. The urge to shriek is very real. I focus on swallowing it. 'They'll kill us,' I wheeze.

'Not without a fight.' Cal glances around for any kind of weapon and leaps up to wrench free a tree branch in easy reach. I don't want him to harm this fascinating living tree and cast about for an alternative.

'No, wait. Over there.' I point to a gun leaning against a tree near the campfire. He nods, a grateful smile gracing his lips, before scurrying stealthily away to retrieve the more convincing weapon. When he returns to my side, he examines it. 'A Fire Bolter,' he says. 'White flame in a stream.'

While we stay low, listening earnestly for what's happening in the clearing, my head begins to feel light and I close my eyes. I hear the whispers. 'Hide, hide, hide,' they say to me.

'Yes, I'm hiding,' I tell them back.

'Hide, hide, hide.'

The ship, roaring overhead, suddenly booms as its thrusters are activated and it zooms straight up and with a tremendous whir is gone. The sky is clear and quiet. Incredibly, it seems the World Council has abandoned its search for us. Why?

'No,' the crew members shout. They scream for it to come back; their screams are so shrill, so desperate they are soon hoarse with their efforts. But the craft does not return. Eventually, they give up and fall as silent as the skies above.

Cal stands. 'It's gone.' He sounds baffled, then bewildered, 'What is going on?'

I stand, too, and find myself gazing through a strange band of light. We are surrounded by it, bathed in its glorious haze.

Jem's crew, huddled on the other side of the clearing, are watching us with grave suspicion. The weapons weighted in their hands are trained on us. I know that Cal is armed, but he is just one person, one gun.

'What...?'

I turn and see. Behind us, floating just above our heads, are the young beings. They are beaming yellows and oranges, creating a barrier of light. The light's vibration is so high, I realise it must have blocked the signals from our nano-bands or interfered with the ship's scanners. Slowly the creatures withdraw their beams, reducing it to just a soft glow.

Cal is staring at them too, unable to comprehend what their presence means.

'You saved us,' I say. 'Why?'

In my mind, I hear, 'Not your time.'

As soundlessly as they had arrived, they take their leave, bouncing and drifting back into the forest, leaving the clearing rather dull and dim in their absence.

'What just happened?' the blue-eyed man of admirable physique demands to know. 'I think you two better sit and start talking.'

'We'll stand,' Cal says, shifting the weapon in his hands. 'This is Britta Tate, Jem's sister.'

'Sister?'

I become the centre of focus. Many eyes begin scrutinising my appearance for any likeness to my brother. I'm not much like him, though we do share some similarities, the shape of our eyes, the pointiness of our chins.

'Are you psychic, like your brother?' The question has come from the woman with the alluring eyes and lips. Unarmed, she is nervously wrapping her long ponytail around her hand. Her hair is brown, though it is tipped silver, suggesting she had once print-dyed her hair that colour and it has almost grown out.

'Of course, she's got the gifts! You saw how those light beings protected her,' the man says and, resting his blue eyes on me, adds, 'Jem could talk to them too. But he went away with one of them and never came back.'

'Jem will come back,' I say, surprising them all.

'We hope that very much,' the woman says sincerely. 'He went to get something. Will he come back with it?' As she asks this, she leans into the blue-eyed man, linking her arm through his.

'I believe he will return with a significant weapon of alien design,' I say.

The crew members exchange glances and they visibly relax.

'Seems we're on the same side. Why don't we sit down and start over? My name's Alagard. I was put in command of this crew and mission. This is my wife, Adelle. Come. Let's sit and all introduce ourselves and then, perhaps, you can explain what brings you here and why that ship was looking for you and, more importantly, why you didn't want to be found.'

They are good questions. I like his directness and welcome his conciliatory tone.

'Let's talk,' I agree.

Guns down, we exchange introductions and a few pleasantries. We are offered a fishy tasting broth, served in large, brittle shells. The soup is warm and peppery and instils a calming effect. I sip at it constantly, breathing in its steam, so that my mind floats and my body releases its long-held tension.

'Take it slower,' Cal says cautioning me. 'I need you with me.'

I smile, ah I smile, such love shining in my eyes. Am I drunk, high, lost?

'Okay,' Cal says, tapping my knee. 'You've really enjoyed that.'

'Yes, I needed it.'

Cal looks concerned. 'You are okay now?'

'Now...' I hold the word in my mind and meditate upon it.

'Looks like I'm doing all the explaining to our new friends then,' I hear Cal mutter.

'If you can.'

Cal takes the bowl of soup from me, despite my protest, then, with a reassuring arm around my shoulders, begins to address the crew, who are eager to learn our story. Cal tells them everything and as I listen, his words sober me. I long for more soup, wanting to disappear into its calming fog, but as I drift back to reality and watch the crew's expressions grow more agitated as they take in the enormity of the current human situation, I realise I have to come back and be in the now, not distant from it and certainly not safe from it. I have to embrace it if I am truly to cope.

It is a sombre monologue that Cal tells. A story of an asteroid less than four months away from Earth, of a father who has claimed leadership of Nattalia to save it from the plans of the World Council, and of our escape from that council determined to thwart our efforts to secure a planet-saving weapon.

There are gasps as they learn eight billion people remain on Earth, awaiting their fate.

'We were told all who wanted to leave would be evacuated,' Alagard queries.

'They were not told about the asteroid until the majority of ships had left with those handpicked for the new planet. There just weren't enough ships. The real chance to save them was in building a rocket to knock it off course, but this plan was sabotaged and the rocket was built to fail.'

In the long, mournful silence that follows, many drink soup

as deeply and as quickly as I had. I watch their eyes glaze, blocking out the pain.

'Miss, you said your brother was coming back. How do you know?' An old man, with chaotic white hair and matching beard, asks. Bent over with age, I notice he is not partaking of the mind-numbing soup, despite the fact he probably needs it more, given his capacity for compassion seems greater than the others. His face is not perfect. He has not sought out a cosmetic surgeon. Instead, he allows natural lines of kindness and friendliness to shape his appearance and expressions. I trust him at once.

'What is your name?'

'Markel.'

'Markel, I tell you that these higher beings of the forest have assured me that my brother will return. They have sent one to bring him back.'

'Where has he gone?' Markel wants to know.

Cal pats my knee and answers for me. 'He's gone to get the weapon. It's far—we don't know exactly where. So how did you come to be stranded out here?'

I give Cal a grateful glance. I would have told them the truth, that my brother was beyond the reach of any known Hatch and this would naturally have alarmed them more.

Alagard tells us their tale. 'When Jem didn't come back to Jucca after many months, we got worried. We proposed a mission to go in search of these forest dwellers to see if we could get some answers. Exploratory missions to this side of Nattalia don't have a good record of success. No one who has come here has returned. And now we know why.'

'What happened?' Cal urges.

'We got this far without mishap then, suddenly, without warning, our ship just shut down. We were lucky to land without crashing. I don't know how we didn't. It came down and we couldn't get it going again. Our droid soldiers stopped working too. They just zapped out. It's as if all our power was sucked out. We've been here ever since.' He spreads out his hands, indicating their camp.

'You didn't try to make your way back on foot?'

Alagard shakes his head. 'No. We wanted to stay near the ship. It still has all our supplies. Look, we wouldn't have made it. The seas are not like those on Earth. They have high swells and are prone to storms. There was no way.'

'You say you kept close to your ship. It's near here?' Cal's voice is slightly higher with hope.

'Don't get excited. Our ship is grounded, useless, not going anywhere—unless you think you've got some kind of magic that can restore it.'

'I don't, but Britta is known to channel the higher forces.'

I feel eyes shift to me with renewed reverence. I don't deserve such worship and become shy of it. Cal's arm tightens around me.

'Well,' says Alagard, clearing his throat. 'You're both welcome to have a look at it.'

We go as a group, treading noisily through the forest. Cal walks up front with Alagard, deep in discussion. I walk with his wife, Adelle, who seems a little distant, guarded. I sense she is nervous of my abilities and is worried I will read her mind. Not that she should worry. She is only thinking about whether to trust me, a reasonable insecurity to have given they have not come across any other humans in the past four years. She is captivating to look at with her golden tanned skin, long wavy hair, and eyes resembling round pools of black olive water.

As the trees thin out, a massive ship looms into view. It is in a C-shape, like the sweet breads on Earth. The ramp to its loading bay is open and I can see inside to the inert droids, the battalion of soldiers, unable to be mobilised.

'We use it for shelter when it storms, but it's hot and stuffy in there. Often, we stay out and sleep beneath the stars.'

'Can I...?' Cal asks, walking toward the ramp.

'Yes, of course.'

Most the crew accompany Cal inside. I choose to wait outside and seek conversation with Adelle. 'You say it just stopped working?' I notice then that beneath a long naval-style jacket she is wearing the EASA uniform, though it is grubby and frayed.

'It was a spiritual force that stopped it,' she says with conviction. 'Those forest creatures, the glowing ones—they don't want us going back to Jucca.' She looks at me warily before her luscious lips curve into a delicate smile. 'They don't want us telling how enchanting it is here. The lands... they have an energy that gets under your skin, you become a part of them. I can't explain it. To be honest,' she leans closer to me, 'I don't want to go back to Jucca. I could live here forever.'

'I feel it too,' I say, returning her smile. She's right. There's a magnetic energy to the lands that binds you to them. Here, more than anywhere, you can feel part of the fabric of the environment. The branches are as precious as your own limbs, I think, recalling my dread when Cal had planned to rip free a branch from a tree.

She reaches her hand out and brushes her fingers through my messy hair. 'You should tie it back. These stringy leaves make good ties,' she says. She strokes my strands into a ponytail and wraps a white tie around it. 'There.'

'Thank you.'

'You are very beautiful without enhancements,' Adelle comments.

'You are a work of art,' I reply.

'But nature is the better artist. I learn this now, here, yes?'

I smile. 'Nature is unity.'

She smiles brightly. 'Something Jem would have said. So, Britta, can you get the forest creatures to make our ship fly? They like you, yes? You talk to them, like Jem?'

'I don't know. There's a lot I don't know. I can try.'

She falls quiet and so do I.

The several men, and two younger women, listening in, nod or smile at me encouragingly. I feel they long to get back to civilisation and hope I can ask the forest dwellers to release their ship from whatever hold they have over it. Even though a war is going on, they would prefer Jucca to this isolated paradise in enchanting lands. They crave contact with other people, with news, with society. Humans do gravitate to other humans, I think.

Wondering if they will have their wish granted, I soften my thoughts and ask to see forward.

I see a ship... white floors... pain, such pain... blood on my hands, dripping. Our return is coming soon. We will go back to Jucca, but at what price? My head pounds with the thought. Careful what you wish for, I hear in my mind, and a light shudder crosses my shoulders. Going back may not be for the best, I realise, though go back we will.

Adelle meets my eyes and sees my anxiousness. 'Don't worry for us,' she tells me, and takes my hand. 'Oh, you didn't train at EASA?' Her synthetic fingers caress my soft ones.

'I did.'

'You kept your hands?'

Before I can reply, Cal and Alagard and the rest of the crew emerge from the ship.

'It's locked up tight,' Cal says, strolling to me, his eyes seeking to make sure I'm safe. 'It's in perfect condition though. Should fly. I don't suppose...' He peers at me sheepishly.

'You want me to communicate with them now?'

He bites his bottom lip. 'Unless you want to stay here?'

Pain is behind my eyes, blinding, horrible, snapping, crippling pain. I push back on it, though my eyes have filled with tears.

'Are you sure you want to go back... to war, to an oppressive World Council, to...?' I can't say it, can't describe the immense pain now gripping my body. My gaze rests on Cal's face. I don't want him harmed. I don't want any of them hurt. I can't say it though. My tongue won't warn them. I don't want to impart bad news.

They observe my tears.

'Britta?' Cal steps closer, takes my hand.

'Tell us what we should do,' Markel puts to me, his slack bottom lip trembling.

I look at him and observe shoulders sagging with age over a buckled body covered in loose, flaky skin. Yet he holds his head of white hair high upon that tired neck, lifting red-rimmed eyes that amazingly are not too old to beseech me, a person much less than half his age, for advice. And I realise he asks not for himself but for his companions who've kept him alive and fed during these years in the wilderness. He wants the best for them.

Such dignity he harbours, such graciousness, such courage. I draw from it, breathe it in.

'We will go back. We have to,' I say.

'Which means you will ask them to help us go back?' Cal asks.

'Is it wise?' Markel asks.

I'm not sure how to answer him. It is hard to know what's wise when the future promises suffering and adversity. When each favour asked will leave a debt owed. I can only follow what I think is right and hope that wisdom comes of it. I nod at the old man.

'It is what it is,' I reply, 'and what will be. So, yes, I'll ask them. First, let's get back to camp. We should prepare for night.'

The light is darkening and my advice is sound.

Cal squeezes my hand. 'You're right. We should get back. If it's okay with you, I'll go back to our cave first. See if there's anything of ours I can salvage. Do you want to come with me?'

'She can walk with us. I'll look after her,' Adelle offers.

He runs his hand up my arm and looks to me for confirmation. 'I can go with them.'

'All right. I'll be back as soon as I can.'

He kisses me, his lips lingering on mine, brushing them with desire, yet I sense his fear runs deep. He is afraid for me.

'I'll be all right. Hurry back.'

'I will. No talking with beings until I do. Okay?'

'Unless they talk to me.'

'Britta...'

'I'll be fine. Go.'

We kiss again, again longer than needed. At last, we separate, my heart going with him.

Back at the camp, the crew heads off to search and gather fuel for the fire, to collect water from the river, and to get food to cook. Some are hoping to catch a fish or two before the light descends. I believe they will; the image of three fish fills my mind.

Promising to be back soon, Adelle and Alagard go together, water containers tucked beneath their arms.

Markel is last to leave, shuffling off in a different direction to the others. He is alone and, to my acute senses, appears to be without clear purpose. What's he up to? Just before he disappears into the thick of the trees, he turns to me and smiles. So, it is farewell. I see it in his eyes. It is not fear that takes him away, just a wise practicality.

'You're not the only one who knows the future,' he says hoarsely and somewhat sadly. 'I'm going to wait this part out. Too old. I'll see you at the end of it.' He doesn't wave, but in my mind he does. I guess he's seen enough in my eyes to lead him away. I feel a rush of relief. He is doing the right thing. He wouldn't survive what's coming next. Will any of us?

With renewed urgency and wanting to make the most of my current solitude, I sit quietly on a spread of leaves and cross my legs. I am not actively going to contact the beings, though I'm hopeful they will reach out to me if I enter into a relaxed state. Becoming mindful of the stillness of the moment, I work to regulate my breath and release my thoughts, which are many. I taste the sweetness of the air and the pollen the air carries. I float with the pollen. Light now with emptiness, I uncross my legs and lie down. After a few minutes of becoming as flat and cool as the earth below my back, I see with gentle observation that I am no longer reclining in the clearing of the camp but drifting above the trees, floating like a cloud over the forest, the lake, the waterfall.

I lift higher into the sky.

With a thought I'm on a ship, forty-five billion light years away.

Tasma is there, waiting for me.

'Have you found Jem, Mum, the weapon?' I ask.

'Yes. They have all been transported to this ship in the hibernation pods. Your mother's crew have awoken. Your brother and mother won't wake.'

I focus on breathing, keeping my emotions neutral. 'Won't wake? Are they... dead?'

'They think they are.'

'Think they are?' I'm confused but I breathe calmly, accepting and not resisting what I'm being told. 'Why?'

'They astral travelled while in hibernation. They've become confused.'

'What can be done?'

'You need to go to them. They'll see you. They watch over you. That's what they do now—watch over family. You can help them to come back.'

'They watch over me... and Dad and Neath?'

'Yes.'

I breathe evenly. 'I see. All right. I'll try to contact them.'

'I can help you. You can do it, now. Just will it.'

I remember a long time ago, Meela had told me there was a

path I would go down that only I could go. This is it. It must be. Though I'm not sure if I can find them in this plane of observation, this spiritual plane of waiting to pass over. Surely, my love for them will lead me there. Trusting in that, desiring it, I concentrate on changing my vibration and passing from the astral plane into another plane. Jem. Lead me to Jem. Mum. Where are you?

'That's it,' Tasma says, its thought coming to me, seemingly from afar. 'They'll see you.'

I am no longer on the ship or in space or anywhere. I am vibration. I am light. I pull my thoughts of myself together, to form, to stay me.

In this loose state, I manage to call for them again, call and search. The light is blinding. I am blind. I float without seeing and suddenly, Jem and Mum are walking toward me.

They look beautiful. They are as I remember them. They are my memories of them. Their smiles are so radiant, their eyes shining with love.

Fair hair, light brown eyes. Fresh faces. Kind. Loving.

Mum wears green, a flowing top and skirt. Is that why I like that colour?

'Britta, what brings you here?' Mum asks. Her voice is like music, reminding me of early memories that brush against my soul. 'Have you learned to visit the spiritual plane?'

'Yes.'

'We've been watching over you,' Mum tells me.

It is as Tasma said. I wonder how much they have seen. Do they know I've been with Cal?

'He's a good man,' Mum answers.

'You chose well,' Jem agrees. 'I was wrong to steer him away from you.'

I see. They know.

'Mum and Jem, you have to listen to me. Your physical bodies are still alive. They are in hibernation on a ship. You are confused. You have astral travelled while in hibernation and your vibrations are different. But it is safe for you to go back now. You must re-enter. You can come back to us.'

'We are gone,' Jem says. 'We are waiting to go to the next plane. It is where the light is strongest. See how it calls to us? We've only stayed here to watch over you and to guide Neath to it.'

I breathe deeply. 'Guide Neath? He died?'

'Yes, in the early fighting. One of the first ships to be fired upon. We're waiting for him to join us.'

'Are you certain? I didn't sense his passing.' I am surprised and upset, but knowing I have to keep up the connection, I try to witness my emotions from a distance and breathe through them. Staying focused, I choose my next words carefully. 'If that is so, Neath can't join you in the way that you think. You're not dead. If you were, Neath would be here now,' I say, struggling to stay emotionless. 'You can come back. You have to believe me. Remember Jem. You went looking for Mum, to bring her back.'

'I failed. We both passed over.'

'No. You succeeded. You found her ship. It has the weapon on it. The weapon needed to defend Earth from the asteroid. You have to wake up. You can. Tasma is with you. Remember Tasma? It can help us. It will know what to do, how to get the weapon to the asteroid. Only you and Mum can talk to Tasma. So, you have to wake up and be shown the way to save Earth. Hurry now. Time does matter on the physical plane. Go back to the time where your bodies are waiting for you.'

'I'm sorry, Britta. We can't. The light calls to us. Soon we will go to it, with Neath.'

'No. If you go into it, you will let go of your bodies. But right now, you are still connected. You are still connected. Find your connection and go back. Do you understand?' My thoughts, pure and strong, are coming all at once on top of each other. 'Do you understand?'

'You want us back,' Mum says. 'But we are gone. Don't grieve for us, or Neath.'

'If Neath is dead, where is he? Why isn't he already here on this plane with you? You're stuck on a plane somewhere in between. You can come back, but Neath can't.' I feel emotional pain in my body and know my vibration is changing. I'll lose contact with them.

I try one last time. 'You are still alive. We need you. Earth needs you. Come back. Please...'

I wake up.

Screams and smoke overwhelm my senses.

What's going on?

Dazed, I sit up and come face to face with a Red Viper.

Behind the menacing droid, the once peaceful camp has been turned into a battle scene of white flames and fallen bodies.

On seeing Cal, I scream.

He's on the ground, battered and bloodied... and not moving.

CHAPTER FIFTEEN

Blood drips from my fingertips and pools on the white floor of the Red Vipers' ship. My recent travels across planes has resulted in too much energy being drawn in through my fingers, rendering them torn.

But my injuries are trivial.

Cal, slumped beside me, is chequered in black bruises from a pummelling I'm glad I didn't witness. Just thinking about it makes me ill. Most disconcerting is the way his swollen arm dangles. It looks broken. He must have put up a good fight. Pain sends him in and out of awareness. When he stirs, he groans, but he hasn't the strength to lift his head.

Like Cal, the members of Jem's crew are also cradling pain and leaning against their seat's restraints in varying states of consciousness. Adelle's red lips are smeared with blood and she is out cold. Alagard's perfect nose has been smashed and pushed sideways.

The only small comfort I can take is that Markel is not among them. His well-timed departure meant he got clear of the Vipers and stayed clear.

What happened? Why didn't the young ones protect us again?

I gaze out the window, seeking a moment's solace. It's night and so there is no view other than blackness to feast upon, and I savour it. Black. A defensive colour, yet one that is waiting to be filled, waiting for the light. Of course, I start to think of Mum and Jem. They say Neath is dead. I find that hard to believe and harder to accept. I don't want to think of my young, spirited brother gone. And while I was disbelieving them, they were disbelieving me. They still think they're dead. If they go into the light, they will become disconnected and their bodies will release them forever. They will die. Being so close to having them back in my life, this is a cruel possibility. I had been afraid to hope, but there's no stopping hope once it gets away from you. In my heart, I know I haven't given up on them, or Neath, or Earth. My hope has so much force, I can't wind it back—not until they are gone, until Earth is gone. Building such hope comes at a price though. If it is dashed, I know it will suck my heart away with it.

The blackness stares back at me like a friend. Its nothingness is restful. I take a breath. Where are we? I wonder if we are passing over the sea, for back to Jucca we will be taken, back to answer to Mandon. He'll want to know about the beings, the weapon, Jem... I won't talk, which means I'll be made to talk. I'm nervous about what method they will use. I'm adept at blocking pain, yet they may reach for alternative means: blackmail or hypnotism. I'm quite susceptible to being hypnotised.

Cal lets out a hideous groan. I respond instantly, turning in alarm, reaching for him. 'Cal?' Biting back tears, I try to handle his lolling head with my palms, trying to offer comfort. He settles and blacks out.

I don't want to think. It hurts too much. My empathy is too acute.

THE HATCH

I look back to the window and seek the emptiness of a dark night. With immense concentration, I focus on Tasma.

It has the weapon. Can it get it to the asteroid? How? As Cal had said, there is no Hatch out there. Yet it seemed confident it could bring Jem and Mum back. If it wants Earth saved, could it, would it do us this incredible service? Or does it just see the human race as a greedy, planet-ravaging species, not worthy of rescuing? Better to reduce our numbers while it has the chance. How can I tell what this higher being wants for us and from us?

I just don't know. My head hurts. I didn't want to think and here I am overthinking, not letting my thoughts flow.

Tears slide unchecked down my cheeks.

Cal may be physically beaten, but I'm just as damaged on the inside.

* * *

We land smoothly and are left to wait to be unlocked from our restraints. Why don't they come and take us? After an unbearably long time, several Red Vipers enter our compartment ,and with callous regard to injuries, yank at locks and straps, letting bodies slam to the floor. Cal's head smacks the white flooring and I squeal. Needing to transport this crippled crew, the Vipers begin to hook each member to a cable and commence dragging the hunched bodies down an exit ramp. The activity elicits curses, groans and pleas. I'm one of only a few who can walk, though we are shoved so harshly, we stumble down the short slope to the landing bay. From there, I'm made to follow the bodies being towed along a series of corridors, my steps treading in the smears of trailing blood.

After an agonisingly long haul, we come to a door. It slides up and reveals a dark cavernous room. Its contents are shocking. Emaciated people are huddled in small groups in the rear corners, cowering away from the door as though nothing good could ever come through it. Their stench greets us, while light from the hall blinds them.

The bloodied crew are dumped inside, littered on the floor like discarded sacks of leaking waste. Cal too. When it comes to me, I'm stopped.

'You, come with us.'

The door slides shut. No. Cal. He needs me. I let out a fierce cry, shuddering at the volume of my own anguish. Cal! Thrashing against my captors, I thrust my body against the door, pounding upon it, smearing it red.

It's a short-lived protest. I'm easily pinned down by synthetic arms and carted unceremoniously further along the hall. Delivered to a cylindrical chute, I'm inserted inside like a capsule and shot up several levels so fast my stomach flips with nausea. Vipers wrench me out at the top and I'm pushed into a room. It's a long room, requiring a long walk. Well-lit by an ever-stretching row of bright lights, I feel exposed and vulnerable. Every cell of my sorrow must be illuminated.

At the far end, Mandon waits. He is seated on a chair; one could say throne, given its expanse and luxuriousness of gold silk and soft padding. Behind him is a wall of glass offering a view to a moon-lit harbour; the light of three moons have the honour of revealing collapsed orange bridges, smashed jetties, and upturned boats.

The war has not been kind to this majestic harbour. No doubt the guns and cannons on the bridge had drawn the bombs.

There are no other humans in the room, though I wonder if Mandon is worthy of being categorised as one. He does not stand as I'm set before him. He does not look at me. I take a ragged breath and wait.

I have to assume that Mandon has much on his mind, for it seems to take him an inordinate amount of time to realise who I am and why I'm here.

'Miss Tate. Yes.' He looks at his nano-band and reads, 'Issue number 3249.'

His artificial eyes lift and stare through me. 'You've been returned, unharmed as per my request. You went with the Granton boy to the other side... in search of a weapon, I believe. Did you find one?'

'Cal Granton was harmed,' I feel a need to point out.

'He's not as valuable as you. Your training cost us much more.' His smile is hideous. 'Let me start again. Did you find a weapon?'

I don't answer.

'Miss Tate, either you answer my questions or I'll start having certain people put to death, starting with your father, followed by your brother, and then your friend, Mr Granton. They are all on level B, guests of the Council, and mean nothing to me. So, did you find a weapon?'

I'm shocked to learn that my father is also in that stench-filled room. I recall the cowering groups, their physical filthiness and distress. There was no mention of Neath. A sick feeling takes hold in my stomach, but I can't think on it. Mandon is becoming impatient.

I'm angry. 'Do I look like I have a weapon?'

'Is there one?' he says, raising his voice, and the red synthetic pupils of his eyes swivel mechanically.

'Yes. You know there is. My mother found it.'

He studies me, considering my answer. 'And where is your mother?'

'On the edge of the observable universe.'

'That far? Interesting.' Unblinkingly, he holds my gaze. 'Why would she strand herself out there? There's no Hatch to get back. So, she and the weapon are beyond salvaging and yet, your brother...'

'Went after her.'

'Yes. Why?' Mandon's face is curious, yet alert. He seems

ready to pounce. I feel his animosity growing as he leans toward me. 'Why?'

'He wanted to bring her back, and the weapon, of course.'

'Of course. What made him think he could?'

I shrug.

'Miss Tate, I don't even need to leave this chair to have those people who matter to you most executed. Now I want an answer. What made your brother travel to a place from which he could never return?'

'He must have thought he could return,' I say, desperately wanting to give an answer to protect the people I care about.

'But how?'

'I don't know. I wish I did.'

'Have... a... guess.'

Mandon lifts his nano-band to his mouth as though readying to give the order.

'He befriended the species on the other side of this planet.'

'Yes. Now we're getting somewhere. The invisible species that has never been sighted but is capable of downing our ships. Tell me about them.'

I don't want to. My mind is clamouring for words. I just need to give him enough to satisfy him.

'They are a peaceful species.'

'And yet our reconnaissance ships and scouts haven't been seen since. They flew over those forested lands and never returned. At a minimum, they've been held against their will. That is not the actions of peacekeepers.'

'They are defensive then.'

'Tell me more. How did they down the ships? With what weapons?'

'They demobilised them with beams.'

'Beams?'

'Beams of light that can stop ships and droids.'

'These beams seem very powerful. How can we stop them? What is their source?'

'I don't know.'

'What do they look like, these defensive creatures?'

'They are transparent. You are right, they can't be seen.'

'But your brother could befriend them. He could see them, hear them?'

'Yes.'

'And you can?'

I nod. I'm afraid to lie, afraid he'll be able to tell and have my father and Cal killed.

'And you haven't as yet asked these invisible creatures how your brother and mother could be returned to you?'

'I did ask. They wouldn't say.'

'But they said it could be done,' Mandon says. He doesn't need me to confirm this. He knows Jem wouldn't have gone forty-five billion light years away unless he thought he could come back.

'The weapon could be on its way to the asteroid now. Could it not?' he puts to me. I see sweat has broken out on his brow.

'That would be a desirable outcome, would it not? Saving Earth from an extinction level strike?'

'Desirable for Earth, certainly. Is this possible?'

'Unlikely,' I say. 'My brother and mother are in hibernation and can't be woken. They think they've passed over.'

'They think they're dead?'

'Yes.'

'Why?'

'They astral travelled while in hibernation and became confused as to their state. This is easy to do.'

'I see... if you say so.' Mandon taps his fingers on the arms of his chair. 'I like you, Miss Tate. I do. You are direct and clear. It's refreshing. You've explained enough.' He looks to the droids at my sides. 'Take her to level B.'

The droids are at my sides and nudging me back toward the door. I struggle to walk. Nerves and fear have grated away at my muscles, leaving my body weak and shaken. When I stumble, I fall hard on one knee. I curse.

'Help her up,' Mandon says.

The droids do so.

'Oh, and Miss Tate?'

I turn back to face him, my fingertips burning.

'What exactly, expressed as a percentage, is the chance your mother and brother will wake up, leave the outer reaches of the universe, and fire the weapon at the asteroid before it can hit Earth?'

'Did you hear the question?' I ask, raising a brow. 'What do you think?'

'I think it impossible. But I'm not the most accurate psychic ever to be trained at EASA. I want your prediction. What do you see?'

I still harbour that resilient hope, but I must factor in practicalities. I try to give an honest answer. 'The probability is low, as low as one percent.'

'One percent?' He nods. 'I'll put fighter ships through the Hatch, get them to scan around the asteroid. If they spy any foreign object, they will be ordered to shoot it down. I don't like to take any chances.'

There it is. An admission that he doesn't want the asteroid destroyed. My anger flares and I can't help retorting, 'No, we wouldn't want the people of Earth to live, would we?'

'It's not about them. It's about Nattalia.'

'Why can't Earth be spared and its population transported here over time?'

'Because people who are free to come and go would go. No Earth and they have to stay.'

It is all true, just as Odell and Cillian had explained. He needs a dependent people to put to work. He wants slaves.

My fury peaks. 'You would leave eight billion to die...' I say, my horror apparent.

'I would not,' he shouts at my accusation. 'Many chose to stay! Many couldn't come. They were too sick, too young to travel, too weak! You have to understand, we've rescued the most able to adapt and that has had its consequences. We took the bulk of Earth's workforce—the growers, the labourers, the medics, the educators. Those left behind are struggling to survive. We've already had news of rioting, disorder, chaos. The asteroid will at least give them focus. I gather it will be a blessing when it finally comes.'

'A blessing?' I am appalled. 'You have created that chaos. You could have stopped the asteroid.'

'To save what? Earth? That dying, dried up, dust bowl.'

'It was recovering. People chose to stay behind because they believed in it. They had a connection to it, its history.'

'Now you agree. They chose to stay. Come now, Miss Tate, we couldn't have taken them all. I assure you we took all we possibly could. The people here are used to having a high standard of living. I needed to protect that. Don't you see? I've saved billions of lives peacefully—and yes, selectively. But I am ensuring human survival of the fittest. An old term but a good one. You'll see, life on Nattalia will far exceed anything we could have known on Earth.'

'Who are you to choose who gets this better life?'

'Who am I? I'm your leader, your elected leader. And I've done what I thought best for the long term. That's what leaders do. They think strategically.'

'The only strategy that I see involves a burgeoning of your financial accounts.'

'You think this is only about me? I'm not the only one who'll benefit. The people of Nattalia will have plentiful food and good, clean air and productive, rewarding lives.'

'Productive for you.'

'Productive for their children, for future generations.'

'What of Earth's future generations, never to exist because of you?'

I've gone too far. It is an accusation on a global scale, painting him as the most sinister killer of all time. His face is pinched with anger, his back rigid. He lifts his nano-band to his lips.

No.

'Cal Granton,' he says with too much satisfaction.

Panicked, I drop to my knees. 'I'm sorry. I've been too harsh. May history look back at you in awe for what you have done,' I say.

'I know you don't mean that,' Mandon says. 'Your arm.'

Blood vessels appear to have risen closer to my skin, showing a criss-crossing of red lines up and down my right arm. I peer at him for explanation.

'The droid put an adhesive applicator on your arm at the start of our meeting. You absorbed a chemical compound that shows up in your blood if you are not telling the truth. You've been honest with me, until now. Your loved ones owe their lives to that, even Cal. But...'

I feel my head buzzing.

'But you will all be put on trial soon enough, for terrorism. The people can judge. Your people will judge. And Miss Tate, I put your chances of survival at say... one percent. Fair odds, wouldn't you say?'

I can't speak. I'm too afraid. What is he talking about? What trial? What terrorism? As long as Cal gets to live a little longer. My breath is coming fast. I feel dizzy.

'May history never recall your name.'

And so I am dismissed. A rough shove pushes me away and I'm directed back down the long room, all the way back to the chute, where I'm shot down at high speed. My anger surges; strong, honest anger, enough to wipe the red lines of lies from my arm. There's nothing more cleansing than true hatred, I think as I hold back my tears, tears of helplessness. For once, I can't see a way out. I'm in the dark, so much so that I think I may as well be in a void, billions of light years away. It's all so very dark.

At the bottom of the chute, I'm delivered to more Vipers that lead me back to the room where Cal and the crew had been deposited. I'm shoved inside.

It is more crowded than I first had observed. There are many prisoners here, over a hundred. Who are all these people?

The door slides shut. Thankfully, the ceiling is glowing softly, offering a dim light. I look around, desperately seeking Cal or my father or, sadly, even Neath.

Suddenly, I hear a familiar voice and Dad is embracing me. I extend my arms, clutching at his shoulders.

'You okay?' Dad keeps asking as I nod rather deliriously at him. His hair is loose and unkempt, and his expression hassled. For a long while, he rests his head on my shoulder and says nothing. I hold his body and feel the trauma he's nursing. He saw the war—too much. I sense his mind's battle to compartmentalise the bad from the inconceivable and to close the lid on that which he needs to lock away.

'Neath?' I bravely ask.

'I don't know. No one tells us anything. I tended the injured. I searched.' He shrugs, pain etched across his face. 'How about you? Cal told us they took you away.'

'I'm okay. Really. It's all right. I'm sorry.'

'We stay together from now on,' Dad says. 'You and me.'

'Yes. I want that too. Cal... he was hurt.'

'This way. Come. I've done the best I can for him. His arm is broken; a neat break. Just the ulna, likely from a blow to the forearm in self-defence. We've tried to elevate it to get the swelling down and I used my belt to strap it to his chest. See here.' In his role as medic, Dad seems calmer, his voice thicker, more in control.

We kneel down to Cal, who is seated on the floor, propped up against the back wall. He's semi-conscious and at first doesn't seem to register our presence.

'Cal.' I kneel and lightly brush the hair from his swollen eyes.

'Britta.' Eyes open, mere slits through blackened lids. There's a snort of relief followed by a grimace as he finds it too painful to smile. 'You're okay.' Eyes close. He swallows hard. 'I thought...' His nose creases, lips overlap. 'I'm sorry. I let you down.'

'No, no, you didn't. I'm all right. We all are. We're all okay. We'll get through this.'

'Where are we?' he asks huskily.

'We're in some kind of prison, in Jucca.'

'Why?' Cal is confused.

Dad crouches. 'Seems we've all been charged with treason.'

'For doing what?' I ask, my anger quick to rise.

Dad hangs his head. I sense reluctance.

'Dad?'

'You won't like it.'

'What?' I shout.

'Shush. Keep your voice down. We're charged in relation to sabotage. We're accused of acting against efforts to stop the asteroid, of wanting Earth's destruction.'

My mouth is open. I'm aghast. I want to laugh, cry, screech. 'But it was them. The World Council! Led by Mandon! They are the ones.'

'Voice down,' Dad reminds me firmly.

'They know I know.'

'Yet you still live,' Neath says with a small grin. I'm glad he hasn't lost his ability to tease.

'Alive, but not free,' I am compelled to point out.

'So, what do we do now? See a way out?' Neath asks.

I hear a heart thumping too fast and, with surprise, realise it's mine. I need to calm down. I'm of no use to anyone in this state. If I'm not calm, I can't think or see ahead.

I peer around, wanting to gauge our surrounds. With my sight now adapted to the dark, I spy Cal's parents at the other end of the room. Odell is lying down. His wife, Cillian, is leaning over him, stroking his damp hair, talking to him. Near them are the bruised and battered members of Jem's crew. Alagard is pacing, his hands cupping his nose. Adelle has come around and is crouched by a young man who is bleeding profusely from his waist. She is trying to make him comfortable. He appears to have been stabbed, possibly shot. Material has been strapped around the wound, but it is not enough to stem the flow of life seeping out of him. I soften my gaze and see his spirit hovering, waiting for the final release. He is dying.

I feel a presence behind me. 'Britta.' The voice is familiar and I am saddened to hear it, here, in this place. No. It can't be.

I twist to face Treesa, the head of EASA. She does not look the same woman we met on the ship of the World Council. Her impressive bird is no longer with her, nor is her confidence or the intrinsic power I had admired. She appears as though she hasn't slept or eaten in weeks. Her spirit is not broken but damaged; it has suffered a tear. I can see it in her slack stance, her dull eyes, her down-turned, weary mouth.

'I'm sorry to see you here,' I say. Beyond her shoulder, there are many other EASA uniforms—her supporters and colleagues and perhaps their families too.

Treesa puts her lips to my ear and speaks just above a whisper. 'Did you locate a weapon?'

There's a spark of fight in her yet and I wish I had more uplifting news.

'Yes... and no,' I breathe and stop to flick a random tear.

'Come now,' she says, though her tone is low and weak. She takes a breath and says more firmly, 'I've always believed in you.

That's why I took you in so young, kept you happy, pushed you to develop the psychic arts. I believed in your mother and brother too. I don't know why he didn't come back.'

'He couldn't.'

Before I can elaborate, there's a loud whoosh and the door to our communal cell slides back. I blink rapidly, trying to shield my eyes from the sudden assault of light. Red Vipers enter. The one in front speaks.

'The trial by people will commence. All stand against the far wall. Line up.'

Without resistance, the prisoners do what they say. Families help to lift the injured and lean them against the wall.

Sadly, for Jem's crew, their youngest member has just passed away and, before they can say their final goodbyes, they must fold back into the line as requested and leave the young man's body for the Vipers to cart away. It is hard for them to do, and Ardelle weeps openly as she is assisted into the queue.

My father takes one side of Cal, the side with the broken arm. I take the other. We get him up and into the line between us. Treesa drops to the end of the queue, among the other uniforms.

Cillian, with Oden leaning on her, tries to join us.

'Cal,' she calls and struggles to move to be with us, but a Red Viper pushes her back. She and Odell are shoved into the front of the line.

Suddenly, I feel like I'm dropping a step and my feet are grabbed. I startle with the shock of it. I look down. The floor tiles have sunken into an indented travelator and clamps have bolted in around my ankles. I can't move my feet an inch. The same has happened to all the prisoners. With a sudden buzzing sound, the travelator begins to move. Several cry out as the motion frightens them. I think I'm one of them.

'What's going on?' Cal asks, becoming more aware. He turns to me and grips my hand.

'We're being taken to trial.'

'Trial?'

'Stay with us,' I say to him.

A larger door slides open and the travelator carries us into the open. The first thing that fills my view is a pale grey sky with skimming plum clouds. Sunrise.

We're in a vast town square. Buildings that once faced the square's plaza no longer stand. Their upper storeys have collapsed in on the first. They lay open and exposed so we can see inside to ash-covered furnishings, partial floors, and smashed appliances. The ground in the square's centre has been ripped up as though a missile has carved a deep and wide trench through its previously smooth paths and gem-studded pavers. On either side of the trench are piles of rubble, mostly comprising fragments of building materials, though I can see split panels, burnt bedding, broken seating, shattered projector lights, cooling units —all smashed, bent, or upturned in an ugly collage of ruin. The worst is the personal items: clothes, dolls, boots, caps, and one destroyed animatronic, a furry brown beast with its head indented.

I hope no one was in those buildings when they were hit by bombs. I see no bodies.

People are gathering around our enforced parade. The travelator stops. The only thing between us and the growing crowd is a single row of Red Vipers. Over the shoulders of the security droids, the people are shouting and spitting, their hatred evident. Looking out amongst them, I see they are not Nattalians. These people are from Earth. They are the refugees and ominously they believe we are the reason for their refugee status. We are the scapegoats. For people will in time ask why EASA didn't stop the asteroid. They will learn that EASA knew about it for a long time. We are the reason it wasn't stopped; our fake terrorism.

A projection of Mandon's head appears as a huge three-dimensional hologram; it is a giant version of himself. I remember Odell telling us that the people of Nattalia regard him as a god. No wonder, if he's been presenting himself on such a scale.

Red eyes, as large as our faces, glare down upon our trembling line-up of prisoners.

'This is trial by people. Good people of Earth. These people knew about the asteroid and they did worse than nothing. They did something. They acted to make sure it was never stopped. They made sure it would hit Earth. They wanted Earth to be destroyed.'

The outcry from the crowd is deafening. Their contorted faces are ugly in their disbelief and condemnation. All the pain of losing Earth is being channelled into hate. So much hate.

I feel my stomach tighten. My breathing is erratic.

Cal's hand squeezes mine. I look to him. His eyes are willing me to stay strong. His chin is up. He is being strong for me. My love expands, though it will not be enough to protect us or to change anything. Love only promises to increase my pain if those I care for are harmed.

It is at that moment that I recall Jem's prophecy, warding off a young Cal to keep clear of his sister because he saw that one day I would be harmed, with this EASA officer at my side. And here we are, side by side, at a trial by hate. I meet Cal's eyes and know he's thinking the same.

'It would have happened anyway,' I manage to mutter, before Mandon's words cut through my thoughts.

'People of Earth, meet Treesa Breenwich, head of EASA.' A light from the travelator switches on, shining on Treesa. 'She was in charge of several missions intending to blast away the asteroid, knock it off course. Yet each mission failed. Coincidence? Here, we have Britta Tate.' I'm lit up. 'Her mother and brother went in search of a weapon to stop the asteroid. Where is this weapon? Britta Tate is the most psychic person we've ever had through the EASA program. She must have known about the asteroid, right? Did she predict it? Did she warn us? No. She knew and said nothing, did nothing. Because her family were hoping to buy land in Nattalia. They were going to use their foresight for their own gain and let billions die so they could live out their lives in comfort.'

The people are shouting again. I catch terrible phrases and can't believe they are referring to me. It is shocking.

Cal shouts back at them. 'She's done nothing. You know nothing. He's lying. She's been trying to help you.' But the more he shouts, the louder they become.

More people join the throng and a familiar pair weave close to the front. I peer at them and after several long seconds recognise Garth and Tilly. Garth has suffered burns to his left cheek. Tilly has her right leg set in a mechanical casing. She must have broken it. They look horrified at what is happening and at what is being said. Guilt keeps their eyes darting around. They are blaming themselves for all the terrors that have befallen the city since they let down the planet's security shield, including this trial.

I try to convey with my eyes that I don't blame them. They chose to shut down the shield to see their families to safety. They did not mean for any of this.

Mandon smiles. 'People of Earth. You decide. Around you is the rubble from the bombing, from the war we were forced to have with Nattalia. The war we had to have because this man, Odell Granton, wouldn't let you land. He would have had you starve and die up there in space. He forced us to go to war. His droids shot down our ships and killed your sons and daughters. Now I ask you to judge. If you think these people and their associates are guilty, pick up a piece from the rubble and throw it. Let them feel your judgement!'

I can't believe what he's saying. Pick up a piece? He's asking this wild, whipped-up crowd, high on anger and rage, not only to judge, but punish! They still have the smoke from the war in their lungs, the fear of death in their veins. Their mentality has become one and as a group they want to strike out. Together, they feel strong, sure and safe in their encouraged violence.

As a few people bend down, clawing for rocks, metal, glass, I see Garth reach for his waist belt. Does he have a weapon? Would he really try to defend us against this crowd and the battalion of Red Vipers? Is he crazy? I shake my head at him, willing him to save himself. Garth hesitates, his anguish apparent.

The first stone hits Odell, chipping skin from his forehead. Many more follow, scraping, cutting, digging, drawing blood. Stones are coming faster, harder, hitting anyone in the line. Those in the crowd, who at first showed some restraint, now join in, scrabbling at the ground for jagged rocks, tiles, glass, metal—whatever they can find.

Some prisoners are targeted more than others. Treesa is one of them. They hold her responsible for the failed missions against the asteroid and want her to suffer for it. Projectiles of all sizes are hurled in her direction, and though she holds up her hands to protect her face, the storm of rubble is relentless. Her arms begin to bleed. Her uniform is slashed open, her skin torn wide.

'Nooo,' I cry, my sorrow cutting deeper than the assortment of missiles 'Leave her. Stop it.' Tears glide down my cheeks. How I long to put myself in front of the screaming woman, to take the pain for her. I can't bear to watch Treesa suffer. This can't be happening, this unfair trial, without a word said in our defence. How can these people let such proceedings go ahead and think it okay to participate in outright murder following such an impromptu, short, and unjust trial, where accusation and verdict are delivered in quick succession by one voice? How can they think it fair and humane? How can they draw blood, not knowing our side, not caring to hear it?

I look to the back. The Nattalians are starting to take an interest and have gathered at the rear, many of them seated astride animatronics, gaining a clear view to the vicious assaults taking place. Yet they do not interfere. They watch with mild interest, some concern, some puzzlement, but it is not enough for them to question the brutish behaviour or to call for it to cease. If anything, they seem entertained. Their superior and dignified stance, safely removed from the baseness of the riotous crowd, allows them the opportunity to snigger at it with something akin to amusement.

The stones begin to come my way. The first one, Cal knocks with his elbow, earning a gash to it. My father blocks the next two. Then the stones rain down. They can't block them all. I close my eyes and lift my hands in what will constitute a useless shield.

Pain tears at me—my head, my arms, my legs.

Then I'm floating out of myself. Have I fainted? Was one of the blows fatal?

I gaze around. I'm on a ship. Jem and Mum are at the controls. The other members of Mum's crew are secured in seating behind them. They are gazing at a Hatch through the front windshield. It is spinning, churning the energy within, but it looks different. The Hatch is sleeker and red in colour. Red?

Tasma appears and sees me.

I instantly want confirmation. 'They are alive?'

'Yes. They came back,' it says. 'You brought them back.'

My heart swells. I still can't believe what I'm seeing, what it means...

'Is my physical self alive?' I ask curiously and marvel at my detachment to such a question.

'Yes.'

I am? How interesting.

'Where is this ship? What is this red Hatch?'

'It is near the void. We built this Hatch out here long before your people built your first.'

'You did?' I'm surprised. 'We copied you somehow?'

'No. Independently of each other, we accessed the same idea from the same plane of knowledge,' Tasma tries to explain.

'I see. Are you going through this Hatch to the asteroid?'

'Yes.'

I look to Jem and admire his sleek form bent over the controls, his concentration absolute. He is fully engaged in scanning numbers scrolling on screens and does not know that my astral self is present.

Suddenly, he remarks in a voice thick with panic. 'I don't know which coordinates to set. The grid puts the asteroid on the border of two sets of coordinates, but which set will get us closest? The wrong one could cast us way out.'

'What choice of coordinates?' I ask, but as soon as the question leaves my lips, I know the answer. I've known it for a long time. 'Tasma, tell him to choose the set of coordinates with the number forty-nine,' I say.

Tasma moves closer to Jem. 'Britta says to pick the set that contains number forty-nine,' it relays.

Jem spins and stares. 'You're talking to Britta? And she knows? Knows for certain?' Sweat is beading and sliding from his upper lip.

'Are you certain?' Tasma asks me.

Jem shouts urgently, 'The choice is thirty-two and forty-nine or thirty-two and fifty. Do I go with the first set? Tasma can you confirm?'

I am not surprised to learn there is a choice with an option containing the number forty-nine. What fascinates me is that the set of coordinates match my issue number at EASA. 3249. I feel a smile elevating my vibration.

Sometimes it is just too great a coincidence to ignore.

'I'm certain.'

Tasma advises, 'She is.'

Jem's hand hovers over the controls for a moment. The ship is starting to grumble and shake. If he doesn't enter coordinates now, they won't go anywhere. The Hatch will merely spit them out back here. He punches at numbers.

I recall Mandon's threat to put fighter jets in the region of the asteroid, but they could not possibly be in place as yet. This ship will reach the asteroid first. They have the weapon and are on their way. I had estimated their chances of success at one percent and I do not believe it was a case of underestimation. I think they are about to attain the incredible.

'Well done,' I say to Tasma. 'And thank you. I'm sorry I won't see it happen.'

Tasma brightens. 'You will.'

I wonder from what plane of existence I will have my viewing.

My eyes open.

A huge rough-edged stone is hurtling toward my face. It looks heavy enough to split my forehead. I brace, staring with horror into my imminent death.

Suddenly, incomprehensibly, the stone cracks and breaks up, dropping at my feet in a pile of loose rubble. I'm left untouched.

My stomach flips. That was close! I taste dust from the broken stone on my lips.

The next objects do the same. They seemingly self-destruct just outside my aura, turning to harmless, minuscule bits on the ground.

I cast my gaze up and down the line. The makeshift missiles are no longer reaching any of their intended marks. Rocks flying toward the stunned prisoners appear to impact an invisible shield around their bodies and simply fall to the ground in a crushed heap.

I look to Cal to express my relief and amazement, only to gasp. I can't believe what I'm seeing. His face is instantly healing as I watch. The immense swelling around his eyes and cheeks is reducing, the colour of his skin returning to its normal tanned complexion.

'Your arm,' I say, completely shocked.

Cal unstraps it and swings it back and forth painlessly. 'Not broken,' he says, and I smile through my tears, leaning lovingly into his recovered arm. 'What's going on?' he asks.

I know without looking but I want to see it. Softening my gaze, I rejoice in the sight of yellow light beaming across the line of prisoners. 'The young ones.'

I watch them delivering their protection and healing. They emit such high vibrations. Their lights change from yellow to peach to pascal green. It's beautiful.

The Earth refugees have stopped throwing at us.

Mandon's smile has gone. 'Who casts this shield? Who interferes with our justice?'

'The innocent cannot be harmed,' Odell shouts, his voice shaking with emotion. 'And we are innocent.'

Mandon yells back, 'The people have judged differently.'

'No,' I say. With Cal's supportive hand against my back, I call out, 'My brother and mother are on their way to stop the asteroid. They have the weapon. They have found a Hatch. They have it and they're going to use it to stop the asteroid. Good people, I do not blame you for your anger but know the truth. My brother and mother will save our home planet. I want nothing more than that.'

The people look to Mandon. Their faces hold confusion, doubt and dare I believe... hope?

'She tells the truth,' Cal says, his voice louder than mine. 'There is a weapon. The mission is on track to stop the asteroid.'

'Isn't it too late?' a lopsided man asks, his bloodshot eyes settling on me.

'No,' I say, certainty in my voice. 'It's on its way.'

Gasps echo. Hands clutch. Chatter is low and cautious.

Mandon's expression doesn't change but his order is chilling. 'Kill them. Just kill them.'

The Red Vipers turn, lift their weapons: high-powered Boela guns that use the waste products of zillet in their fire streams.

Screams ripple down the line to my left and right. We can't run. Our feet are still shackled to the travelator. Some try to crouch, though it is a pathetic attempt to avoid blasts that will be fired at close range.

Garth and Tilly whisk out their guns, but they are two against many. They will die defending us.

I don't flinch and neither does Cal. We stand tall and take strength from each other. Can the light shield protect us against such powerful weaponry? We don't know. I believe the young ones will try, and I believe in them to keep us safe if they can. But there are so many Vipers, so many guns, directing such intense radioactive force straight at us.

Inside, I say a quiet goodbye and ignore the tremor of sadness, threatening to quake me apart.

Triggers are jerked back in a frightening act of mass execution.

Nothing. I feel nothing. Unharmed. Whole.

I think I smile.

The guns of the Red Vipers are jammed and as they inspect their weapons, they themselves power down, becoming inert in an array of odd angles.

Mandon sees his security force fail and seethes. Without another word, his oversized projection winks out. I take it as the first sign of retreat.

Garth and Tilly run to the controls at the front of the travelator and find the mechanism to unlock our ankle clamps. We are free.

Cal's parents hurry to him and they embrace. I find myself in the arms of my father.

Dad is quick to ask, 'Britta? You said your mother and brother. Does this mean...?'

'Yes, yes it does. Mum is alive and Jem too. They are coming back to us. They both are.'

Dad pales. The news is too much for him. He sits, and Neath and I kneel beside him.

'They said she was dead,' he says. 'I believed her gone.'

'I did too,' I tell him. 'But she's very much alive.'

He nods, smiling, believing. 'I never stopped hoping.'

The hologram chamber beeps as another huge projection uploads—not of a person, of space. Stars twinkle against the lightless fabric of the universe and in the foreground blazes a rocky mass, forging a path, leaving a white tail.

I gather the young ones have somehow changed the channel and are letting us see the asteroid. They are projecting what they can see.

I will see it stopped.

We all watch, our breaths held. If it wasn't threatening Earth, it would be deemed magnificent in its barrelling, headstrong journey, ever thrusting onward until such time as it collides with a worthy opponent.

That opponent will not be Earth. It is the weapon. Tasma's weapon.

It takes a while to emerge, but suddenly it is there, small at first—a defiant glow that gets closer and closer.

The people of Earth are holding hands. Their uplifted eyes are glued to the three-dimensional projection playing out in front of us. Cal and I look at each other and there is no longer hope but triumph stamped across our faces. We know the ending. Jem and Mum have done it. Tasma has done it.

The gap between the asteroid and weapon is closing. It seems they are running for each other, wanting to embrace in a defining collision. None of us move. We wait and watch. The weapon is like a fireball, not even a third of the size of the asteroid, but when it slams against it, the asteroid easily splinters, cracking in two. We watch two large rocks sail in different directions, amongst a shower of broken bits.

The wide arc they take sets them on a different course. Earth will be spared.

We cheer and embrace and cry.

I turn to Cal and our kiss is mirrored across the crowd as couples turn to share and seal their joy with loved ones.

Cal's lips are firm, pressing victory against me, and I kiss back, relishing the taste of elation.

The victorious moment is infinitely glorious in contrast to what could have been.

And how differently things could have gone. Without the help of higher beings, without the energy that delivered to me the number forty-nine, without the red Hatch, we may not have had this moment. But all those incredible things did happen, were always going to...

As I peer out at the celebrating throng, my gaze softens with exhaustion and in that moment a lone figure, pale with a soft glow, appears in the centre of all the joyous chaos. He smiles and lifts his hand, not in greeting, but in farewell. Neath.

I can't smile back. I'm overwhelmed with sadness. No, Neath, no. I warned you.

In my mind, I hear him telling me, 'It's all right, Britta. It was for the best. I had to show Mum and Jem that they weren't dead. Only I could do that, Britta. See, I did something right, in the end.'

I look up at him. His expression is one that begs understanding and forgiveness.

I nod. 'You did well. You saved everyone really.'

'We did.'

'Yes.'

'Well, I best be off. I'll be seeing you.' His presence fades before my eyes and it is as though he is taking a piece of my heart with him.

'Love you,' I whisper.

Every kind of emotion weighs heavily on my heart and yet there is a sense of order that I haven't felt in a long time and I'm left to ponder the simple elegance of it, while I let my tears roll.

CHAPTER SIXTEEN

Mandon and his council depart the planet in the chaos of the ensuing festivities. His plans become known and condemned, ensuring his name is written and recorded into the darker chapters of human history.

Even the people of Nattalia who would have benefited from such plans of exploitation express outrage at the extent to which he had been prepared to go. They had never envisaged that he would ensure Earth's ruin for the sake of Nattalia's gain.

Garth and Tilly make their peace with us after countless apologies. While I am quick to forgive, Cal takes longer. He had expected greater loyalty from them. To earn his trust, they work harder than most in the clean-up armies that sweep through the city, labouring to rebuild and restore the town devastated by weeks of intensive bombing.

My father and Neath help too, though in different capacities. My dad lends his healing skills to the city's hospital, while Neath helps to repair robotic machinery.

During this time, Cillian and Odell willingly hand over the reigns of leadership to EASA, until democratic elections can be held. Neither of them will run for office. They dream of going back to the forests and of building a place of their own by a river, living a quiet and peaceful life. After weeks of contributing to the city's clean-up, they head off to explore the lands and to decide on a site. Cal goes with them. It is their time to connect, to catch up on lost years.

It is hard for us to part. Our love is evolving rapidly, almost as though we have loved before and are reigniting old flames. He has only just left with his parents and yet I miss him already. I feel incomplete. After so much time together, I've come accustomed to having him around. Of course, I could not have stopped him from going, not when I knew how much he needed that time with them.

While helping Cal's parents hire a craft for their land hunting exercise, I learn that Alagard and Adelle have also rented a ship. It seems they have returned to their campsite on the other side, searching for an old friend. I hope they find him.

Treesa reluctantly heads up the new caretaker government and resists pressure to stand for the top job of Nattalian leader. It is with some comfort that I foresee she will eventually succumb to this pressure. She will make a fine and fair leader of Nattalia for many years to come, her bird ruling by her side. I don't tell her this though. She'll come to the decision on her own soon enough.

My father lends his healing skills to the city's hospital and, of course, I also help with the clean-up. Technologies that would have been used to scan for buried survivors have been destroyed in the war and so it is to my psychic abilities that they must turn. With a courage I didn't know I possess, I walk the streets, only stopping before destroyed houses or buildings in which I sense life, signalling for the rescue crews to start digging. Sometimes, among the rubble, I see confused spirits standing nearby and I offer to take messages from them to their surviving relatives before helping to guide them on their way to the next plane. Somehow, I find the strength to relay these messages to grieving loved ones, awaiting news of the rescue efforts. It is by far the hardest thing I've had to do, and yet I feel I must. No technology can step in here to help.

I save over three hundred lives and bring messages of comfort to many more.

When not working to support the rescue crews, I spend time alone, meditating and astral travelling, visiting Mum and Jem. They are four years away from a Hatch, outside of Earth, and so our family has a long four-year wait until we can be reunited. I know it won't be the same. I'm not a little girl or a pesky sister anymore. And Neath won't be with us, not physically.

Mum tells me I've learned much. I disagree.

'With more insight, I would have found you sooner,' I tell her. 'We could have spent more time together.'

'I didn't want you to worry about me,' Mum says. 'You were young and emotional.' She sits in a relaxed, meditative state, her hair shining in the light. I want to bury my face in her hair and kiss her pale cheeks. I rejoice in knowing that one day I will.

'You reached out to Jem,' I say pointedly, trying to flatten my tone so it doesn't come out like an accusation.

'I did. He was older and able to act. But look what happened. He, too, was betrayed and could have been killed.'

I shudder. She's right. It was never going to be easy to do anything without Mandon knowing about it. His eyes were everywhere.

'I searched for Jem,' I say, remembering my training at EASA and the long searches my roaming spirit conducted. 'And I knew you were there, sometimes.' I recall whispered words, a touch, a feeling...

'Whenever I could I was watching over you or your father or Neath. I missed you all so much.' Her image shimmers as her emotion disrupts our connection. She quickly breathes in, calms and, recovering, smiles at me. 'You found me at the right time. It all happened as it should.'

'As it should,' I repeat. Yes, still so much to accept and learn.

* * *

The weeks pass. I visit Cal. He can't see me, but I watch him. I am there on the day his parents find their dream site. It is on the slope of a valley, near a small community of huts and will suit them perfectly. I watch their happiness, their surety in claiming their spot, their plans to purchase it. I see Cal sharing his parents' joy, talking about their future, the home they will build.

Yet he is unsettled. Despite his smiles, I know he misses me as much as I miss him. He wants to be planning our future. I sense his desire to return to me soon and I can't wait for him to be back.,

I too am unsettled. I not only miss Cal, but I struggle with a greater sense of incompletion for there is a question that haunts my sleeping and waking hours.

Why did Tasma's species help us? This question only becomes louder, more persistent, until one morning, as though beckoned, I set out beyond the city's natural borders toward the forests in search of an answer. I take Ray-Ray. The suns are high and the air cool and crisp, nipping at my skin. I neglect to tell my father or Neath where I'm going. It happens so spontaneously that I just don't think to do it. I walk far and long and enter the forest without any hesitation. I am being called. I stop when I feel I should. The sunlight passes through the high canopies, shining on tubular flowers and the slow, large insects that hover over them. Ray-Ray sits, computing by my body language that it's time to halt and stay. I sit next to him. I close my eyes and answer the call.

When I catch a slight movement, I look up. Tasma is there.

I smile, relieved. 'Good morning.'

'Yes, it is.'

'I want to thank you.'

Tasma shines. 'You want to know how to thank us?'

I am pleased our interaction is coming straight to the point. 'Yes. Are you ready to tell me? What do you want in return for all your help?'

'You can't see it?'

I open my mind, trying to look forward. I see a house. I hear the word 'home'.

I fish for understanding. 'You want to go home?'

'No. Our home has no future.'

I feel sorry. Has something happened to its planet? 'Where is your home?' I ask, wanting to know more.

'Our home is beyond the void on the edge of your observable universe. Your mother and brother skimmed the edges of this void—a lightless, cold spot, a pressure point, where our universe is leaning on yours.'

'Beyond the void... your universe.' I'm thrown. My mind can't see it.

'Yes.'

'Your home... Another universe?'

'Yes. Ours is dying. It's collapsing in on itself. It won't happen for a long time, but we know we must move on.'

'Is that why you've come here?'

'We came through the void, looking for an alternative universe. Now we want to move here, but our young ones can't traverse the void. They haven't mastered vibrational change. They can only go astral for short periods, disappearing into one of the lower planes, then they must return to the physical plane.'

'But there are young ones on Nattalia. How did they get here?'

'They were created here, born here, to see if this environment will suit. It does, very well.'

'It does. Your young ones kept us safe.'

'They will always work with you if they are here. We need a

place to bring them, a place to teach them. We want to bring them here.'

'Is that why you built a red Hatch out there and need a ship?'

'Yes. One Hatch and one ship to start and if that works well, many ships. We will teach you to build ships capable of withstanding the void's dynamic properties. It can be done. Nattalia has the minerals that will allow for such ships.'

'I see.' I am stunned. It wants us to build ships that can move through voids into alternative universes, which is helpful for them, but I don't know if we are ready for such a leap. If the ships can travel through voids, where else can they go?

'You will only be given passage and knowledge when you're ready,' Tasma relays, hearing my inner concerns.

I smile wanly, hoping it is right.

'There are many families in our universe that don't want to wait for their young to grow old to come here. We age slowly. I am thousands of years old. The families are waiting for the ships.'

'How many of you are there?'

Tasma's lights are bright. 'Adults will mostly coexist across several planes. Our young will be less than the trees of the forests. And we can work with you to keep this planet healthy and safe.'

This puts my mind at ease. They will be low impact and supportive of environmental sustainability. They've already proven themselves peaceful and protective. I feel the love in its words and smile. 'You know you could have taken them anywhere.' I think of the trillions of inhabited stars and planets they could have selected. I've seen so many beautiful and adaptable places in my astral travels. It must have too.

'But we heard through your communication waves that Nattalia is the most liveable planet in the universe,' Tasma says. 'We wanted the most liveable.'

I'm confused for a moment, then I recall the advertisements, the propaganda aimed at getting everyone to migrate to Nattalia and to choose it for the pro-development campaign.

'You chose Nattalia because of our messages?'

'Yes, and when we came here, we saw they are true and it has the resources we need for the ships and people who can help us build them.'

'You need us?'

'You are adept at physical creation.'

'That may be true, but humans are often guided by fear and greed. Many humans would like to see this planet developed and mined beyond its limits. Mandon certainly planned for that.'

'We saw that. But now he is gone. A woman with a symbolic bird will lead and you will see that the ships are built. You will help us as we've helped you.'

Tasma is right. I will do whatever I can to see them repaid. It is important to keep balance and order when it comes to giving and taking. We owe them... at least a place for their young to grow. 'I will do what I can to help you.'

'Yes. You will come.'

'Come?' I don't understand.

'To our universe, to collect the first passengers.'

Fear shoots through my veins. 'You mean, through the void to your universe?'

'Yes.'

'I don't know...' I'm overwhelmed by the thought. It just seems so far, so unreal, so beyond anything I can really imagine or prepare for. I don't know how to tell it that I don't think I'm up for it.

'You want to help us.' Its lights are changing to warmer colours.

'I do. I just, I don't know. I don't know how I can. What use I'd be! We, humans, we're not that strong,' I say, unable to comprehend why it would want me along.

'You don't think we can learn from you?'

'I think you will find my abilities... disappointing.'

'Your perceptions are unique.'

'They are?' I consider it. 'So, you are willing to teach me things, if I teach you things?'

'Of course, that's why we're here.'

'I see.' Slowly, I start to accept and then warm to the concept. There is much I want to learn.

'What is this device with you?' Tasma asks, indicating Ray-Ray, which has curled up in sleep mode beside me.

'It is our family pet. We built it drawing on the characteristics of two animals that we humans are fond of.'

'Why do you have it?'

I look at Ray-Ray and play with its soft ear. 'It does small errands for us, helps keep watch, guards our home, makes us laugh, helps us relax. What it symbolises is calming. The vulnerability and friendship of friendly animals, amusing animals, calms us. I don't expect you to understand any of this.' I feel ridiculous. Ray-Ray is like a loveable toy. What would a species like Tasma know about toys, our relationship with animals, our need for security?

The lights running beneath Tasma's skin change colours from pink to orange to yellow to a pale blue and I'm mesmerised by it.

'So, you are interested in our world,' I say, embracing the idea of being a teacher. 'Let me think... Why don't we begin with something simple. What's your favourite colour?'

I ask this knowing that my favourite is green and I'm curious to see if Tasma's will be the same.

'Colour?' it muses. 'What is colour?'

I feel its confusion. I watch its lights change from blue to green.

It doesn't know colour even though it shines within it. In that moment, I realise how much we do have to teach, just as much as we have to learn.

But do I really have to get on a ship and go where no other

humans have gone before just to acquire more knowledge? As I pose the question, the great human explorers of our past come to mind. They risked just as much for the sake of learning for all. Besides, I've explored the far reaches of our universe and other planes while in my astral state. This won't be so different, will it? Except, when I'm astral, I can always come back into my body with a single thought...

As I consider this future path, my mind fills with green—a shining, bright, green light.

So, that's it, is it?

Ready or not, I must be going.

ACKNOWLEDGMENTS

I would like to thank my husband, René Ranke, for his help with *The Hatch* and for proofreading my early drafts. As an avid reader of texts in the fields of metaphysics, cosmology, quantum physics, analytical psychology, and ontology, he was able to contribute scientific knowledge to my writings, for which I am very grateful.

I also thank my editor, Nathan Phillips, for his sound advice and encouragement.

A huge thank you to Odyssey Books publisher, Michelle Lovi, for believing in my historical fiction novels, *Port of No Return* and *Wanderers No More,* and for staying with me as I crossed genres to science fiction to publish *The Hatch*. I would like to take this opportunity to acknowledge Michelle for her efforts and support of emerging authors, particularly in Australia and New Zealand.

My interest in science fiction has always been there, though in more recent years I've had greater exposure to the genre through reading books and viewing films with my two sons, Louis and Jimi. I thank them for those many shared hours of inspiring entertainment.

There are other acknowledgements that I'd like to make in relation to referencing some of the concepts in *The Hatch*.

In order to set my story across the far reaches of our known universe, I introduced the Hatch, a technology that could facilitate deep space travel. In development of this concept, my husband turned my attention to research being undertaken at the Large Hadron Collider in Switzerland, which involves the study of collisions between high energy particle beams and how such collisions could lead to the creation of miniature black holes. It was this body of research that led to the creation of the Hatch.

To power up the 'Hatch', I drew from the discovery by Canadian PhD student Matt Shultz of Queen's University, Ontario. He is responsible for finding two massive suns with magnetic fields in a binary system where the magnetic lines of force were gigantic at the duos common centre.

The Hatch facilitates deep space travel when a computer-guided ship enters a tear in space/time, where space has bent back on itself, and the craft is able to pop back out instantaneously at a pre-programmed destination. This notion of curved space/time refers to the three-torus cosmological model proposed in 1984 by Alexei Starobinsky and Yakov Borisovich Zel'dovich at the Landau Institute in Moscow.

My work also relies on long-held Eastern philosophical thought around the existence of other planes and dimensions and the heightened use of a sixth sense, as well as other paranormal activities such as astral travel.

Through my life-long inquiries and explorations of the psychic arts and languages, I have come to accept that there is more to our universe than what we can perceive through our five senses. In writing *The Hatch*, I have at times borrowed from the teachings of Ram Dass (aka: Prof Richard Alpert), who has often referred to other dimensions as different channels co-existing in varying vibrations.

I have written about energy patterns, synchronicity, signs, and prophetic experiences, imagining a future where an advanced understanding of such concepts could expand our knowledge and guide our way. Such imaginings have underpinned my writings of this novel, which takes the reader not just beyond Earth but into a world of higher abilities.

ABOUT THE AUTHOR

Michelle Saftich was born in Brisbane, Australia. She holds a Bachelor of Business/Communications Degree, majoring in journalism, from QUT. For more than 20 years, she has worked in communications, including print journalism, sub-editing, communications management and media relations.

In 1999, she won a national award for Best News Story at ASNA (Australian Suburban Newspaper Awards).

She spent 10 years living in Sydney; and two years in Osaka, Japan, where she taught English.

Her debut novel, *Port of No Return*, was released in 2015 and was inspired by her father's family story. Its sequel, *Wanderers No More*, was released in 2017.

Her most recent novel, *The Hatch*, explores similar themes to her previous works, of migration, family and adaptation, though instead of looking to history for inspiration, she has looked to the future.

Michelle is married with two sons. She is currently a member of the Queensland Tarot Guild.

www.michellesaftich.com

facebook.com/msaftich

twitter.com/MichelleSaftich

ALSO BY MICHELLE SAFTICH

Port of No Return

Wanderers No More

Lightning Source UK Ltd.
Milton Keynes UK
UKHW010603060120
356421UK00001B/24/P